NOBLE MAN

DATE DUE

1496			

NOBLE MAN

This book is a work of fiction. Names, characters, businesses, organizations, places, events and incidents either are the product of the author's imagination or are used fictitiously. Any resemblance to actual persons, living or dead, events, or locales is entirely coincidental.

Book and Cover design by www.LiteraryRebel.com

First Edition: September 2015

Dedication and special thanks:

This book is the result of a lot of hard work and effort. I could not have done it without the support of some amazing people. I would especially like to thank Marte Gruber who gave me valuable feedback on the first draft, the designers at www.literaryrebel.com who provided Noble Man with an amazing cover, and the editors who caught most of my typos.

CHAPTER ONE

JACOB NOBLE'S LAST OFFICIAL MISSION FOR THE CIA started out like so many others. His plane landed in Doha shortly before sundown. His entry Visa listed him as a security analyst for a non-existent data solution firm headquartered out of San Jose. If anyone bothered to call the phone number, they'd speak to a very pleasant secretary who would confirm Noble's identity. It made the perfect cover. With cybercrime on the rise, companies in the Middle East were snapping up security consultants in effort to safeguard their systems from attack.

A customs agent compared Noble to his photograph. Lean and hard with tan skin and shaggy hair, he looked more like a surfer than a computer expert. He wore a sport coat, faded denims, and scuffed loafers. A rumpled t-shirt proclaimed, *"Don't Monkey with My Tail."* His wallet contained fake ID and credit cards to match his cover. Despite never having set foot in San Jose, he had a ticket stub to the movie theater on Roosevelt Boulevard. There was even a well-read note from a fictitious girlfriend folded up behind his driver's license.

He passed through the bustling international terminal, collected his baggage from the carousel, and made his way outside. Heat hit him like a sucker punch to the gut. It was early May and already hot enough to melt the tarmac. Beads of perspiration trickled down his forehead. A patch of sweat formed between his shoulders.

From Hamad International Airport he took a cab to a four-star hotel on Al Awarsi Street. It was just expensive enough for a programmer from Silicon Valley. Noble deposited his fake luggage in the room and went back downstairs. He made a point of asking the concierge for directions to a trendy nightspot. Outside he took another cab into the heart of the city. This time he dropped the tourist act. He gave the driver directions in Arabic to the Qatar News Agency south of Al Waab Street.

He tipped the driver and spent the next twenty minutes performing what was known, in tradecraft circles, as a surveillance detection route. He wandered the crowded neighborhood in the blistering heat, stopped at various street vendors, took turns at random, and doubled back to throw off pursuit. Barkers called to him. Livestock brayed and honked. The pungent aroma of Arabian spices attacked his nose. Satisfied that he had not been followed, Noble ducked into a travel agency on Abu Bakr.

A squeaky ceiling fan stirred the oppressive heat. A few faded posters clung to the walls. Noble's shoes stuck to the floor and made loud peeling noises with each step. Everything about the office was designed to ward off potential customers. A pudgy Arab with tired eyes slouched in a swivel chair reading the evening edition. He peered over the top of the paper as Noble entered. "Hello, my friend. Welcome to Qatar. Are you interested in a tour of our beautiful country?"

"Actually, I'm here to meet a friend," Noble said, using the prearranged code. "Goes by the name Finch."

The Arab folded his paper. One hand disappeared beneath the desk. With a smile he said, "The Englishman?"

"American," Noble said.

His hand reappeared. "Take the stairs all the way to the top."

Noble nodded, pushed through a beaded curtain, and mounted a narrow staircase to the third floor. At the landing, he caught snatches of whispered conversations through a flimsy wood door. He knocked. There was a pause from inside and then, "Who is it?"

"Muskrat," Noble said.

Supposedly a computer spit these operational codenames out at random. Muskrat was innocuous enough. He'd also been Starlight, Rosepetal, Babydoll, and Debutante. Noble was convinced some wit back at Langley was picking names that tickled his funny bone.

The door opened to the end of the security chain. Jesús Torres's grinning face filled the gap. He was a short Hispanic man with a neatly trimmed goatee and impeccable teeth. He glanced past Noble into the empty stairwell, then closed the door, removed the chain, and opened it again. "Welcome to the party, amigo."

Five men, equipment, and sleeping mats crowded the small room. In one corner, they had set up a makeshift listening post. Antennae bristled from the back of a clunky electronic tower powered by a cyclical battery. A black-and-white satellite photo of Doha covered a foldout table in the center of the room. The air stank of strong Arabian coffee and cigarettes.

Noble locked and chained the door. "Bring me up to speed. How's our cover?"

"Intact," Nathan Horn told him. He sat atop a plastic food crate in front of the communications equipment with a headphone pressed against his left ear. A toothpick protruded from the corner of his mouth. "Our assets on the ground haven't picked up any chatter. There are rumors of a rebel uprising in Saudi Arabia. Nothing to worry about."

Noble rotated the satellite picture to face him. The target building was circled in green. The primary extraction route was marked in red. Blue marked the secondary route. "Walk me through it," he said.

Hassan Ahmad, the team's only Arab, plucked a clove cigarette from his mouth. He blew smoke at the ceiling where it formed a lazy blue halo around a naked bulb. "We drive to the target house. There's a pair of SUVs waiting downstairs. The trucks are stolen so leave the keys in the ignition when you are done.

"Myself, Horn, and Sutter go in the front door. Noble, Torres, and Randall go in through the back. The layout inside is relatively simple. First floor is one large room with a corner office and a toilet. The top floor is a little more complicated. Four bedrooms and a bath. Be sure you clear them."

"Opposition?" Noble asked.

"Light," Hassan said. "Just the seller and his two hired guns. The goods are held inside a wire cage on the first floor.

Once the hostiles are down, Torres drives the getaway truck to the front door. Two minutes to neutralize the bad guys and three to load the cargo. We're in and out in five minutes."

Noble turned his attention to Torres. "How's our extract?"

Jesús gave him a thumbs up. "The truck is parked a block away, and the boat is sitting at the dock, gassed up and waiting on passengers."

Paul Sutter, a former member of the United States Navy's top-secret Developmental Group, looked like a long haul trucker with receding hair and soft eyes. He asked, "How long from the target building to the dock?"

"Ten, maybe fifteen minutes depending on traffic," Torres said.

Lucas Randall whistled through his teeth. "Lot of time to be out in the open." He was a veteran of Iraq, Afghanistan, and a score of top-secret operations around the globe. If there were too many moving parts in an op, Lucas would be the first to point it out.

Noble agreed but shrugged. "Not much we can do about that." He had spent the last six months fine-tuning this op, planning every detail. He had invested too much to walk away now. He checked his watch. It was 2120. "We move at 2200 hours. We hit the house at 2215. Anyone have objections? Now is the time."

No one spoke.

"Let's go kill some bad guys," Noble said. He held out a fist. Torres bumped it.

CHAPTER TWO

For the next fifteen minutes, the cramped hotel room was a flurry of activity. The team cleaned and inspected weapons, wrapped electrical tape around grenade pins, and tested their ear mics. Noble checked the action on a Kalashnikov rifle. He worked the charging handle several times to be sure the bolt was free of snags and then pulled the trigger on an empty chamber. Satisfied, he fed a magazine into the weapon and gave it a slap to be sure it seated properly. He shed his sports coat, slipped into a tactical harness, and then collected five extra mags and a flashbang grenade.

Hassan had bought the gear through back channels after arriving in Qatar a week earlier. It was all local and would trace back to illegal arms dealers in the United Arab Emirates. The vehicles had been boosted from a local construction company. Only the communications equipment in the corner was American. As soon as they left, the local asset manning the desk downstairs would dispose of it and scrub the room.

By 2135 the six men were armed and ready. They had checked and rechecked their gear. Now all they could do was wait. They cracked jokes to ease the tension. The minute hand on Noble's Tag Heuer moved with agonizing slowness. Lucas chain-smoked. Torres did free-weight squats to keep his blood up. Horn managed a digital farm on his cell phone. At 2200 the group rose without a word; they moved in silence down the stairs and out the back door to the waiting SUVs.

They drove through crowded markets and narrow alleys. Qatar is a combination of the old and new. Modern high-rises loom over shanty towns. Polished BMWs and beaters held together with duct tape throng the major arteries. The locals use their horns incessantly.

Torres was behind the wheel of the rear SUV. Dust caked the front windshield. He triggered the wipers, cutting a path through layers of grit. Noble rode in the passenger seat with his AK-47 between his knees, sorting through contingencies. A host of things could go sideways. As the team leader, it was his job to prepare for eventualities. Black ops into friendly countries require surgical precision and absolute deniability. Officially, Qatar was neutral on the world stage. Noble and his team were breaking dozens of international laws and, if caught, the United States government would disavow them.

The target house was a two-story sandstone structure in a quiet neighborhood. It had faded blue shutters and stout metal doors that screamed "*Go Away.*"

Torres split off from the lead SUV and turned down a

narrow dirt lane that ran behind the building. The alley was littered with trash and lit by the spill from a few barred windows. The light from the headlamps fell on a half-starved mongrel nosing through the trash. The dog tucked his tail and ran as the SUV entered the alley. Torres parked and cut the engine. Noble released his seat belt. Lucas, slouched in the backseat, used the butt of a cigarette to light another. The noxious cloud filled the SUV. Noble cranked down the passenger side window for a breath of dry desert air. The heat, even at ten o'clock, was oppressive.

Torres looked in the rearview mirror. "How do you not have cancer?"

"Gotta die of something," Lucas said.

"Do you have to take us with you?" Noble asked.

Torres laughed.

The tension inside the vehicle mounted as the minutes ticked past. Noble focused on his breathing, keeping his heart rate regular so when it came time to pull the trigger his hands would be steady. At 2210 Sutter keyed his mic. His voice came over the net in whisper. "Boss, we got a problem. Looks like the buyer's here early. A car just pulled up, followed by a van."

The first tickle of fear started at the base of Noble's skull. He opened his mic. "Talk to me."

"Three men are getting out of the car. Looks like the drivers are staying with the vehicles. Be advised; the party crashers are wearing Uzis on shoulder rigs."

Noble chewed the inside of one cheek. Operations had a habit of going bad at the last minute. A buyer showing up a day ahead of schedule might mean nothing or it might mean the entire operation was blown. Counter intelligence work was a wilderness of mirrors. There were layers within layers.

The Green Berets had taught Noble to improvise, adapt, and overcome. Failure was not an option. All that changed when he joined the CIA's Special Operations Group. The Company teaches their agents that when there is doubt, there is no doubt. Keeping your cover intact is mission one. Sometimes it's best to walk away.

Sutter came over the mic and asked, "How do you want to play it, boss?"

Noble weighed his options. He could abort. Doing nothing meant watching twenty-three women loaded up and carted off to be sold as slaves. They would be used, abused, and then discarded like trash. It meant standing aside and allowing innocent people to suffer. That option didn't sit well with Noble. He looked across at Torres.

"They'll disappear into the market," Torres said. "We won't get a second shot at this."

"We are changing the op," Noble spoke into the mic. "My team will breach and secure the first floor. Sutter, as soon as you hear us pop the back door, your team will take out the drivers and then come through the front. I'll lead my team up stairs to secure the second floor while you load the goods on the truck. Any questions?"

"Roger that," Sutter replied. "Let's rock and roll.

CHAPTER THREE

Noble climbed out. Torres and Lucas followed. They left the doors open. The muffled thump of a slamming car door would draw unnecessary attention. The keys were in the ignition. With any luck, a thief would happen by and take the vehicle for a ride, helping to muddy the trail.

Noble moved along the alley in a half-crouch with Torres close behind. Lucas brought up the rear. They stacked up at the back door of the target building. Noble gave a hand signal. Lucas hurried forward, letting his rifle hang at the end of its sling, and went to work affixing adhesive blasting strips to the door frame. He was one of the best operators in the business. In a few short seconds, he had placed the strips, set a charge, and retaken his place at the end of the line. He counted down from five on his fingers.

A deafening *whomp* blew the door and most of the frame into the room, killing one man instantly. His mangled body went tumbling across the floor like a broken marionette.

Noble was moving before the metal door hit the ground. He ducked through the shattered frame into a swirling cloud of dust. The explosion had destroyed most of the overhead lighting. One neon bulb managed to survive. It flickered and buzzed. On Noble's left, a door opened onto a stairwell. On his right, a chain-link fence sectioned off half the room. Five men hunched up their shoulders like turtles trying to retreat inside their shells. Four were armed. Noble ignored a gunman directly in front of him and moved to his right, into the far corner.

Ignoring a thug with an automatic weapon goes against natural instincts, but taking down a room full of bad guys is a delicate ballet. It requires precision movements. If Noble paused long enough to kill the tango in front of him, he would foul up Torres immediately behind and that would roadblock Lucas. All three of them would bottleneck in the open doorframe. Instead they fanned out into opposite corners of the room, forcing the enemy to divide their attention.

The closest gunman shook off the shock of the blast, tracked Noble, and pressed the trigger. The Uzi spit a stream of bullets. Lead impacted the wall over Noble's shoulder with hard cracks.

Lucas came through the door last and silenced the Uzi with a short burst from his AK-47. Bullets stitched the guy's chest and drove him backward. He died shooting holes in the ceiling.

Noble trained his weapon on an Arab in a five-thou-sand-dollar suit with impeccable hair and a gold wristwatch. He shouted orders in Farsi, "Get down on the floor! Get down on the floor, now!"

Torres and Lucas caught the remaining tangos in a cross fire. Their twin AK-47's cut down the bad guys before they had a chance to mount a counterattack. The fight was over before it began, but the Arab in the suit wasn't cooperating. Noble kept ordering him onto the ground. Instead of hitting the deck, the man reached a hand into his suit jacket.

Time slowed. A thousand possibilities raced across the surface of Noble's mind. The man could have a gun, a grenade, or a detonator. The simple press of a button could kill Noble, his team, and the hostages. To wait was to invite death. Noble couldn't afford to find out what the Arab had under his jacket.

He squeezed the trigger. His AK-47 kicked. The muzzle flashed. The shot ripped the back of the man's head off. His knees buckled. He landed flat on his back.

The other team breached. The door blew off its hinges, and they poured into the room, weapons up, looking for targets.

"First floor clear!" Noble yelled.

The acrid stench of cordite hung in the air, mingling with the smell of human offal. Spent shell casings littered the concrete floor. Noble's ears were ringing from the explosions. He spared a glance through the chain-link fence. Dirt-stained, terrified faces stared back. Most of them had their hands over their ears. Others had curled up in an effort to avoid stray bullets.

Noble checked the dead suit. His blood and brains painted a grisly tapestry on the dusty floor. He clutched a gold money clip along with a laminated Identification Card in his lifeless hand. Instead of kissing the ground like he'd been told, the idiot died trying to show his I.D. or maybe he was trying to bribe them.

Noble shook his head. "Moron."

Sutter's team took control of the first floor, and Hassan went for the transport truck parked at the end of the block. Noble lead his team up the steps. Most of the rooms stood empty. Behind a door at the end of the hall, they found a girl huddled on a threadbare mattress. She looked about ten years old, with tangled blonde hair and dark circles around her eyes. A few crumpled candy bar wrappers winked in the dim light. Noble crossed the room, scooped her up, and moved back to the stairs with his team in tow.

"Boss, you'd better take a look at this," Sutter said as Noble reached the first floor. He knelt over the body of the buyer, examining the laminated I.D. card.

"What's up?" Noble asked.

Horn and Hassan had loaded most of the girls onto the truck. A few needed to be carried. Sutter indicated the dead buyer with a thrust of his chin. "This guy is a ranking member of the Majlis al Shura."

"Not anymore," Noble said. He had a sinking feeling in his gut, like he had just drawn the proverbial short straw. "Take his papers and get the rest of those girls on the truck."

Taking the I.D. would delay identification, but heads would roll. The Majlis al Shura acted like an Islamic Parliament, drafting legislation and passing laws. It didn't surprise Noble to learn that a Qatar politician was involved in the slave trade, but it meant he had executed a standing member of government.

He ignored the sinking feeling in his gut and carried the little girl outside to the waiting truck. He let his AK-47 swing on its harness while he hoisted himself and the girl into the passenger seat. Hassan slid into the driver seat next to him. The rest of the team climbed in the back with their terrified passengers. Hassan shifted into drive with a grinding of gears. The big transport lurched forward, throwing Noble against the seat back.

"This thing going to make it?" Noble asked.

Hassan rocked his head to one side. "We're about to find out."

The girls in the cargo bed huddled together in groups, watching the armed men with naked fear and trying to decide if their situation had gotten better or worse. The girl on Noble's lap spoke in Russian. He turned in his seat and asked Lucas, "What's she saying?"

"She wants to see her mother," Lucas translated.

Noble looked down into a pair of hopeful eyes set in a dirt-stained face. It felt like someone driving a nail into his heart. "Tell her she's safe now."

Lucas frowned. "We are door kickers, boss, not psychi-atrists."

"Just tell her," Noble said.

Lucas smiled and spoke Russian. Noble didn't know what he said, but it worked. The tension went out of her little body. She rested her head against Noble's chest. He stroked her hair.

It was a breach of protocol. Noble's job was to eliminate bad guys and rescue hostages. He and his team were under strict orders not to make any claims to the victims. The girls came from all over the world. Even if the CIA returned them to their home countries, many were orphans and would never see their families again. They had been rescued from a short and bitter life as sex slaves only to become wards of the state.

Hassan pulled the truck onto Salwa Highway, grinding gears the whole way. He drove straight through the heart of Qatar. Noble kept listening for the wail of police sirens. He checked the rearview mirrors every few minutes. A dark van with tinted windows followed them for several miles but finally turned off at the circle road.

They reached Dhow Harbor unmolested. A rusted trawler bobbed on the wine dark waters of the bay. Hassan parked next to the dock. The engine died with a tired cough. The truck's tail pipe farted out a black cloud.

"I think you killed it," Noble remarked.

Hassan flashed him a hand sign.

Lucas dropped the back gate, and the girls were herded from the truck onto the boat. Sutter climbed into the wheelhouse and revved the engine. The screw bit into the water. The trawler ferried the girls and their rescuers out to sea where a company ship, under the guise of a research vessel, waited to carry them all to Hawaii. In less than seven hours, they'd be in international waters under escort by the United States Navy. Everything had gone according to plan—everything except for the one idiot who got himself killed refusing to cooperate.

Noble couldn't shake the feeling that he had turned a corner, that he had made a mistake in a business where mistakes could be deadly. He replayed the action in his head over and over and told himself he had done the right thing.

CHAPTER FOUR

FOUR YEARS LATER

Weekends were always busy at the shelter. Friday nights were the worst. That's when young prostitutes in the Philippines, staring down the barrel of another grueling weekend, slipped their handlers. Twenty or thirty would find their way, by word of mouth, to the shelter on Makati Boulevard in the heart of metro Manila. By the following weekend, two-thirds of the new girls would return to a life of prostitution. Others would overdose and still more would choose suicide. It was a small remnant that managed to clean up and carve out a life for themselves.

This Sunday evening they had seven new girls, all of them strung out, in need of food and fighting the urge for a fix. Three were in such a bad state of withdraw that they had to be taken to the hospital by ambulance. A fourth was on suicide watch after trying to cut her wrists with a plastic knife during dinner.

Besides the new arrivals, the water heater was on the fritz, two of the regular volunteers were sick, the kitchen was out of rice again, someone had stolen the DVD player from the rec room, there had been two fist fights, the dead-bolt on the backdoor was busted, and the electric bill was a week overdue.

At the center of the storm was Bati Malaya Ramos. She hustled from one emergency to the next in a futile attempt to bring order from chaos. It was a losing battle, but one that she fought every day, seven days a week.

She had the back door open and was trying to remove the broken deadbolt with a Philips head. Her tongue was stuck firmly in the corner of her mouth as she worked. A new deadbolt lay on the cheap linoleum still inside the plastic. Bati's short, dark hair was windblown. She was wearing the same khaki shorts and white blouse from yesterday.

"I just got off the phone with a repair man," Nawa told her. "He said he can't come until Tuesday."

Bati wrestled with a stubborn screw. "Did you tell him we are a charity organization? There are two dozen girls here who won't be able to shower until it's fixed."

"He didn't seem to care."

"Try another. See if you can get someone here by tomorrow at the latest." Bati broke the final screw loose and breathed a sigh of relief.

"And the new girl who tried to cut her wrist says she wants to leave."

"We can't hold her against her will," Bati said.

"Oh, and did you know the kitchen is out of rice?"

"I'm going to the grocery after I change this lock."

Nawa hurried off to call more repairmen.

Bati stripped the broken deadbolt off the door and then

17

pried open the new packaging. The sharp plastic sliced her fingertip. She winced and sucked the blood.

Samantha Gunn stuck her head around the doorframe. She and Bati had started the shelter together. Hard to believe it had been nearly two years. At the moment, she looked as stressed as Bati felt. "Did you know the kitchen is out of rice?" Sam asked.

"I'm going to the grocery as soon as I get this lock changed."

"Any word on the water heater?"

"Not until Tuesday."

"What if we need a new one?" Sam asked. "We don't have the money. We are stretched to the breaking point."

"If that's the case, we'll figure something out," Bati told her.

Sam raked both hands through her straight, black hair. "I'll see about a coin laundry for getting clothes washed."

"Take the money from petty cash," Bati told her.

"I've got a jar full of coins at the apartment," Sam said. "I'll use that."

"Thanks, Sam." Bati held the new deadbolt up to the old hole and found a match. At least something was going her way. "Oh, Sam? The girl who tried to cut her wrists is talking about leaving. See if you can get her to stay."

"Will do," Sam said. She started to leave and stopped. "By the way, the jerk is here."

Bati opened her mouth to respond, but Sam fled before she could say a word. They had been around that particular block a dozen times and agreed to disagree. She shook her head and returned her attention to the door. She threaded the new screws into the deadbolt and tightened them. She tested the lock. The bolt shot into place.

Diego appeared in the back hall with his hands stuffed deep in the pockets of his cargo shorts. His flip-flops made a rhythmic clack on the cheap linoleum. "We were supposed to meet for dinner half an hour ago," he said by way of greeting.

Bati looked at her watch and groaned. "I'm really sorry, babe. I've just been swamped. You know how weekends are around here."

"Come on," he said. "Let's get out of here and get some food."

"Give me a few minutes, okay? I need to take care of a few things."

Diego rolled his eyes. "You are always busy."

"Don't be that way," Bati said.

"The world isn't going to stop if you eat," he said. "Let's go. I'm hungry."

Bati held up her hands in surrender. "Okay. Let me clean up here and get my purse." She grabbed the empty plastic that the deadbolt had come in, along with the broken lock and the screwdriver. She piled it all onto a cluttered supply shelf and then went to her office for her purse. She couldn't eat without her insulin syringe.

Diego followed her, making long-suffering sighs the whole way. Bati ignored his attitude. He could be such a child when he didn't get his way. But then, most men were like that. Diego could also be really sweet when he wanted to be. That was the side Sam never saw.

Bati took her purse from a locked drawer in her desk and pecked Diego on his stubbly cheek. He had been trying, unsuccessfully, to grow a beard for weeks. "Where are we going for dinner?"

"It's a new place," he told her. "Friend of mine told me about it."

They left by the back door. Bati didn't like the girls to see her with a man. So many of them had developed a deep mistrust of men after being used like puppets. Who could blame them?

Bati threaded her arm through Diego's as they turned the corner onto Tayuman Street. "So what's the name of this new place?"

"Uh... I forget. It's not far."

Bati's brow knit. She didn't remember any new restaurants opening in the neighborhood. She started to ask more questions but never got the chance. A rusted old heap of a van jumped the curb onto the sidewalk. "Look out!" Bati screamed,

Diego leapt clear.

The front bumper missed Bati by inches. Brakes squealed, and the tires locked, leaving skid marks. A primer gray door rolled open. Two men with guns and pantyhose over their heads leapt out. Bati's knees turned to rubber. She opened her mouth to scream, but no sound came out.

"Leave her alone!" Diego launched himself at one of the attackers and got hit in the nose with the butt of a pistol. Bati heard the bone break with a wet crunch. Diego's head snapped backward, and his feet shot out from under him. He landed flat on his back, clutching a broken nose and moaning.

The scream that she had been working on finally made its way up from her lungs and echoed along Tayuman

Street. People stopped and turned. One of the masked men grabbed Bati around the waist. He tossed her into the back of the van. She landed with a bone-jarring thud on the metal floor. The two attackers jumped in behind her and rolled the door shut with a bang. The driver stomped the gas.

CHAPTER FIVE

SAM GUNN WAS TRYING TO TALK A SOBBING HOOKER out of running back to her pimp. Detoxing at the shelter would be hard, maybe one of the hardest things the girl had ever done, but going back would be worse. The girl had curled up in a corner of the ratty sofa in the rec room. Tears streamed down her cheeks. Several of the other women who had been living at the shelter for a while offered encouragement.

"If you go back now, you'll take a beating," Sam told her.

She palmed a rope of snot away from one nostril. "He'll find me. I know he'll find me."

"You'll be safe here," Sam said. She wanted it to be true. The shelter was supposed to be a safe place. But Manila was the Wild West, at least compared to America. More than once, a pimp or club owner had shown up looking for a girl. Jealous boyfriends and angry fathers were also a regular occurrence. They had to call the police once or twice a month, and local law enforcement took their time responding. No one cared much. Prostitutes are third-class citizens in the Philippines.

Sam heard the shriek of tires and a scream from Tayuman Street. The sound of that scream left a chill in her heart. The small hairs at the back of her neck stood on end. She left the sobbing woman in the company of the resident girls and stepped outside.

There was a commotion at the end of the block. People were on their cells and pointing. Sam hurried along the sidewalk to the corner. There was no sign of a traffic accident or anything out of the ordinary. She stopped a few people passing by and asked if they had heard a scream. No one seemed quite sure what had happened. Some said a van had jumped the curb. Others said a man got beat up. But there was no van and no man that Sam could see. She walked back to the shelter, but she couldn't shake the nagging feeling in the pit of her stomach, like something terrible had happened.

The hustle of running the shelter drove the incident from her mind. There were groceries to buy, laundry to be done, and suicidal girls to babysit. It wasn't until she woke up the next morning and found Bati's bed unslept in that Sam began to panic.

CHAPTER SIX

Fear coursed through Bati's veins as the van swerved through traffic, dodging jeepneys, panel trucks, and Toyotas. She didn't know she was screaming until one of the kidnappers belted her across the face. The scream died, cut like knife through string. Her cheek burned.

"Keep your mouth shut and maybe you won't get hurt," he said.

Bati held up both hands in surrender. "Okay. Okay. Don't hurt me."

The driver used his horn and ran a red. Tires shrieked on asphalt. Bati heard the telltale crunch of bumpers coming together. The truck rocked on its springs as the driver swung a corner. The engine labored.

The kidnappers forced Bati onto her stomach and wrenched her hands behind her back. They looped a yellow zip-tie around her wrists. The heavy gauge plastic bit into her skin. She winced. Then they rolled her onto her back. One of the men had an oily shop rag. The other peeled a length of gray duct tape. One man pinned her shoulders to the floor while his partner tried to stuff the smelly rag in her mouth.

Blind, unreasoning panic gripped her. As the kidnapper forced the rag into her mouth, Bati chomped down on his finger. Her teeth bit through the bone with a crunch. Warm blood burst over her lips.

He reeled backward. Blood shot from the stump of his finger in bright, crimson arcs. "She bit my finger off!" he screamed. "She bit my finger off!"

In the confusion, the other man relaxed his grip on her shoulders. She spit out the oily rag along with the severed digit and lunged for the backdoor of the van. She didn't go two steps before the kidnapper caught her. He slammed her back down. Her chin impacted the floor. Lights exploded in her vision.

She knew she had to fight, to escape, but the information wasn't getting to her legs. The kidnapper pressed her face against the floor of the van, and with his other hand, he worked the button on her shorts. He hauled them down over her legs. Then he wadded and stuffed them in her mouth before slapping a piece of duct tape over her lips.

Bati lay there with her shorts in her mouth, her pink cotton panties showing, and tears spilling down her cheeks. Terror was a weight pinning her to the floor of the speeding van.

The man with the missing finger finally stopped screaming. His eyes focused on Bati. His lips peeled back from clenched teeth. "Little slut!" He lifted his foot to stomp her head.

Bati curled up in a desperate attempt to shield herself.

She squeezed her eyes shut and waited for his boot to come down.

His partner pinned him against the wall of the van.

"She's a ten-thousand-dollar payday," he said. "You want to kick her to death?"

He struggled to break free. "She bit my finger off!"

Over his shoulder, the driver said, "Buy a prosthetic with your share of the money."

He struggled for another moment, but reason finally won out. They wrapped the severed stump in the oily rag and then used the duct tape to keep the makeshift bandage in place. The van had stopped. Bati heard a fog horn's mournful cry and knew they must be near the water.

The uninjured kidnapper glanced out the front windshield. "What are we doing at the docks?"

"Change of plans." The driver produced a pistol and shot the uninjured kidnapper through the head. Blood splattered Bati's face and chest. She screamed into the gag.

The driver climbed between the seats "Help me get her to the boat."

The kidnapper with the missing finger grabbed a fist full of Bati's hair and jerked her into a sitting position. "Try anything, and I'll rip out your throat."

CHAPTER SEVEN

LADY SHIVA DABBED HER BRUSH IN YELLOW AND MIXED it with blue until she had just the right shade of green—the vibrant color of the summer grass on the steps of the Banaue Rice paddies north of Mount Pulag. She wore white socks and a baggy, paint-splattered shirt that hung half way to her knees. Her hair was piled on top of her head, held in place by a rubber band. With her tongue stuck in the corner of her mouth, she delicately added the marshy rice plateaus to her latest painting.

Most of her works were nature scenes; the Philippine countryside she remembered from her earliest childhood. Unframed canvases depicting mountains, thatched huts, and meadows were stacked against the walls of the simple art studio. The occasional portrait could be seen peeking out between the landscapes. The floor was scuffed hardwood, and the walls were cracked plaster. In the daytime, she painted under the skylight. Tonight she worked by the diffused glare of a light box she'd bought secondhand from a professional photographer.

She stepped back to survey the canvas. There was a knock at the door. Without taking her eyes from the painting, Shiva shouted, "Come."

Oscar entered, closed the door behind him, and stared at his sneakers. He had a cauliflower ear on the left side. The pulpy, disfigured flesh was proof of countless hours spent in a boxing ring. A sleeveless shirt revealed muscular arms. His usual swagger was gone, replaced by cowering obedience, which could only mean bad news.

"Well?" Shiva asked. "Where is she?"

"There was a problem," Oscar said. He refused to meet her gaze. He stared at a painting of the ocean instead. "The men I sent to pick her up are... missing."

"Missing," Shiva repeated. Her mouth turned up in a humorless smile. She pulled the rubber band out of her hair, re-gathered her tangled black tresses and bound them up again. As she did, the hem of her shirt climbed up. Oscar's eyes flicked to her naked thighs and then back to the painting.

"I waited," he said. "They never showed. I called. They aren't answering their mobiles. I even-"

Shiva cuffed his cauliflower ear with an open palm, cutting off his stream of excuses like a knife blade. "Stupid boy." She grabbed his cauliflower ear and twisted. Oscar bore the torment in silence. "Stupid, silly boy. I should have left you in the gutter where I found you."

She let him go and went back to her painting. She found a rag and dried her brush with more vigor than necessary. "What about the boyfriend? What's he got to say for himself?"

Oscar put a hand to his ear. "He isn't answering his phone. I checked his apartment. He isn't there."

"Find him," Shiva ordered. "If he doesn't know who has the girl then find out who does."

"Yes ma'am." Oscar slunk from the room with his head down and his muscular shoulders drawn up like a dog with its tail between its legs.

Shiva took the paintbrush in both hands, bared her teeth, and exerted all her strength in an attempt to snap the wood. A vein stood out in her forehead. The muscles in her slender forearms bunched. The wood refused to bend, much less break. She hurled it down with a curse.

CHAPTER EIGHT

Bakonawa Ramos gazed out over a sea of people crowding the main ballroom at the Willard in Washington D.C. The walls were paneled in dark wood, contrasted by green marble pillars. Crystal chandeliers hung from the ceiling like alien egg sacs. The women wore thousand-dollar gowns dripping with diamonds. The men sported black tie. Ramos stood on stage, resplendent in a hand-tailored tuxedo from Old Bond Street.

He had notes, but he didn't need them. Cue cards were for politicians—people reading someone else's script. Ramos spoke with conviction on a subject he knew intimately.

"Ladies and gentlemen, all over the world—right now— human beings are being bought and sold. According to the latest U.N. statistics, sex trafficking is a 36.2-billion-dollar industry. There are over 30 million people being trafficked as we speak. Over 80 percent of them are women, and 60 percent of those are minors. Most of these children are never heard from again. They disappear into an underground slave market that extends all the way from Southeast Asia, the Middle East, and Europe to South America and right here." He tapped the podium with two fingers. "In the United States of America. They are used like puppets and then discarded like trash."

He paused to let that information sink in. Several women gasped in shock and disgust. The small noises split the silence-like outraged shouts. Ramos nodded sympathetically.

He continued with his presentation. A projector threw grainy black-and-white images onto a screen behind him. Special Operations teams took the pictures during classified raids. Photos of half-naked, underfed children stuffed in cages like animals drove home the reality of the situation.

"Tonight, each and every one of you has the ability to make a difference," Ramos told the audience. "Every single dollar helps save a life. I hope you'll give generously."

Applause filled the hall. After his speech, Ramos milled through the crowd, thanking people for their support and donations. A senator from California grabbed his hand and pumped it enthusiastically. "I'd really like get you out to the West Coast for a fundraiser in my district," the senator said. "We've got deep pockets in California, and I can promise an appearance by Angelina Jolie."

Ramos smiled. "It would be my pleasure. Every bit helps. Let me put you in touch with my secretary, and she'll set up the details." He scanned the crowd, spotted Amanda Purdy, and waved her over. "Amanda handles all my speaking arrangements. I honestly don't know what I'd do without her. Mrs. Purdy, this is Senator Granger from California."

While Amanda hashed out the details with the senator, Ramos worked his way through the crowd to a redhead in a sea-foam green dress with sequins. She had a bright smile. She obviously took care of herself, and she wasn't wearing a ring.

He straightened his bowtie and passed a hand over his thinning hair. After Bati had graduated from college, Ramos found his thoughts turning more and more often to marriage. At fifty-two he was still young enough to have another child, maybe a son to carry on the family name.

The redhead greeted him with a smile.

He introduced himself.

"Heather Rainier," she said and offered her hand. "I think it's marvelous what you are doing to help victims of human trafficking."

"I couldn't do it without people like you," Ramos told her. He shifted the conversation from human trafficking to more pleasant matters. She laughed at his jokes. Soon he had forgotten all about his thinning hair and enjoyed her company instead. He was just about to ask if she had plans for Friday evening when Fredric Krakouer, his head of security, appeared over his left shoulder.

Heather took one look at Krakouer and retreated a step. Krakouer gave the impression of a man ready to do violence. He had a jutting jaw, a shaved head, and a puckered scar across the bridge of his nose. He ignored the girl, leaned in, and whispered. "I've got the head of Manila law enforcement on the phone, sir. He says it's urgent."

Krakouer held out a mobile.

Ramos offered Heather a tight smile. "Would you excuse me?"

He took the cell, located the nearest exit, and stepped into a carpeted hallway lined with potted plants and antique chairs that looked uncomfortable. The door clomped shut, cutting off the low rumble of conversation from the ballroom. Ramos put the phone to his ear. "This is Bakonawa Ramos. To whom am I speaking?"

Cold fear pumped through his veins as the Director General of the Philippine National Police Force explained that Bati had been kidnapped off the street a block from the women's shelter. Ramos went to one of the antique chairs, gripped the arm and lowered himself onto the seat.

"What do you want me to do, sir?" the Director General asked.

A vein pulsed in Ramos's forehead. "I want you to do your damn job and find my daughter!"

A young bellhop in hotel livery happened by at that moment. He stopped and hesitated, torn between the desire to help and to avoid trouble. One look from Krakouer sent the kid scurrying on his way.

Ramos hung up, tugged his bowtie loose, and opened the top button on his collar. The cold in his veins turned to poison, a witch's brew, seeping into his limbs and slowly working its way toward his heart. The thought of his little girl at the hands of his enemies made him want to vomit. He looked up at his head of security. "I want you on the first plane to Manila."

CHAPTER NINE

THE GULF OF MEXICO IS THE FINAL RESTING PLACE for hundreds of sunken ships. The warm body of water attracts hurricanes, and as a result, the ocean floor is littered with Spanish galleons, Civil War ships, and merchant vessels of every kind. Over the years, these shipwrecks have been a gold mine, literally, for explorers. Most of the treasure has been hauled away, but the silent wrecks remain beneath the placid surface as eerie reminders of the ocean's violent and unpredictable nature.

Less than three miles off the coast of Saint Petersburg, Florida lays the skeleton of an anonymous corvette dating back to the eighteenth century, dubbed *"the Lost Girl."* Historians have long debated the identity of the ship. The man who found her, a Florida native and professional treasure hunter named Henry Nester, salvaged nearly a quarter million in French livre from her holds. Once the silver was gone, interest in the wreck died down and *"the Lost Girl"* was left to her watery grave.

Jacob Noble, in red swim trunks with a yellow oxygen tank harnessed to his back, slipped into the sunken corvette through a gaping hole in the hull. He had a dive knife strapped to his calf and an underwater Nikon around his neck. He clicked on an LED flashlight and shined it around the gun deck. A school of brightly colored fish darted past him to open water. Noble watched the school disappear and then turned his attention back to *the Lost Girl.*"

She had surrendered to the depths so quickly that the crew had no time to abandon ship. Skeletal remains bobbed in the current. An octopus had taken up residence inside a yellowed ribcage. Thick green barnacles covered the brass cannon. Noble peered through the viewfinder on his underwater camera. The flash sent more tropical fish speeding away.

A current caught him and forced him up toward the ceiling. Noble let his camera dangle at the end of its tether and used his hand to stop himself from slamming into the overhead beams. Underwater currents could throw an unwary diver into a bulkhead with enough force to break bone or knock him unconscious.

He checked his dive computer. He had another thirty-two minutes of air. He took his time, exploring *the Lost Girl*" and snapping photos of anything he found interesting. The cannon made good material, as did the bow of the ship where barnacles were slowly claiming a wooden mermaid. Once he had what he came for, Noble took a few minutes for himself, enjoying the peace and solitude that could only be found in the silent depths.

Four years ago, after the CIA tossed him out of the Special Operations Group, Noble had been tempted to get drunk and stay drunk. Everything he had worked and trained for was gone in a flash. The world he thought he knew lay in a thousand tiny shards around his feet, and the bottom of a bottle looked mighty enticing. But he had seen too many other guys take that road after leaving the teams. Guys who he used to know and respect had ended up broken shells. Instead he took his camera and his boat and made a go at underwater photography. It didn't take long before he had a photo published in *Diver*.

It was good, honest work, even if the royalty checks were few and far between. He was good at it. It should have made him happy. But it didn't. He felt at loose ends with himself like a man in a foreign city where he didn't know the language. He felt out of his element.

He had gone over the attack in Doha countless times over the last four years. He asked himself over and over again if he had done the right thing. Could he have done anything different? At first it had all seemed so clear, so cut and dried. Now, four years on, it didn't feel so black and white. He found himself questioning whether he was really the team leader he thought, or if he had been reckless. He wished he had one last mission, one more chance to prove himself. He wanted to find out if he was a Special Operator unjustly discharged by the Company, or a screw-up.

With ten minutes left on his dive computer, Noble started for the surface and spotted a prowling bull shark. Attacks off the coast of Saint Petersburg were rare. Hungry predators were occasionally attracted by vacationers splashing in the shallows, but most sharks kept to the deeps. Swimmers didn't have much to worry about. Divers were another matter.

Giving the hunter a wide berth, Noble put on extra speed, using his flippers to propel himself through the water toward his wooden sailboat, *the Yeoman*. All of his attention was on the bull shark, and he almost missed the dinghy bobbing in the *Yeoman's* wake. He was five meters directly below the hull when he spotted the telltale shape of the smaller craft outlined against the shimmering green of the surface.

It might belong to a fisherman who had run into trouble and motored for the nearest vessel in search of help. There was an even better chance it belonged to a foreign operative with an automatic weapon and a score to settle.

Noble had kept a low profile for the last four years, but a determined hitter could have tracked him down. And as to who... Hell, Noble could think of a dozen people who wanted him dead.

He had six-and-a-half minutes of air left in the tank, and his only weapon was a dive knife. That didn't leave him a lot of options. A knife requires stealth, and it's hard to be sneaky in flippers and an oxygen tank. There was also the bull shark.

The seven-foot sea monster had circled back around, gliding effortlessly through the water less than seven meters away. One alien eyeball studied Noble with malevolent intent, like something out of a science fiction movie. The old-time fishermen said sharks could smell fear. Right now, Noble believed it. His heart was trying to beat its way out of his chest. He could hear the blood rushing in his ears.

Forced to choose between a bullet and being eaten by a shark, he decided to take his chances on a bullet. He

37

continued his ascent, and the bull shark followed, getting closer with every lap.

Noble paused under the hull of *the Yeoman* to drop his tank. He took a deep breath, released the plastic clips, and shrugged out of the harness. The weight of the oxygen tank carried it to the ocean floor trailing bubbles.

He pulled his knife and clamped it between his teeth before surfacing between the dinghy and *the Yeoman*. Hearing returned. Water lapped gently against the polished wood hull. Gulls cried overhead. Hawser lines creaked. The sun beat down, glinting on the surface of the water, and the smell of salty ocean air filled his nostrils.

Noble grasped the dinghy's gunwales and pulled himself up for a peek. It was a seven footer painted light blue with an onboard motor and a pair of oars, but no sign of the owner. He let go of the dinghy and turned his attention to *the Yeoman*. He couldn't see onto the deck from this angle, but no one started spraying bullets. So far so good.

He filled his lungs and ducked under the surface. The bull shark was less than four meters away now. It could close that distance in seconds. Noble fought the urge to panic. He wanted out of the water and fast, but panic gets soldiers killed.

He used the underside of *the Yeoman* to pull himself along, located the anchor chain, and hauled himself hand over hand out of the ocean. He didn't breathe a sigh of relief until his feet were out of the water as well.

He thrust his head over *the Yeoman's* bow. The deck was empty. Everything was just as he'd left it. His visitor must be below decks.

In the distance, he could see Treasure Island. It was a

strip of white sand and brightly painted hotels on the horizon. Three miles looked tantalizingly close, but he would never make it that far against the current with a curious bull shark nosing around.

Noble slipped over the gunwale, kicked off his flippers, and belly crawled across the sunbaked deck toward the cabin windows for a look inside. It felt like crawling over the surface of a hot frying pan. His bare skin squeaked against the wood.

The noonday sun turned the windows into bright mirrors that showed Noble his own reflection. He would have to cup his hands against the glass if he wanted to see anything. He paused, imagining himself putting his face to the glass and catching a bullet. A hitter could be sitting inside waiting for him to pop his head up, but it couldn't be helped. He swallowed his fear, pulled himself the last few inches, and rose up to his elbows for a look.

CHAPTER TEN

WHAT HE SAW THROUGH THE SUN-DRENCHED GLASS
made him curse. Matthew Burke sat wedged between the
galley table and the bulkhead, drinking Noble's coffee,
eating a plate full of his eggs and bacon. Noble didn't mind
the eggs or the coffee, but eating another man's bacon
crossed a line. He sheathed the knife and stomped around
to the cabin door. "I just dumped a two-hundred-dollar dive
tank on the ocean floor because of you."

Burke picked a bit of food from between his teeth with
one thick pinkie finger. "Good to see you, too."

Burke was a Georgia boy, born and raised in
Savannah by his grandmother. At six foot four and nearly
three hundred pounds, he looked like a baby bear
squeezed inside a garish, yellow Bermuda shirt. In college
he had played inside linebacker for Georgia Tech and
spent a lot of time in the weight room. Now the only
thing he pushed was paper. Long hours behind a desk
were taking their toll. He had started to go gray at the

temples and the lines around his eyes were deeper than Noble remembered.

When the mission in Doha went bad, Noble turned to Burke. As Noble's mentor inside the Company, Burke should have gone to bat for his protégé. Instead, Burke watched in silence while the Director hung Noble out to dry. Now he sat on Noble's boat as if nothing had happened.

Noble went to the cabinet over the sink and drew out a .45 caliber pistol hidden between a box of protein bars and instant oatmeal. "I ought to put a bullet in you."

Burke speared eggs with his fork and shoveled them into his mouth. "Go ahead."

Noble centered the front sight on Burke's chest and pulled the trigger. The hammer fell on an empty chamber with a hollow click.

Burke put the fork down and managed to look offended. "I'm hurt. You were actually going to shoot me?" He reached into his shirt pocket, brought out the magazine, and laid it on the tabletop.

"I knew it was empty," Noble said. "The weight wasn't right." He laid the handgun on the countertop, poured a cup of coffee, and slipped into the bench across from Burke.

"What if I had left one in the chamber?"

"Sloppy tradecraft," Noble said with a shrug. "A bullet in the chest is less than you deserve."

"Come on, Jake. You killed a politician."

"He was neck deep in human trafficking and had ties to Hamas."

"He was unarmed," Burke said.

"It was the heat of combat. He had his hand in his

jacket. When there is doubt, there is no doubt." Noble jabbed a finger across the table at Burke. "You taught me that, remember?"

Burke held up both hands. "Sometimes ops go sideways. You knew the risks when you took the job."

Noble scrubbed his face with both hands.

On the bench next to Burke lay a file with EYES ONLY stamped in red across the cover. He picked it up and dropped it on the table.

"What's this?" Noble instinctively reached for the file. On top of a slim pile of papers he found a black-and-white 8X10 of an Asian girl with bright eyes, a wide mouth, and straight black hair. The photo was an enlargement of a student ID from Yale.

"That is Bati Malaya Ramos. She was abducted twenty-nine hours ago."

"Daughter of Bakonawa Ramos?" Noble asked.

Burke nodded.

Ramos was a well-known champion in the fight against human trafficking. As a diplomat, he campaigned to raise awareness and funds to battle trafficking rings all over the Middle East, Asia, and South America. Behind the scenes, he fed info to the CIA. He had been instrumental in the mission that ended Noble's career.

"The daughter's a crusader just like her old man. After graduating Yale, she moved to Manila where she opened a Christian shelter for women. You know the type of place I'm talking about. They try to wean the girls off drugs, introduce them to Jesus, that sort of thing. Everyone from the traffickers to crooked police tried to shut her down. A combination of Daddy's money and sheer tenacity kept the operation running."

"Then she has enemies," Noble said.

"Looks like the kidnappers knew who they were after, too," Burke said. "They snatched her a block from the shelter. She was walking with her boyfriend, a local by the name of Diego Hawa. No one has seen him since."

"What do the kidnappers want?" Noble asked.

"We don't know yet. Ramos has gone dark. We found out about the kidnapping through other channels."

Noble chewed the inside of one cheek. "We should have been his first phone call."

Burke nodded. "And if he's not talking with us, we have to assume he's talking with the kidnappers. You and I both know if he gives in to their demands, they'll kill the girl."

Burke dislodged himself, took his empty plate to the sink, poured another cup of coffee, and sat back down with a grunt of effort. "The Director is worried that if Ramos loses his daughter, the goose will stop laying golden eggs. Ramos feeds us a lot of actionable intel. We want you to go over there, find Bati, and bring her home."

A wry smile turned up one side of Noble's mouth. Burke had manipulated him. People who went to work for the Company were puzzle-solvers by nature; it was in their blood. Noble was no exception. Put a problem in front of him, and he would lie awake at night until he solved it. Burke handed him a puzzle and let Noble's instincts take over. Noble closed the file and passed it back. "I don't work for you anymore."

Burke cradled his coffee mug in both hands and propped his elbows on the table. "The Company is prepared to offer you $150,000 if you can bring the girl back alive."

Since the debacle in Vietnam, the United States government had not been overly kind to the men and women who protect their borders. They hadn't even given Noble a severance package when they cut him loose. According to the Director, he should be happy he wasn't going to Leavenworth. Now they were offering him $150,000 for a single job. Mighty generous. He whistled. "Sounds a little too good to be true."

"Time is against us," Burke admitted. "Bati is type-one diabetic. If she doesn't get insulin soon, she'll go into a diabetic coma and die. If we play by the book, the girl doesn't stand a chance. We need someone who can bend a few rules."

Noble snorted and shook his head. "And if it all goes sideways, the CIA can deny any involvement."

Burke conceded the point with a shrug. "South East Asia is your territory, Jake. No other agent knows that corner of the world better. If anyone has a shot at bringing Bati home alive, it's you."

Noble leaned back in his seat, raked both hands through his hair, and exhaled. He didn't want to be manipulated by the Company into mercenary work. It was a slippery slope. Once he started down that path, it would be hard to turn back.

"How much do you make taking photos for *Deep Sea Diver*?" Burke thrust his chin at the July issue on the countertop. One of Noble's pictures graced the front cover. Photography put diesel in the engine and coffee in the cupboard but didn't leave much left over. Most nights Noble had to catch his dinner.

Burke tapped a thick, black finger against the stack of unpaid medical bills in a brass holder shaped like an octopus. "Do it for her."

That comment pushed Noble to the tipping point. "Get the hell off my boat."

Burke drained his coffee, stood up, and went to the cabin door. "The clock is ticking on this girl's life, Jake. We need your answer by sundown."

Burke stepped topside. Noble sat at the galley table and refused to move until he heard the onboard motor crank. Then he got up, reloaded his weapon, and watched through the window until Burke and the dinghy disappeared from sight.

CHAPTER ELEVEN

Noble motored around the southern tip of Saint Petersburg and docked *the Yeoman* in its slip at South Yacht Basin. His father had been a sailing man. He bought *the Yeoman* when Jake was twelve. Together they spent the next nine years painstakingly restoring her. The old wooden schooner stood out amid the floating parking lot of glaring white fiberglass hulls bristling with modern antenna arrays.

Jeremiah Noble had spent twenty years in the Navy and another ten with a commercial shipping outfit. When he dropped dead of a heart attack at fifty-seven, Jake inherited the ship. During his time with the Green Berets, he had used her to unwind after grueling fourteen-month tours in Iraq and Afghanistan. After Burke recruited him into the Special Operations Group, Noble had put her in dry dock. Work with the Company didn't leave much time for anything else. His team was either on a mission, gearing up for a mission, or planning a mission. All that changed after being unceremoniously drummed out of the company.

Noble burned through his savings account, had to give up his apartment, and *the Yeoman* became his home.

He toyed with the idea of selling her but never gave it any serious thought. He needed it for work as an under-water photographer, at least that's what he told himself. The truth was *the Yeoman* symbolized the last piece of his father. It was the only thing he had to hold onto. Noble would never willingly give up the old girl.

He changed into linen slacks, suede lace-ups, and a white cotton button down. It was late September. The mercury in Saint Petersburg hovered just under 85 degrees Fahrenheit. Noble slipped a Bersa .380acp into a leather holster at the small of his back. The Argentinian-made semi-automatic was small enough to conceal and packed enough punch to get him out of a scrape.

In the parking lot, he pulled the cover off a 1970 Buick GSX hardtop. It needed a new carburetor and the transmission was ready for an overhaul—Noble didn't have the money—but the engine was solid. It turned over on the first try.

He cranked up the air conditioner, pulled out of the parking lot, and turned onto Bay Shore, enjoying the feel of the big V-8 engine. Noble liked old machines, machines made to last, made with character and class. Driving, sailing, flying—these were activities to be savored in Noble's opinion. And the best way to do that was in a vehicle he'd re-built with his own two hands.

That good feeling evaporated, however, as he turned into the parking lot at Saint Anthony's Hospital. He found a spot in the shade and entered through the emergency room doors. A dozen people occupied hard plastic seats.

Some sipped vending machine coffee. Others thumbed messages into smart phones. A mother bounced a two-year-old on her knee, making shushing noises. Her eyes were rimmed in red. The smell of disinfectant clung to every surface, trying in vain to mask the lingering scent of death and heartache.

Noble took the elevator to the second floor and spotted Doctor Lansky coming out of a patient room with a clipboard stuck under one arm. He wore glasses and walked with his head thrust forward like an overgrown vulture. Lansky recognized Noble and pushed his glasses up the bridge of his hooked nose. "Mister Noble, I'm glad you are here."

"How is she today?"

"She is feeling better."

"Any change?" Noble asked.

He paused a beat. "Maybe we should talk in my office."

Lansky led the way to a small room lit by lifeless fluorescents. Medical degrees hung on the walls. The doctor sat behind his desk, and Noble sat across from him.

"I think it is time to bring in hospice, Mister Noble," Lansky said.

Noble gripped the arms of the chair. "Are you saying there is nothing more you can do?"

"Your mother's treatment has exceeded the cap on her medical coverage. I'm afraid any further treatment would have to be paid for out of pocket."

"You didn't answer my question."

Lansky sighed. "We could try another round of chemotherapy. But out-of-pocket expense is very costly, and there is no guarantee that it will work."

"Do it," Noble told him.

"I'm afraid that's not up to me," Lansky said. "The hospital won't authorize any more treatments until they know who is going to pay for it."

Noble's knuckles turned white. He spoke through clenched teeth. "I'll get the money. Just make sure she gets the treatment."

Lansky pressed his lips together, but nodded. "I have to prepare you. If this doesn't work, it's only a matter of time."

"I understand." Noble heard the words coming out of his mouth. His hands and feet felt disconnected from his body. He swallowed a hard lump in his throat. "Is she awake today?"

"Awake and telling me all about the Apostle Paul."

"Yeah." Noble rolled his eyes. "He's one of her favorites."

Lansky forced a smile. "I'd better get on with my rounds."

Noble shook the doctor's hand and then made his way to room 214. He paused with his hand on the latch. Part of him wanted to turn around, drive back to the marina, get on the boat, and sail until he ran out of gas. Losing his father had been hard enough. Noble had been deployed to Afghanistan at the time. He got home two days after the funeral. Dad was already dead and in the ground. It all happened so fast. In a way, it was a good thing. Disaster struck and then Noble got on with the process of healing. This was different. Watching his mother waste away felt like living with a demon eating his soul. He took a deep breath and pushed the latch.

It was a dual-occupancy room painted pale green.

Machines beeped and hummed. Sometimes Jake wondered if those machines had a purpose or if they existed to break up the silence.

In the bed next to the window, Mary Elise Noble sat up with a Bible open to Ephesians on her lap. She had an IV in one arm and a half dozen wires snaking out the armholes of her hospital smock. Her hair was gray. Her frail chest labored for every breath, but her eyes still had the spark of life in them.

She smiled. "How did your pictures turn out?"

"I think I got some good stuff." He tried and failed to get comfortable in the hard plastic seat next to the bed. "Lots of cannon with barnacles. Magazines love that sort of thing. How are you feeling?"

"Grateful," she told him. "Every day with the Lord is a good day."

It wasn't quite the answer he was hoping for. He pinched the bridge of his nose. "If God is so damn good, how come there is so much evil in the world?"

She planted her boney hands on the mattress and made an effort to push herself up straighter in bed. "He made men like you to stand up to evil."

The words drilled right to his core. The idea that he might be God's answer to evil, ordained by a higher power, struck Noble as strangely poetic. It was also the very same reasoning extremists had used to justify some of history's worst atrocities. The Caliphates who attacked Spain and got the ball rolling on the First Crusade believed they were ordained by God. What made Noble any different?

Besides, if God did exist, Noble had an altogether different question he wanted answered. Forget all the megalomaniacs of the world. They could kill each other from now until doomsday for all Noble cared. He wanted to know why a loving God would let his father and now his mother die.

Mary Elise Noble reached over, took her son's hand, and squeezed. Her skin felt like dry paper. A sad smile formed on her lips. As if she could read his thoughts, she said, "We take the time given to us and make the best of it."

Noble sat in brooding silence.

"They want you back?" she said. It was more of a statement than a question.

"Yeah," he said. "How'd you know?"

"I'm your mother," she said. "And you get all quiet before a mission."

He grinned.

"Is it bad?"

He hitched up his shoulders. "Bad enough."

"When should I start to worry?"

"A week," he told her.

She nodded. As a Navy wife, she had gotten used to long absences. At least Dad had been able to say where he was going and when he'd be back. Jake could only give her vague time frames and promise to be careful.

"When do you have to leave?" she asked.

"Right away."

He wanted to say more. He wanted to tell her how much he loved her. He wanted to say he couldn't bear to lose her and beg her to get better. Some nights, lying in his bunk and feeling the ship roll on the ocean, he begged a God he didn't believe in. He shook his fists at heaven while tears spilled down his cheeks. He pleaded, cursed, and cajoled. Waves lapping against the hull was the only answer he ever got.

He placed a kiss on the back of her hand. "I'll visit soon as I get back."

"Be careful," she said.

"I will."

On his way across the parking lot, Noble dialed Matt's number and put the phone to his ear. Burke picked up on the first ring. "You in?"

Noble unlocked the Buick and stood in the open door with his elbows propped on the roof. "I get half up front."

"Done," Burke said. "Be at the Birchwood in two hours."

CHAPTER TWELVE

Across from Straub Park in downtown Saint Petersburg, commanding a view of Tampa Bay, stands the Birchwood Hotel. Built as apartments in the 1920s, it has since been renovated and now looks like someone turned a Spanish mission into a posh nightclub. The top floor is an open-air bar called the Canopy where singles go to hunt.

Noble strolled into the air-conditioned lounge and found Burke in a corner wearing a summer weight suit and sipping a fruity cocktail with a little umbrella in it. Noble sat across from him and indicated Burke's choice of drinks with raised eyebrows. "You look ridiculous."

Burke smiled around the stem of a curly straw. "I'm secure in my manhood."

"You'd have to be," Noble remarked.

Burke reached into a leather attaché case and produced a sealed package. "The alibi shop worked around the clock putting together a legend on such short notice. All your documents are inside."

Next, he brought out a small black kit containing syringes and a battery-powered tester. "Your sugar kit," he explained. "All diabetics carry one. Your passport lists you as type one. You're cleared to travel with those. Don't lose them."

Noble picked it up and turned it over in his hands. He didn't know much about diabetes. "How long can Bati last without these?"

Burke shrugged. "Hard to say. Diabetes is different from person to person. Our best guess, according to her medical profile, is four or five days. She always carried a shot in her purse. But who knows if the kidnappers let her take it."

"It's already been thirty-two hours," Noble said. "She'll be well into day three before I even land in the Philippines."

"That's why we hired the best," Burke said. He reached into his jacket, brought out a Samsung, and passed it over. It would be preprogrammed with numbers that matched Noble's cover identity in the Philippines, plus photos and apps that backed up his legend. Noble passed Burke his real cell phone and took a moment to thumb through the Samsung.

"What time is my flight?" he asked.

"You fly out of Tampa International at 7:15. You'll need to memorize your legend in flight."

Noble consulted his Tag Heuer. It was already ten minutes to four. "That doesn't give me much time to pack."

"Don't waste it talking to me," Burke said. He picked up his cocktail and slurped the last of the pink mix from the bottom of the glass. The straw gurgled.

Noble had his mission, and the clock was ticking. He gathered up the sealed package with his passport and papers along with the insulin kit, stood up, and started for the door.

"Jake?"

Noble stopped but didn't turn around.

"Sorry about the way things turned out."

"Me too," Noble said and walked away.

CHAPTER THIRTEEN

BURKE FLAGGED DOWN THE WAITRESS, ORDERED another strawberry daiquiri, and then used Jake's phone to put in a call to the Deputy Director. He sat back and counted eight rings before a voice filled the line.

"This is Clark S. Foster. To whom am I speaking?"

It was the kind of nasal voice that assaulted the ears. Burke could picture Foster at his desk dressed in a bow tie, tweed coat, and coke-bottle glasses riding low on the end of a long nose.

"It's Burke."

The waitress returned with his drink. Burke thanked her with a smile.

"Mr. Burke, I didn't recognize the number."

"I'm calling from Noble's cell," Burke told him.

"Highly unorthodox, Mr. Burke."

"My battery is dead," Burke lied.

Seeing an unknown number on his private line, Foster had run a trace. That's why it took him so long to pick up.

He could end the trace, but it would look suspicious to the listening intelligence officers. There was a long moment of silence and then Foster said, "I trust you have good news?"

Burke took a moment to appreciate a leggy blonde on the arm of an older man. "Noble's on board."

"I hope you are right about this." Foster had switched into PR mode. "The director wants that girl home safe by any means necessary."

Burke rolled his eyes. Bureaucrats in the intelligence community were less than useless; they were liabilities. "If anyone can find her, it's Jake."

"I trust your judgment," Foster said, still performing for the recording. "I expect regular updates."

"Yes, sir." Burke ended the call.

He put the phone on the table and picked up his drink. Burke believed in the mission of the CIA—someone had to keep tabs on the bad guys—but he had no illusions about the people he worked for. They were politicians. The likelihood of bringing Bati home alive was slim and, after the snafu in Doha, Foster wasn't about to send any of his own people, but he'd been ordered from on high.

Foster was a bureaucrat, plain and simple. He had no field experience. A Harvard graduate, he had come up through SIGINT, got lucky on a few operations and rubbed all the right elbows. His appointment was purely political.

While Foster was busy trying to insulate himself, Burke was looking for a way to bring Noble back onto the reservation. The kid was probably one of the best SOG agents Burke had ever recruited. It pained him to watch Jake get tossed out in the cold.

When the director of the CIA ordered Foster to mount

a rescue operation, Foster dragged his heels. He tried desperately to pass the buck. He knew the operation had a slim chance of success. The resulting failure would be a black mark on his otherwise unblemished service record. Burke saw the opportunity he had been waiting for and submitted Noble's name. The kid could get the job done, but if it went sideways they'd both swing. A hard knot formed in Burke's chest. He took a long sip of his strawberry daiquiri and tried not to think about all the things that could go wrong.

CHAPTER FOURTEEN

FREDERICK KRAKOUER ARRIVED ON THE 10:45 FLIGHT to Manila, dressed in khakis and a polo. He was tired and slightly drunk on Dos Equis. He collected his duffle from the luggage carousel and made his way through the airport to the car rental, eager to pick up Bati's trail and punish the people responsible. Saving the girl was the job; busting a few heads along the way was icing on the cake. But first he paid a visit to his Philippine girlfriend.

Maria lived in six-floor walkup with paper-thin walls and loud neighbors. Krakouer met her five years ago during one of Ramos's annual trips. She danced at a club called Sour Grapes. She was rail thin and double jointed with a flat bottom, but she was pretty enough in her own way. She had other boyfriends. Krakouer knew about them. It did not bother him. What he and Maria had was strictly business. She knew when he was in town, the others had to wait. He found a parking spot on the street, climbed six flights of stairs, and hammered on number 603.

Maria opened the door, saw who it was, stepped out into the hall, and pulled the door closed. "I have company."

"Get rid of him," Krakouer said.

"Maybe we could go somewhere else? A hotel?" She grasped Krakouer's hand and smiled. "I'll take real good care of you, baby."

Krakouer gave her a hard stare. "Get rid of him or I will."

Before she could say anything else, a Filipino man in shorts and sandals opened the door. He looked Krakouer over and scowled. "Who is this guy, babe?"

Maria drew her shoulders up and stared hard at the ground.

"Get lost." Krakouer jerked a thumb over his shoulder.

The guy was six inches shorter and forty pounds lighter, but that didn't stop him from wagging a finger under Krakouer's nose. "Think you can do whatever you want with your American money? Mess with me, and I'll kill you."

Krakouer grabbed his index finger and twisted. The knuckle separated with an audible pop. The guy opened his mouth to scream, but never got the chance. Krakouer hit him with an uppercut. His teeth clapped shut, his head rocked back, and his knees buckled.

He sprawled out on the ground in a semi-conscious daze.

Krakouer took a moment to study him like a farmer trying to decide what to do with a lame cow, then he proceeded to pummel him. Each punch fell with a meaty crack. Droplets of blood dotted the floor and the front of Krakouer's blue polo. Maria stood with her back pressed against the wall, her face turned away, and her eyes squeezed shut. Her boyfriend was unconscious and bleeding when Krakouer dragged him out of the doorframe onto the landing. He shoved Maria inside the apartment and kicked the door shut.

Maria summoned up her courage. "You didn't have to-"

Krakouer shut her up with a slap. "Take off your clothes and get in bed."

She did as she was told. He followed her into the bedroom. He wasn't gentle. When it was over Maria lay on the far side of the bed with her face to the wall. Krakouer smoked a cigarette. He had been rough with her, but she deserved it. Women needed a firm hand. Krakouer learned that watching his father knock his mother around. The first time one of Krakouer's girlfriends started to mouth off, he had cracked her a good one right across the face.

He could still remember the sound and the way she looked afterward. He thought for sure she would walk out on him. Amazingly enough, she stuck around. She took several more beatings and eventually learned to behave. From that day on, Krakouer had never hesitated to discipline one of his women.

He stabbed his cigarette out on the bedside table and dressed. He took a few bills from his wallet and dropped them next to the cigarette butt.

The stairwell was empty except for blood splatters. A trail led down the steps. The guy must have crawled away while Krakouer was servicing Maria. Krakouer went downstairs and climbed into his rental.

In the last decade, Internet cafes had sprung up all over metro Manila. Krakouer thought of them as nightclubs for nerds. The Infinity Cyber Café on Taft had three floors dedicated to everything from simple business needs to state of the art gaming.

Krakouer made his way up to the second floor where teenagers stared at glowing screens, sipping Mountain Dew and chain-smoking cigarettes. It was like stepping into a dimly lit cave. He spotted a skinny kid with a pathetic attempt at a mustache, wearing a Seven Nation Army t-shirt, hunched over a computer terminal. His hacker name was Gage. What his real name was, Krakouer didn't know.

Krakouer took the empty computer terminal next to Gage, reached across and tapped a bunch of random keys. On screen, Gage's army man made wild loop-the-loops. Before he could recover, another player blew him up with a rocket launcher. Gage threw both hands into the air. "Dude! Seriously?"

"I'm looking for the missionary chick," Krakouer told him. "The one who got kidnapped. Know anything about that?"

Gage had restarted his game and was busy mowing down bad guys with some kind of futuristic laser rifle. "Your boss usually pays me for information."

Krakouer grabbed Gage's crotch and squeezed. The kid's eyes tried to bug right out of his skull. He hunched over the keyboard and let out a pathetic moan. Everyone else in the room had headphones on. They were too focused on their games to notice Gage twisting in pain and whimpering.

"Her boyfriend sold her out to Lady Shiva," Gage spluttered. "He's a lowlife gambler. Owes several large to bookies."

Krakouer let him go. "Keep talking."

"Shiva never got the girl. She disappeared. Shiva thinks Diego double-crossed her. Everyone in town is looking for him, including the cops. Find him, you'll find her."

"Got an address?"

Gage tabbed out of his video game, brought up an Internet browser, and jabbed at the keys. Sweat beaded on his forehead. His hands shook as he worked. "He's got an apartment on K-1." He gave Krakouer the apartment number.

"If you find out anything new, call me right away. Understood?"

Gage cupped his crotch in both hands and nodded. "Yeah, Okay. Fine."

Krakouer gave him a pat on the back hard enough to knock the kid face first into the keyboard and then he got up and walked out.

CHAPTER FIFTEEN

THE YELLOW ZIP-TIE BIT INTO BATI'S FLESH. DRIED blood crusted both wrists. Her long black hair hung in damp tangles. She lay curled up in the hold of an empty cargo ship. Dirt and grime had turned her pink panties gray. The cold metal floor gave her goose bumps. Thick rust layered the walls, and the corners were shrouded in darkness. Her only light came from a weak bulb fixed to the bulkhead.

She didn't know how long she had been in the ship. The kidnappers had dragged her, kicking and struggling, onto the freighter, shoved her into the hold, and slammed the hatch. The bolt had shot home with all the finality of a judge's gavel. After that, Bati had sat with her back to the wall and listened to the steady churning of the engines and the rush of water.

She spent the first few hours sobbing through the shorts stuffed into her mouth. Unreasoning panic and terror gripped her. The fear of what these men might do next drove out rational thought. She knocked her head against the metal floor in an effort to get rid of the awful images in her mind. Eventually the panic subsided. The fear lost some of its urgency. Then she turned to prayer. First she prayed for rescue. Then she began to question. Why would God let this happen to her?

She got no answers.

The engines had stopped some time ago. A foghorn bellowed in the distance. Bati sat up enough to check the inside of her naked thighs for the red streaks that would mean her system was turning septic. Her skin was still a healthy tan, but that wouldn't last. She laid her head back down.

So far the kidnappers hadn't fed her. It was a blessing in disguise. Food would spike her blood sugar, and she had no insulin to counteract. She had a syringe in her purse but didn't know if the kidnappers had kept it or left it in the van. Sooner or later her blood sugar would start to climb, and she would need that insulin shot.

She heard muffled voices outside the hold. She sat up, put her back to the wall, and pressed her knees together. Her heart galloped inside her chest. The locks released with an echoing clang, and the door groaned open on tired hinges.

The kidnappers high-stepped through the hatchway. They had removed the pantyhose, and Bati got a look at their faces. The short, stocky one had found a proper bandage for his missing forefinger. He had lost a lot of blood, and it showed on his face. He glared at Bati. The other man looked all business. He had a pistol tucked in the waistband of his black trousers. "Help me get her in the car."

Bati tried desperately to communicate through the gag. If she could only explain about diabetes maybe they would understand and let her have the insulin. But neither man paid her wordless moans any attention. They grabbed her by the arms and hauled her out of the hold. Cruel fingers dug into her flesh.

The shipping freighter had moored inside a massive dock house. Early morning sunlight streamed in through holes in the walls. A few small windows were covered over with old newspaper. A dark sedan waited at the end of the pier with the trunk open. Bati lashed out with her feet, growling through the shorts jammed in her mouth. It did no good. The two men picked her up and forced her inside the trunk. The lid came down with a *thump*, shutting out the light.

CHAPTER SIXTEEN

NOBLE EXITED THE INTERNATIONAL TERMINAL AT Ninoy Aquino Airport wearing a gray suit over a white button down with a carry-on bag slung over one shoulder. He paused on the sidewalk long enough to take in his surroundings. A passenger jet roared overhead. Taxis jockeyed for position. Horns bleated. The smell of industrial smog and waste mingled together into a pungent sweet aroma. A hint of ocean breeze hid beneath the stench like a lover's perfume. His heart beat a little harder. He hadn't realized how much he missed the thrill of an operation until now.

It was just after two in the afternoon. The sun beat down, and the hunt was on. Bati had been missing for sixty-six hours. Time was running out. Noble had to work fast. His first order of business was to arm himself. He used the burner cell provided by Burke to place a call to an old friend in Manila Branch who owed him a favor.

A gravelly voice filled the line. "Hola."

"It's me," Noble said. "I'm in town for a few days. I'm going to need a good pair of walking shoes."

"When?"

"Meet me at the Arch in thirty minutes," Noble said.

There was a pause and then a heavy sigh. "You could have called ahead."

"It was a spur-of-the-moment trip," Noble told him. "Can you make it?"

"I'll be there."

Noble slipped the phone in his pocket and ignored the green airport taxis for a white city taxi, which had just dropped off a woman and her young son. Noble slipped into the back seat. The cracked leather upholstery groaned under his weight. The interior of the cab smelled like boiled cabbage. The driver, a rail thin Filipino with a mop of unruly hair, took Noble for a tourist and tried to overcharge. It was standard practice for a white face coming out of the international terminal.

Noble told the driver to run the meter and gave directions in Tagalog.

"You speak Filipino?" the driver asked pointlessly.

"A little," Noble lied.

The driver worked his way through the congested airport traffic and merged onto Carlos P. Garcia Avenue headed toward Marikina in the northeast. "Where did you learn Tagalog," he wanted to know.

"Business school."

"You speak it well."

The driver kept up a running dialog the whole way. He

asked a string of questions that Noble answered with vague generalities, laying down the cover story worked up by the alibi shop. His name was Todd Michaels. He worked for an import business and had been in Manila many times over the last ten years. No family, but he had an on-again, off-again girlfriend in Quezon. He slouched in the seat and tried to look tired from a thirty-two-hour flight. It didn't take much acting.

The highway looped past the American cemetery. A massive circular sward of green with row upon row of headstones memorialized the men who fought and died here in World War II. The stone crosses glowed white under the harsh midday sun.

Thirty minutes later, the driver dropped Noble off in front of the Marikina Arch. It wasn't much to look at, just a Spanish-style wall with a clock set in the face, but at night, when it was lit up, it took on a romantic appearance. There was a fountain in front in the middle of the square, but it wasn't flowing. Try as he might, Noble had never figured out the fountain's schedule. It seemed to come on at random and never at the same time each day.

Manny was already there, sitting on the low wall of the fountain, snacking on a cup of sweet taho. He had dripped chocolate syrup down his shirt. He was a middle-aged man with a potbelly and a pockmarked face. A brown paper sack sat beside him on the wall.

Noble joined him, taking a seat on the fountain with the paper sack between them. A crowd milled around the arch. From the nearby park, Noble heard the peculiar crack of tennis balls shuttled back and forth across the court and the energetic grunts of the players.

"Welcome back, my friend," Manny said through a mouthful of taho.

"How have you been?" Noble asked.

He shrugged. "I've got a bad case of the gout. The ex-wife takes everything I make in alimony, and I'm forced to sell black market merchandise to former Company men just to pay the rent. Take my advice, don't get married."

"Hadn't planned on it."

"How long will you be in town?"

"A few days," Noble told him.

"Does it have anything to do with the missing girl?"

"I'm just taking in the sights," Noble said.

"You know the head of Manila branch is breathing fire," Manny said and chuckled. "He thinks our office should have been assigned to the girl. He knows the company is bringing somebody in to find her, but he doesn't know who."

"Are you going to blow the whistle?"

"And admit I'm in contact with a blacklisted agent? I have enough troubles." Manny thrust the cup of taho under Noble's nose. "Do you want any of this?"

Noble waved him off. He nodded to the sack. "My shoes?"

Manny inclined his head. "Need anything else?"

"If I do I'll call," Noble told him. He handed Manny a wad of pesos and took the sack. "So long, old friend."

"Happy hunting."

A shoebox filled the sack.

Noble clamped it under one arm, hailed a cab, and gave the driver an address. Bati's boyfriend had an apartment on K-1. Diego hadn't gone to the police after his girlfriend was snatched, and he hadn't been home either. Hardly the actions of an innocent man. He might as well have signed a confession. The local authorities wanted him for questioning in connection with the kidnapping. Noble decided to start with Diego's apartment in the hopes that he would find something the police had missed.

CHAPTER SEVENTEEN

NOBLE SAT BEHIND THE DRIVER'S SEAT SO HE COULD
open the shoebox without being observed. Inside he found a
compact .45 caliber Armscor pistol with tritium night
sights, two extra magazines topped off with hollow-point
ammo and a leather holster.

He grinned. "Thank you, Manny."

"Excuse me?" The driver glanced in the rearview.

"Nothing," Noble said. He leaned forward and tucked
the holstered weapon in his back waistband, pocketed the
extra magazines, and crammed the empty shoebox into the
floorboard. When he looked up, he recognized the neighborhood. "Drop me here."

"You don't want to get out here." The driver waved
away the idea. "It's not a very nice part of town."

"Stop here," Noble ordered.

The driver, after a shrug, put on the brakes.

Noble paid, opened the door, and slung his carry-on
over his left shoulder. He wanted to be sure no one was

tailing him, and this was a good place to run a surveillance detection route. More importantly, he wanted to reacquaint himself with the neighborhood. Places are a lot like people; each has its own unique personality. Noble wandered the streets, getting a feel for the maze of rundown apartments and corner stores. Cars clogged the intersections. Kids in cheap plastic sandals chased each other. In the distance, a jackhammer rumbled. Shadows stretched as the sun made its way across the sky.

A young man dressed in knockoff designer wear approached Noble with a toothy grin. "Hello, my friend. I work at the hotel. Do you remember me? Are you lost? I can help you."

It was a regular con the locals ran on unsuspecting tourists. A man would claim he worked at their hotel and that he recognized them. He'd offer to help them find their destination or the best shopping. Instead he would lure them into a dead-end alley where his buddies would relieve them of their money and valuables.

"Try someone else," Noble said.

The young con hurled curses at Noble's back as he walked away.

He turned the corner onto K-1 Street and knew right away that his instincts had paid off. It was a good thing he hadn't let the cab driver drop him in front of the building. He wasn't the only one interested in the boyfriend. The street was full of people watching Diego's front door. There was an Asian girl in a white Toyota parked directly across the street. Coffee cups decorated her dashboard. A pair of thugs parked two car lengths behind her in a beat-up minivan with balding tires. And a white guy with a scar

73

across the bridge of his nose sat in a dark sedan at the end of the block. He had parked with his bumper facing away from Diego's building and used the rearview to watch the front door. He was the closest thing to a professional in this little farce.

The hard cases in the minivan were hired muscle. The driver had short-cropped hair and a cauliflower ear. He looked like he knew how to handle himself. The fatty in the passenger seat was strictly window dressing. Who sent them and why was the only question.

The big foreigner in the dark sedan was either international law enforcement sent to investigate Bati's disappearance or a Company man. It wasn't unheard of for the CIA to send spies to watch their spies.

The girl was a big question mark. She had black hair and dark eyes, but her features weren't Filipino. Spend enough time in Asian cultures, and you begin to recognize the subtle differences. At a guess, Noble would say she was Chinese. She wasn't a cop. He was sure of that. She might be a reporter.

He redirected his steps without slowing down. It forced him to cross in front of the dark sedan, but that was unavoidable. To stop and turn around would look suspicious. He passed the front bumper and locked eyes with the driver. Noble nodded at the brutish face behind the steering wheel. The driver returned a sullen stare.

Noble circled the block in search of a back entrance. A narrow lane between buildings gave him access to a trash-strewn alley full of stray cats and one cast-off engine block. He found the back door to Diego's building and let himself in. The lobby was a sad affair, just a narrow hall with cracked linoleum. A row of mailboxes and stairs led to the second floor. A tabby cat napped on the fourth step. She opened one eye as Noble approached. He stopped long enough to scratch under her chin. She rewarded him with a loud, contented purr.

Diego lived in number three. A notice from the police was taped to the door requesting he report to the local precinct for questioning. Noble crumpled the note and shook his head. He took a pair of picks from the lining of his wallet. It took him thirty seconds to scrub the lock. He inserted the tension tool and then raked the tumblers into place. It wasn't very subtle but would open most doors.

At first, Noble thought the place had been ransacked, but closer inspection proved the owner was simply a slob. Dirty clothes and crushed soda cans littered every surface. The smell of soiled socks assaulted his nose. Video game wires snared up the floor and a high-definition television hung on one wall. The apartment was a one-room efficiency with a futon and what real estate agents call a kitchenette. Diego could walk away from this pad and only be out the cost of a few game consoles.

Noble dumped the wastebasket and sorted through the trash with his foot. He found crumpled betting tickets and a matchbook for a popular horse track in Quezon.

He stuffed the match book in his pocket and then checked out the rest of the apartment. His search failed to turn up anything else of value, not even a photograph. He still had no idea what this guy looked like. Finding one stranger at a track full of strangers would be next to impossible, but it was the only lead Noble had to go on.

He went to the window overlooking the street, bent one

of the cheap plastic shades, and peeked out. The girl in the white Toyota held a pair of binoculars up to her eyes. Noble snorted. "You've got to be kidding me," he said to the empty room.

They weren't even a small pair of low-key binoculars. They were the big jobs that tourist from Michigan take on bird-watching expeditions. "Somebody's seen too many cop movies," Noble said.

The hired thugs in the van watched the girl with growing suspicion. The fat one in the passenger seat kept motioning to the white Toyota. Noble didn't need to hear the conversation. They were trying to figure out how she fit into all this and what to do about it.

Noble couldn't see the black sedan from this angle, but he didn't need to. A guy like that would wait for the other players to show their hand.

He let go of the blind. The reporter—if that's what she was—had just stumbled into a world of trouble. If Noble didn't intervene, there would be two missing girls instead of one. Saving her meant showing himself to the other players. It would put him at a serious disadvantage. Noble chewed the inside of one cheek and weighed his options.

CHAPTER EIGHTEEN

Noble exited the front of the building, crossed the street, and circled the front bumper of the white Toyota. The heavies in the minivan took notice. The girl lowered her binoculars and watched him walk around to the passenger side. When it was clear he was going for the door, she triggered the locks and then fumbled for the window button. In her panic, she pressed down instead of up. She quickly corrected her mistake. The windows started up with an electric whir. Noble grabbed the glass in both hands and wrenched. There was a loud shriek. The window popped off the track and the pane of glass slipped down inside the doorframe.

The girl snatched her purse out of the passenger seat and darted a hand inside. "I've got pepper spray."

"I've got a gun," Noble said. He opened the door from the inside and climbed into the passenger seat. The heavies got out of the minivan and approached the Toyota. Noble pointed to the rearview. "You know those guys?"

Her hand stopped digging through the purse. She glanced into the mirror. "What guys...?" Her voice trailed off. She shook her head. "No."

"Hand me that," Noble said, indicating the binoculars in her lap.

She hurried to obey.

The fat one stuck his head in the open passenger window. "You're in the wrong neighborhood."

Noble swung the binoculars. The heavy aluminum frame broke the fat man's nose with a hard crack. Blood burst from both nostrils, leaving red raindrops on the side of the white Toyota. He staggered away, clutching a hand to his gushing nose.

His partner hammered a fist against the driver's window. "Open this door or I'll tear it off!"

"Drive," Noble ordered.

The girl twisted the key in the ignition. She threw the car in gear, cramped the steering wheel, and stamped the gas pedal. The Toyota lurched forward. The thug was forced to leap back or have his toes run over. The front bumper clipped the tail end of a Hyundai. Plastic crunched, and the Hyundai's alarm shrieked in protest. Noble reached over and took the steering wheel, helping to steady the nose of the Toyota.

"Did I just hit that car?" she asked.

"Yup." At the corner, he hauled on the wheel, forcing her to hang a right.

The Toyota slewed through the turn and missed an oncoming jeepney full of passengers by inches. Horns blared. The driver of the jeepney hurled a curse. The girl spun the wheel, and the car jerked back into the right lane.

"Calm down," Noble told her.

She took a deep breath, held it, and then let it out slowly. Her knuckles turned white against the steering wheel. "Are you going to hurt me?"

"No." He stuffed his carry-on in the floorboard and brought the matchbook out of his pocket. "You know this place?"

She nodded.

"That's where we're going."

"Who are you?" she asked. Her American accent was perfect. She either went to school in the states or was born there. She wore a simple black tank top over dark denims and ankle boots. Noble bet if he checked the labels they would be American as well. He wanted to know what she was doing in the Philippines and how she was connected to the disappearance of Bati Ramos.

"Why were you watching Diego's place?"

"I don't know what you are talking about," she said.

"Drop the act. You were watching Diego's apartment. I want to know why."

She looked like she wanted to crawl down into the seat and disappear.

Noble made an effort to soften his voice. "Okay. Relax. Let's start with your name."

She took her eyes off the road long enough to steal a glance in his direction. "Samantha Gunn."

"Gun?" Noble made a gun with his thumb and forefinger.

"Two Ns," she said. "My father is from San Diego. My mother is from Hong Kong. Your turn."

"My name is Jake," he told her. He couldn't say why he

used his real name instead of laying down his cover identity. He wanted Samantha to trust him, and the truth has a way of disarming people. "Why were you watching Diego's apartment, Ms. Gunn?"

"My friend was kidnapped. I think Diego had something to do with it." After a moment, she shook her head. "I told Bati he was no good. I told her, but she wouldn't listen."

"What makes you say that?"

Samantha shrugged. "Diego's a scammer."

"He's a conman?"

"No. Nothing like that." She shrugged. "He spent all his time on the Internet trying to make a fast buck on those work-from-home sites. You know the ones I'm talking about? He never had two dimes to rub together. When he did manage to make a little money, he would gamble it away." She motioned to the matchbook. "Is that why we're headed to the horse track?"

He inclined his head. "How do you know Bati?"

"We've been best friends since our freshman year at Yale. We run a shelter for battered women." She looked at his carry-on in the floorboard. "You taking a trip?"

"Just got off a plane in fact."

"Why are you looking for Diego?" she asked.

"I want to find Bati."

"Why?"

Noble ignored that question.

"Do you really have a gun?" she asked.

"Yes."

"Why?"

He gave her a hard look.

"Okay," she said and took another deep breath. "How do I know you aren't..."

"A bad guy?" Noble suggested.

"Yeah."

"I didn't have to save you from those thugs back at Diego's place." He cocked a thumb over his shoulder. "It would have been a lot easier for me if I hadn't. Now they know I'm here and that I'm looking for Bati. I gave up the element of surprise and lost the initiative."

She glanced in the rearview like she expected to see the beat-up minivan on their tail. "I guess I should thank you."

She was a cool customer. Even a small altercation left people shaking from the adrenaline spike. Her hands didn't tremble on the wheel, and she hid her nerves better than most. It said a lot about her.

"You know what Diego looks like?" Noble asked.

"You know for a guy who doesn't like answering questions, you sure ask a lot of them."

Noble waited.

Samantha rolled her eyes. "He dated my best friend. Of course I know what he looks like."

"Good," Noble said. "I'll need your help."

"Do I have a choice?" she asked.

"No."

CHAPTER NINETEEN

BATI, TRAPPED INSIDE THE TRUNK AND BREATHING petrol fumes, felt like her head would split right down the middle. The car rumbled over unpaved roads and pounded through potholes. Every jolt brought her closer to vomiting. She was afraid to puke with the shorts stuffed in her mouth. She would choke on her own spew. That made her think of Jimi Hendrix. Hadn't he died choking on his own spew? It was a crazy thought. Here she was, trapped inside a trunk and thinking about dead rock stars. She was losing it. She had to keep it together. That's what she kept telling herself. *Keep it together.* Daddy was a diplomat. Someone, somewhere, was looking for her. She just had to stay alive until they found her.

The car hit another pothole. Bati groaned. She curled up in an effort to minimize the impacts and concentrated on not puking. Bile crawled up her stomach toward her esophagus where it would make that last mad dash to escape.

Gravel crunched beneath the tires. The car slowed and

stopped, and the engine died. Bati heard the doors open and close. The hood latch released. Light blinded her. She squeezed her eyes shut.

The kidnappers dragged her from the trunk. The rough treatment opened the floodgates. Her stomach convulsed, sending the contents north. She hunched forward and made a chugging noise like someone shaking a jug of expired milk. Her eyes tried to bug right out of her skull. Streamers of hot sluice shot from both nostrils.

The kidnappers let her go. Gravel skinned her knees. The vomit kept coming, filling up her mouth and pushing out through her nose. She strained at the zip-tie around her wrists in her panic, struggling to free her hands as the bile backed up into her throat.

One of the men ripped off the duct tape. Bati spit shorts and a mouthful of vomit into the gravel, sucked in a lungful of air, and threw up again. The muscles in her stomach quivered from exertion. Her legs shook. Ropes of snot hung from both nostrils. The taste filled her mouth. Her throat burned. Tears spilled down her cheeks. She crouched in the gravel, trying to spit out the taste and blink away tears.

It was twilight. The sky had turned hot and red. They had brought her to an abandoned rock quarry. Stone walls, twenty meters high, surrounded them on three sides like a massive horseshoe. A building of corrugated steel hunkered in one corner of the site. The ceiling had collapsed in several places. Abandoned mining equipment lay scattered around the yard, along with a few old metal carts on miniature railroad tracks. One gigantic dump truck, slowly turning to rust, rested on bald rims. A sign advertised the company responsible for the dig, but the sun had bleached out the letters.

The kidnapper with the missing index finger nudged Bati in her ribs with his boot. "Are you done?"

In response, she retched up another wave. This one was more of a dry heave. She coughed, spat, and gulped fresh air. When she felt she could talk without losing any more of her stomach contents, she said, "Please. I need my insulin."

"Shut up."

They picked her up, dragged her into the building, and deposited her on a dirty concrete floor. Large sacks of crushed gravel were stacked waist high against the walls. A sagging conveyor belt entered the building from the quarry. Smaller conveyors branched out through the processing plant to several pulverizing machines wired to dead motors. A thick layer of grit covered every surface.

Bati lay with her head on the floor and her knees pulled up to her chest. Growing pressure behind the eyes told her she was in danger of diabetic shock. Being manhandled and bounced around inside a car trunk hadn't helped any. If she didn't get a shot, she would fall into a coma and die. The thought sent fresh waves of terror through her body. "I'm going to die unless I have insulin," she said. "Please. I'm no good to you dead."

The uninjured kidnapper studied her with expressionless eyes. Bati had started to think of him as the leader. The other man followed his orders.

She licked her cracked lips. "Please. I have insulin in my purse. Please."

"Go get the purse," he said.

The man with the missing finger shot Bati an acid look, but marched outside into the sunlight.

Bati closed her eyes and put her head down. They had saved the purse. It was a small victory, but she felt like she had just crossed the finish line of a triathlon. A bright spot of hope, like a hot air balloon lifting up into the sky, swelled in her chest. She was going to get her insulin. That was something.

The short one came back with the handbag. Eyeliner, mascara, and blush clattered across the floor as he emptied the contents. A compact hit the ground. The mirror cracked. He found the insulin pen and passed it to the boss.

"Where do I inject it?" He thumbed off the plastic cap.

"Let me do it," Bati said.

He shook his head. "I don't think so. Tell me how to inject it or you can lay there and die."

"In my thigh," Bati told him.

He held her down with one hand and jabbed the needle into her thigh. Bati winced and then relaxed. It would take a few minutes for the insulin to work, but waves of relief were already spreading through her. She had managed to reset the clock on her life.

When it was done, the leader tossed the used syringe. It came to rest an arm's distance from where she lay. Bati watched him walk back to the open door and stuff his hands in his pockets. The other man joined him. They conversed in low murmurs with their backs to her. She glanced at the discarded hypodermic.

She might be able to use the needle. She wasn't sure how or where, she'd figure that out later. First she needed to get her hands on it.

She sat up and put her back to the sacks of crushed rock piled against the corrugated steel wall. The movement caught the kidnappers' attention. They turned. Bati hung her head and tried to look dejected until they returned to their conversation. She waited several minutes and then slowly stretched one bare leg to her right. She managed to put her heel on the insulin pen and carefully rolled it across the ground until she had it between her feet. One of the kidnappers glanced over his shoulder. Bati held her breath. When he looked away, she started working the hypodermic back toward her bottom.

CHAPTER TWENTY

It was dark by the time they reached the horse track. Noble directed Samantha Gunn to a parking spot around the south side of the building near an emergency exit. From this angle, he could see the first turn of the track through a chain-link fence. A pack of horses tore around the curve. The jockeys stood in the stirrups. Hooves kicked up tufts of dark earth. Towering banks of arc-sodium lights created artificial daylight. They reminded Noble of his days playing high school baseball.

He had pitched his junior and senior year. He never had the arm to go pro, and he probably knew it even then. But like all the other guys on the team, he had entertained fantasies of opening for the Tampa Bay Rays. When that didn't work out, he joined the Army.

Samantha put the Toyota in park and turned off the engine. "What's the plan?"

"Find Diego." Noble opened his door. "Pop the trunk. I don't want my carry-on stolen."

"Too bad *someone* broke the window," Samantha said. She keyed the button for the trunk release. Inside Noble found a pair of jumper cables, a small emergency medical kit, and a folded blanket.

Samantha saw him studying the contents and shrugged. "I like to be prepared."

Noble gave an approving nod, closed the trunk, and strode through the lanes of parked cars toward the entrance. Samantha had to jog to keep up. A cheer, mixed with a few boos, rose from the stadium. An announcer's voice boomed from loud speakers, declaring the winner.

"Once we find Diego," Samantha asked. "What then?"

"Find out what he knows."

"Do I want to know how you plan to do that?"

Noble shook his head. "Nope."

They pushed through a crowd of chain-smoking men milling in front of the betting windows. The place stank of sweat and broken dreams. Crumpled tickets crunched under foot. Several television screens showed close-ups of horses fidgeting in the starting gates, waiting for the next race.

The track had security. Young men in poorly fitted gray uniforms strolled through the crowds with their thumbs tucked in their belts. They had 9mm handguns on their hips and radios clipped to their shirts. Their focus would be on breaking up drunken fights and preventing robbery, but a pair of foreigners poking around might arouse even the sloppiest security team. Noble peeled several notes off a stack of pesos and handed them to Samantha. "Place a few bets."

"Why?"

"Because we want to fit in," he told her.

She went to a window, placed bets at random, and handed half the slips to Noble.

"Now we look like a couple enjoying an evening at the track," he told her. "Any sign of Diego?"

She shook her head. "So we are a couple now?"

"That's right," he said as they made their way up a flight of steps to the spectator stands. "Been going steady about six months."

"You take me to the most romantic places," she remarked.

A gun barked, and the gates opened with a clang.

A sea of Filipino men with black hair and tan skin packed the stadium, roaring at the jockeys and waving race tickets in the air. The girls wore tight dresses and a lot of makeup. The smell of cheap cigarettes and fresh-clipped grass filled Noble's lungs. He scanned the crowd, not knowing what he was looking for, but keeping his eyes open for anything odd or peculiar.

On the field, horses and jockeys sprinted around the turns and down the final straight-a-way. The announcer narrated with auctioneer cadence and growing excitement. Even with native level proficiency, it was hard for Noble to understand the scratchy stadium loud speakers. He only picked up every other phrase. "Old Blue comes out strong... here's Grand Lady catching up at the turn... Easy Does it pulling ahead... Old Blue retakes the lead! The final stretch... neck and neck! Old Blue wins by three-quarters of a length!"

"Hey look!" Samantha held up one of her tickets. "We won."

Noble wasn't listening. He had spotted a lanky Filipino

in baggy blue jeans and a wrinkled t-shirt, sporting a recently broken nose covered by a bandage. When Old Blue crossed the finish line, the man crumpled his ticked and tossed it in disappointment. Noble pointed. "Second row. Is that Diego?"

Samantha's eyes narrowed. "That's him."

During Noble's surveillance training at the Farm, one of his tradecraft instructors had talked a lot about a human's sixth sense—that tickle right between the shoulder blades, or the uneasy feeling at the base of the skull when someone is watching you. Sometimes it's nothing more than a feeling deep in your gut that tells you something isn't right. Brighter minds have theorized that these instincts are hardwired into us as part of our survival instinct. The subconscious mind, they said, picked up on subtle clues that our rational mind missed or rejected. Everyone had it, but civilians, living their work-a-day lives, had no need for it. As a result, it faded into the background.

Cops and criminals tend to be more in touch with their primal instinct. They need it to survive. So it didn't surprise Noble when Diego turned and looked directly at them. He must have felt that tickle between his shoulder blades.

Samantha gasped, threw her arms around Noble, and pressed her lips into his. It was the worst thing she could have done. Tangling up in a kiss works in the movies, in real life two people making out draws attention. If she had watched the horses and smiled, Diego might have over-looked them. On the other hand, the last four years had been a bit of a dry spell for Noble. He allowed himself to enjoy the kiss while watching Diego from under partially closed lids. Her slender body pressed against him, and her lips melted into his. He felt the locked tumblers on his heart move.

Diego went for the stairs.

Noble broke off the kiss. Samantha's eyes opened. Red splotches colored her cheeks.

"You've seen too many movies," Noble said.

Her brow furrowed. It looked more cute than angry. Noble found himself suppressing a grin. "Come on, *Jane Bond*. Diego's on the move."

He took her by the hand and pushed through the crowd. He almost lost Diego at the bottom of the steps. Wrinkled t-shirt and baggy jeans were a common fashion statement at the track. Diego made the mistake of looking over his shoulder. The white bandage on his nose was a dead giveaway. Unfortunately so was a white face in a crowd full of Asians. Diego spotted Noble and broke into a jog. He hurried past the betting windows and the refreshment stands, along the concourse and turned a corner.

By the time Noble reached the turn, Diego had disappeared, but the door to the men's room was swinging shut on a pneumatic hinge.

Samantha pointed. "I think he went into the bathroom."

"No kidding?" Noble remarked. "He's almost as bad at this as you."

"Hey," Samantha said.

Noble dragged her to the men's room. Samantha started to protest. He ignored her and threw the door open hard enough to bounce it off the wall in case Diego was hiding on the other side. The door rebounded with a hollow boom.

There was a row of sinks on the right, stalls on the left, and an open window on the far wall. It was just big enough for a small man to climb through. Noble stepped into the bathroom. Diego rushed in from the left with a wild haymaker.

CHAPTER TWENTY-ONE

Noble brought his forearm up to block and threw a jab. His knuckles re-broke Diego's nose with a wet crunch. Diego's head snapped back. Blood burst from both nostrils. He barked in pain. Noble hooked his right heel behind Diego's lead foot and delivered an open-hand strike to the throat, putting Diego flat on his back in the middle of the men's room floor.

A middle-aged man in a mismatched suit stood at the urinal with his hand still on his zipper. Noble fixed him with a hard stare. "Get out."

He pulled up his zipper and fled.

"Watch the door," Noble told Samantha.

She put her back against it.

Diego rolled onto his hands and knees, leaving large red drops of blood on the sea-foam green tile. Noble kicked him in the ribs. He didn't hold back. He let Diego have it. The top of his foot connected with a heavy *whomp*, lifting Diego an inch off the ground and putting him on his back.

Samantha drew a sharp breath.

Diego gave a long, shuddering moan that sounded like an old car trying to start. The neon lights turned him a sickly shade of green. Sweat sprang out on his forehead. Noble knelt down next to him. "Where is she?"

"I don't know," he groaned. With his sinuses full of blood it sounded like, bah ont ngo.

"Who has her?" Noble asked. "Give me a name."

"I don't know."

Noble gripped Diego's broken nose and twisted.

Diego screamed in pain.

"Who's got her?" Noble demanded.

Diego opened his mouth to speak. Someone tried to enter at the same time. The door opened half an inch before Samantha forced it the other way. "Um... Occupied!" she yelled.

Noble returned his attention to Diego. "Tell me what I want to know, and the pain stops."

"Lady Shiva," Diego said and spat a mouth full of dark blood onto the floor. "Lady Shiva has her."

Noble had heard the name before. Shiva was a shadowy figure in Manila's underground sex trade with a ruthless reputation and a flair for the dramatic. She acted as a sort of human-trafficking middleman, importing young girls from the provinces and selling them to sex clubs in the city. The CIA had been trying to build a file on Shiva for years and didn't even have a photo to go with the name. She always managed to stay a step ahead.

Samantha had apparently heard the name as well. She covered her mouth. The color drained from her face. A little squeak, like chalk on a blackboard, escaped her throat.

"What happened?" Noble asked. "You get hard up for cash?"

Diego nodded and wiped blood from his nose, smearing it over his chin in the process. "I owe twenty grand to a loan shark."

Noble let out a low whistle.

"You little weasel!" Samantha threw herself at Diego with balled-up fists.

"Hey!" Noble caught her around the waist and pushed her back. "Watch the door."

She glared at Diego but put her back against the door.

"You got in deep and then you found out your girlfriend was the daughter of a Filipino diplomat. You figure she has to be worth at least twenty grand," Noble said, filling in the rest of the story. "Have I got it right so far?"

"I changed my mind at the last minute," Diego said. "I wasn't going to go through with it. I tried to stop it, honest."

"You're a real humanitarian," Noble said. "Once you decided to sell, you had to look for a buyer. Who put you in touch with Shiva?"

Diego shook his head. "He found me."

"Try harder," Noble said and reached for his nose.

"I swear." Diego moaned. "He's a local fighter. One ear is all curled up. Goes by the name of Oscar."

Noble turned to Samantha. "Sound familiar?"

She nodded. Someone else tried to enter. She put her shoulder against the door and shoved with her legs.

Noble grabbed a fistful of Diego's wrinkled t-shirt and gave him a shake. "Where do I find him?"

Diego hesitated.

"I'm going to start breaking fingers," Noble said.

"Talk to the owner of Club 10," Diego told him.

"If I get there and find a welcome party..."

Diego held up a bloody palm in surrender. "I swear on my mother's grave."

Noble left him bleeding on the tile floor, took Samantha by the arm, and steered her out the door.

"That's it?" Samantha said. "He gets a pass?"

Diego deserved jail time at the very least. Leaving a loose thread might come back to haunt him, but Noble didn't have time to deal with Diego. "Guys like him get theirs in the end. They always do."

Right now he was more worried about security. One of the guards saw him and Samantha emerge from the restroom and went to investigate. Noble cursed under his breath and picked up the pace.

"What?" Samantha asked. She glanced over her shoulder in time to see the guard push open the bathroom door.

"Don't look," Noble told her. "Keep walking."

Her body tensed.

"Stay calm," Noble told her.

The guard found Diego in a bloody heap on the floor, pulled a silver whistle from a draw cord on his belt, stuck it between his lips, and blew. A shrill scream echoed along the concrete corridor.

Noble broke into a run. Samantha sprinted to keep up. The young security guard gave chase, running with one hand on his Beretta pistol. They flew along the main concourse, weaving through the crowd. Noble stiff-armed anyone unlucky enough to get in his way. They reached an intersection, and Samantha turned toward the main entrance. Noble grabbed her arm. "Not that way."

She was too scared to ask questions. Noble guided her to the south end of the concourse. They rounded a corner. Noble spotted a plastic trash container with the horse track's logo stenciled on the side in blue. He let go of Samantha's arm, grabbed the can and swung it.

The security guard rounded the corner in time to get hit in the face with the trashcan. His head snapped back. His feet shot out from under him. He landed flat on his back. The trashcan rolled across the floor, spilling half-eaten pretzels, crumpled paper, and crushed beer cans. Noble and Samantha sprinted away.

Noble spotted a glowing red EXIT sign twenty meters ahead, but another security guard stood between him and freedom. This one wasn't much more than a kid, nineteen maybe, with pimples and a buzz cut. The guard planted himself in front of the emergency exit, placed one hand on his gun and the other out in front of him, palm up, like he was directing traffic.

CHAPTER TWENTY-TWO

Noble could have solved the problem with the pistol in his waistband, but innocent people would get hurt if bullets started flying. And the security guard was only doing his job. Besides, Noble had been doing this long enough to know who was willing to pull the trigger and who would hesitate. Shooting holes in paper targets is one thing. Shooting holes in another human being is different. The kid's eyes told the whole story; he had taken a job at the track because it was easy work and he got to carry a gun. It made him feel tough. He probably never expected to see any real action.

Noble sprinted directly at him. The kid ordered Noble to stop. When that didn't work, he pulled the Beretta and racked the slide. That's when the gravity of the situation hit. His courage wavered. By the time he recovered, Noble had closed the distance.

He caught the barrel of the weapon in his right hand, forced it up to the ceiling and brought his left hand down on the guard's wrist at the same time. He twisted the gun around, forcing the kid to let go or have all the tendons in his wrist snap. The kid chose to let go.

The move took less than a second. The young security guard stepped back and started to raise his hands in surrender. Noble struck him a blow to the temple with the Beretta. The kid's knees buckled, and his eyes rolled up. He'd probably have headaches for the rest of his life, but he would live.

Samantha watched the whole thing with her eyes wide and her mouth open. She looked from the gun in Noble's hand to the unconscious security guard and let out a trembling breath.

Noble released the magazine. It clattered across the floor. He racked the slide, ejecting the round from the chamber, and tossed the empty Beretta into a corner.

"How did you..." Samantha started to ask.

"Later," Noble said. He slammed open the emergency exit door, and the alarm let out long, ear-splitting whoops.

Samantha leapt through the open door. Her Toyota was directly ahead.

Noble followed her to the car. She dug the keys from her pocket while she ran and pressed the button. The doors unlocked with a chirrup. Noble snatched open the passenger side and piled in beside her. She got the car started, threw it in gear, and roared out of the parking lot, weaving through traffic. Noble let her get three blocks and then told her to slow down.

It took another city block, but she finally eased up on the pedal and relaxed her grip on the wheel. They passed a kilometer in silence before Samantha said, "You took the gun right out of his hands. How did you do that?"

"Hang a left at this intersection," he told her.

She put on the indicator. "And the exit," she said, more to herself than Noble. Her mind was putting together the pieces. "You knew exactly where we'd come out. Like you had it all planned." She turned to him. "Are you some kind of..."

"Spy?" he offered.

She nodded. "For America?"

He inclined his head. "Bati's father is a Filipino diplomat to the United States."

"I know," Samantha said. "Starting the shelter was Bati's idea. Her father gave us the startup capital on the condition that she used a fake last name. He said he had enemies in the Philippines."

"That's putting it mildly. Take another left up here."

"Is that why Lady Shiva kidnapped Bati?" Samantha said. "To use against Ramos?"

"That was my first thought," Noble admitted. "But something doesn't add up."

"What do you mean?"

"Diego said Oscar contacted him, and I believe it." Noble considered the implications as he spoke. "Bati's cover was already blown. Someone else knew who she was."

Samantha's hands tightened on the wheel. Her knuckles turned white. "Who do you suspect?"

"I'm not sure yet," Noble admitted. "There's something else; the thug with the cauliflower ear, Oscar, is Lady Shiva's muscle. If Shiva already had Bati, why would her men be staking out Diego's apartment? It doesn't make any sense. Unless something went wrong. Someone got Bati first. Shiva thinks Diego double-crossed her."

Samantha took a hand off the wheel and pushed hair out of her eyes. "You're right," she said. "But if Lady Shiva doesn't have Bati, why are we trying to get to her?"

"She's the only lead I've got."

They rode in silence the rest of the way into San Juan. Samantha parked two blocks down from a brightly lit building with a neon sign that read "CLUB 10" in blue. More clubs lined the bustling boulevard with names like Envy, eXclusive, and Locale QC. The whole block pulsed with competing base lines. Well-dressed Filipinos thronged the sidewalks along with western businessmen in expensive suits looking for underage prostitutes and cheap blow.

Samantha turned off the engine. "What's our next move?"

"This is where you exit stage left," he told her.

"I can help you, Jake," she said. "I've lived in Manila for two years. I know my way around. I know the language."

"I'll manage."

"You never would have found Diego without my help."

He turned in the seat to face her. "You think this is a game? You think we're in a movie? Before this is over, people are going to get hurt, probably even killed. One of those people might be me."

She set her jaw and spoke through clenched teeth. "I know that, Jake."

"My job is to find Bati," he said. "I can't do that if I'm trying to protect you."

Her face crumpled. Tears spilled down her cheeks. "It's my fault."

"What?"

Her voice cracked. "It's my fault Bati got kidnapped." She dropped her chin to her chest and squeezed her eyes shut.

"I'm listening," Noble said.

"I slipped up," Samantha said between sobs. "I mentioned her father to one of the volunteers at the shelter a month ago. It just sort of came up in the course of the conversation. When I realized Bati had been kidnapped..." She hitched up her shoulders and let them drop. "It's my fault, Jake."

Noble was still trying to decide what to say when she twisted in her seat and threw her arms around him, burying her head in his shoulder. The move caught him off guard. He sat there, unsure what to do.

Small lapses in security spread like cancer. Plenty of good agents have been killed because of a simple slip of the tongue. He could have told her it wasn't her fault and that everything would be all right. Samantha had messed up and gotten her best friend kidnapped, probably killed. That couldn't be an easy thing to live with. He didn't bother to lie. He put an arm around her and let her cry.

Tears soaked through the shoulder of his suit jacket. When she had finally gotten it all out, Noble said, "I'm going to get her back. That's my job."

Samantha sniffed, nodded, and wiped away the tears.

"You want to help?" Noble asked.

Another nod.

"Let me see your phone."

She dug in her pocket and handed over an iPhone. Noble dialed the number to the burner Matt had given him.

It vibrated twice in his pocket. "Stay put and watch the front of Club 10. As soon as you see Oscar, or anyone else that feels suspicious, you text me right away. Understood?"

She sniffed and gave a thumbs up. "Got it."

Noble got out and crossed the street. First he had given Samantha his name, which was bad enough, now he was letting her tag along on a rescue operation. Living alone on his boat all those months must have driven him insane. It was the only explanation.

Samantha had handled herself exceptionally well for a civilian, but she had yet to be in any real danger. Noble had an idea she would do all right if push came to shove, in fact, he suspected she had the makings of a decent field agent, but his interest in her was far from professional. She had an Ivy League education and intelligence—the two rarely went hand in hand. She also had a gorgeous face and a runner's body. Not to mention courage. Not many people would take the law into their own hands. Most folks went home, had a good cry, and hoped the authorities could sort it all out in the end. Samantha was ready to take on the most notorious underworld criminal in Manila to save a friend.

None of that explained his decision to allow an untrained civilian to participate in a covert op. She had done her part and found Diego. Now she was a liability. Noble entered Club 10 determined to set up the meeting with Oscar and then cut Samantha loose. It was the smart thing to do.

He could feel the baseline in his bones. The music threatened to shake his teeth right out of his skull. Strobe lights flashed in time to the music, attacking his retinas. He paused in the entrance long enough to allow his eyes time to adjust.

A troupe of young girls, dressed in dark blue bikinis, police hats, and plastic nightsticks, danced on a raised platform to the pounding rhythm. Most of them probably came from small villages. Poor farmers would sell their daughters to "recruiters" who promised a decent job at a hotel. Once in the city, alone and penniless, the girls were forced into prostitution. The recruiters weren't picky either. Noble had seen girls as young as four and five working the nightclubs.

Sex trafficking had become a major source of revenue for metro Manila. Every year tourists poured into the country on "sex vacations." Most of the offenders came from the Middle East or other Asian countries, but a good number of westerners made their way here in search of underage prostitutes. The Philippine government publically condemned prostitution and human trafficking—both were technically illegal—but off the record, the government turned a blind eye. Prostitution kept tourist dollars pouring into the country. Occasionally the police would raid a club and make a few arrests to keep human rights activists happy, but it did nothing to stem the flow of women trafficked into the city.

Most of the crowd in Club 10 was Filipino, but several white businessmen prowled the floor. A knot of western college kids had a VIP table in one corner, blowing through mommy and daddy's money, completely oblivious to the fact that they were supporting modern slavery.

Noble made his way to the bar, caught the attention of a bartender, and ordered a Cerveza Negra. He paid and pretended to drink. Crowded clubs are security nightmares;

it is impossible to keep track of so many people all at once, you have to shout to be heard and there are multiple exits.

When the song ended, the girls came off the stage to mingle with the crowd.

One spotted Noble. She was fifteen or sixteen and still had baby fat. "Hello, handsome man." She flashed him a smile that never touched her eyes. "Maybe you buy me a drink, yes?"

"Maybe next time," Noble told her.

She made a pouty face and walked away.

The lapse in music provided Noble the opening he needed. He signaled the bartender. "I need to speak with the owner."

The barman wrinkled his brow. "He's busy."

"I want to buy some merchandise," Noble said. "A friend of a friend said the owner of Club 10 could put me in touch with Oscar. You know the one I'm talking about? Boxer with a cauliflower ear. Works for Lady Shiva."

He was throwing out bits of true information in hopes that the bartender would add to what little he already knew. It was an intelligence-gathering technique called fishing.

The barman didn't bite. "Who should I tell him is asking?"

"Mr. White," Noble said.

He considered that for a moment, then told Noble to wait. Noble sipped his beer and watched the barman disappear through a door marked private.

CHAPTER TWENTY-THREE

Samantha sat clutching her phone, watching the front entrance of Club 10. The busy sidewalk would make it difficult to pick out Oscar. She had seen him only once, briefly. She bullied her exhausted brain into remembering the hurried glimpse of his face. At the time, her only concern had been escaping before he could break the glass and drag her out of the car. It was only a few hours ago, but it felt like days. It was like trying to remember the name of a person she met at a party and then never saw again. His face kept slipping away. She knew he had a cauliflower ear, but from this distance, small details were hard to make out.

She reached for the cup of coffee in the center console and tried to take a sip. It was empty. She returned the cup and pressed the heels of her hands into her eyes. How long had she been awake? How long had Bati been gone? She felt around on the floorboard. Her fingers located her purse under the passenger's seat. Inside she had two of Bati's Insulin pens and a spiral bound notebook. Samantha flipped through the battered pages. Bati had been abducted at 8:22pm on Sunday. She checked her watch. It was now 9:37pm on Wednesday. She made a note. Bati had been missing over seventy-two hours. Three days.

Not missing, Sam reminded herself, kidnapped. And it was her fault. She had slipped up, and Bati paid the price. Sam tried not to think about all the terrible things that might be happening to her friend right now. A single word went through her thoughts like a scratched record.

Rape.

Images flooded her mind's eye. If she let them, the pictures would consume her, drive her mad. She would be a sobbing wreck in a corner somewhere, no use to anybody. She fought to keep the images at bay and stay focused on what she was doing here and now.

The kidnappers probably wanted money. That's what Sam told herself. Bati's dad was a diplomat. He was rich. The kidnappers wouldn't hurt her. Samantha hoped.

Her thoughts turned to Jake. What did she really know about him? He claimed to be working for America, but she had only his word to go on, and he wasn't exactly chatty. But Samantha wanted to believe him. Mostly because she didn't want to believe she was alone, fighting a losing battle. Jake was clever and resourceful. He might lack subtlety, but he made up for it with brutal efficiency. His looks didn't hurt either. *How could she even think about Jake like that while her best friend was missing?* Sam ran a hand through her hair.

Her thoughts circled around in an endless loop. She forced her attention back to the front of Club 10, spotted a westerner, and did a double take.

He had a face like a steam shovel. A scar ran across the bridge of his nose. And he was looking right at her. Sam had seen him before. He was some kind of bodyguard for Mr. Ramos. She had only met Mr. Ramos face-to-face on a handful of occasions, and the bodyguard had always been hanging around in the background.

He turned and disappeared into the crowd.

Questions crowded Sam's brain.

What was he doing in Manila? Was he searching for Bati? Had he recognized her? If so, why was he walking away? Maybe he hadn't been looking at her after all. Or maybe he hadn't recognized her. To him, Samantha would be another Asian face in a sea of Asian faces.

Before she could answer any of those questions, someone slumped against the driver's side window. Samantha's heart tried to crawl out through her throat. She bit back a startled cry. Her first thought went to panhandler. They were all over Manila. She started to tell him she had no money, but it wasn't a beggar.

It was the boxer with the cauliflower ear. He had a small semi-automatic pistol in his hand. The barrel was pressed against the glass. He kept the gun close to his belt to shield it from people passing by, but the muzzle was pointed at Samantha's chest. He bent down to peer at her through the glass. "Open the door."

CHAPTER TWENTY-FOUR

THE NEXT DANCE NUMBER WAS THE SAME GIRLS IN THE same bikinis, but they had switched their police hats for sailor caps. The crowd didn't seem to mind. Noble sipped his drink and kept his eyes off the skin. The beer turned room temperature while he waited for the owner. It was taking too long. Noble flashed back to that first, all-important, lesson of counter intelligence; when there is doubt, there is no doubt. He chewed the inside of one cheek.

His instincts told him to abort, but he had no other leads. Walking away meant giving Bati up for dead and losing seventy-five-thousand dollars. And his mother needed that money. To find the girl, he would have to keep teasing at this thread and see where it went. Against his better judgment, Noble signaled for another beer and continued to wait.

Ten more minutes slouched past before a potbellied man in a garishly colored silk shirt, gold chains, and flip-flops emerged from the back room. He had seen too many old episodes of Miami Vice and probably thought big-time drug dealers actually dressed that way. His lips turned up in a peevish little smile. "You are American?" he asked, yelling to be heard over the music.

"That's right," Noble yelled back. "My employer is setting up a club in Malaysia and needs some girls. A friend said you were the guy to talk to. He said you could put me in touch with sellers. We're only interested in top-of-the-line merchandise. Cute and young. My employer is willing to pay top dollar."

The owner smiled that peevish smile again. "I think I can help you. Follow me."

Noble tossed a few pesos on the beer-stained bar top and followed him through the door marked private. They stepped into a crowded storage space. A desk had been wedged between shelves stocked with booze, bar snacks, and replacement bulbs. Oscar was there. So was Samantha. The boxer leaned against the desk and had a semiautomatic pistol pressed into Samantha's side.

The club owner swung the door shut, cutting off Noble's retreat.

Samantha stood with her fists clenched and her shoulders hunched. Tears rimmed her eyes. "I'm sorry, Jake. He snuck up on me."

"Don't sweat it," he told her. "Happens to the best of us."

He kept his face expressionless, but fear flooded his veins like ice water. He sorted through his options. The music was loud enough to cover the sound of a gunshot. Oscar could murder them both without raising an alarm. Noble could stand there and die or draw his weapon and risk hitting Samantha. Either way it was a losing proposition. At best he could take Oscar with him. Noble made up his mind to do just that.

But instead of gunning them down on the spot, Oscar thrust his chin at an emergency exit. Their chances of survival in a dark alley improved only slightly, but they weren't dead yet. Noble planned to keep it that way as long as possible. He showed his empty palms and moved to the door.

Oscar followed. He kept Samantha between them and pressed the pistol into her ribcage. Samantha walked hunched over with her face pinched like the barrel burned her skin.

Noble stopped at the door. There was a sign that said: WARNING. EMERGENCY DOOR. ALARM WILL SOUND.

"Go on," Oscar ordered.

Noble pushed open the door.

The alarm did not sound.

The club owner let out a girlish giggle. "Good-bye, American. Enjoy Manila."

CHAPTER TWENTY-FIVE

A BLACK BENTLEY MULSANNE GLIDED ALONG THE gravel drive, the quarter-million-dollar suspension handled the rock quarry's uneven terrain effortlessly. A pair of dusty gray Mercedes-Benz G class SUVs followed. The Bentley's Xenon headlamps illuminated the dilapidated crushing facility and the kidnappers standing in the open door. They shielded their eyes against the light.

The Bentley stopped. The SUVs pulled up along either side. Five men in tactical vests, armed with assault rifles, piled out of the SUVs and fanned out to recon the area. They communicated to each other by way of state-of-the-art, closed-circuit radios—the same system used by the United States Presidential Secret Service.

The driver of the Bentley got out and opened the back door. Eric Tsang emerged wearing a tailored suit from Saville Row and handmade deerskin loafers. He had a Bluetooth in one ear. "Daddy loves you too. Don't stay up too late, Okay?"

"Hai."

"Put mommy on the phone, ching," Eric said.

He heard his seven-year-old daughter drop the handset on the glass coffee table with a bang and then her little feet hammered the polished hardwood floors. Her voice sounded like it came from the bottom of a well as she hollered for her mother. "Mai mai!"

It was amazing how much noise such a tiny person could make.

Eric stood in the open door of the Bentley while his security team finished their sweep. His brother Tiger waited on the other side of the car, bored and rolling his eyes. He was a decade younger with spikey hair, baggy pants, and a pair of clunky headphones around his neck. Half the time they were not even connected to a music player, but the headphones were a mainstay, part of his façade, like the tiger tattoo on his forearm. He gave Eric an impatient look and then motioned to the crumbling building and the waiting kidnappers.

Eric ignored him.

A moment later, Eric's wife picked up the phone. He heard her take a long drag from a cigarette and exhale. "What?" she asked.

"Don't let Yan Yan stay up too late," Eric said. "She's got school in the morning."

"Why don't you come home and put her in bed yourself," Shelia Tsang said.

Eric turned and walked away from the car, putting his back to his employees. "I'm working," he said. "So I can pay for all your fancy clothes and lavish vacations."

Sheila laughed. "Yes, you love me so much." She took

another drag from her cigarette. He could hear the soft crackle of burning paper. "That's why you haven't touched me in months."

"I'd touch you more often if you stopped smoking those cigarettes," he said. "Maybe get on a treadmill. That wouldn't hurt either."

"Go to hell, Eric."

"Don't you hang up on me-"

The connection died. Eric cursed and jerked the Bluetooth out of his ear. He was tired of Shelia and all her drama. In the beginning, it had been a lot of fun. They could spend hours just talking, and the sex was phenomenal. Back then, Shelia had been bright, funny, and ambitious. Now all she did was spend Eric's money, smoke cigarettes, and snort blow in between back-to-back episodes of reality television. He would divorce her, but there was Yan Yan to think about.

Another problem for another day, Eric told himself.

He slipped the Bluetooth in his pocket and fixed a smile on his face. "Gentlemen," he said walking up to the crushing facility. "Let's see the merchandise."

Paeng held up a hand with a blood-soaked bandage on it. "The slut bit my finger off," he said.

Eric's smile never faltered. "Sorry to hear that."

"I think it deserves a little extra," Paeng said.

"Ten thousand was the agreed-upon price."

"That was before I had my finger bit off," Paeng said.

Fau flashed his partner a warning look.

Tiger crossed his arms over his chest and blew a bubble with his chewing gum. "How'd you like to have your head cut off?"

Fau clutched at the pistol in his waistband. Eric's security detail responded in kind, training their automatic weapons on the kidnappers.

"Everybody relax." Eric held up his hands. "You lost a finger. In this business, that is considered a job hazard. Maybe after this you should change careers?"

"You could be a guitar player..." Tiger said in a deadpan voice. "Oh wait."

The security team grinned.

Eric chuckled. Every once in a while his little brother came up with something witty to say.

Paeng fumed.

Eric dropped the smile. "Ten thousand was the agreed-upon price. You can take it, or this gets ugly." He motioned to his security team with their automatic weapons.

Fau and Paeng stepped aside.

Eric moved past them into the crushing facility. Bati Ramos sat with her back against sacks of crushed gravel. Her hands were zip-tied behind her back. She had no pants and no shoes, just a pair of dirty pink panties. She drew her knees tight to her chest in an attempt to hide her nakedness.

Eric knelt down, pushed a lock of hair out of her face, and smiled. "Hello. Have they been treating you well?"

She didn't answer.

He brushed his fingertips along the outside of one naked thigh. "You are a very beautiful woman," he remarked.

Bati shrank from his touch.

"Don't worry," Eric told her. "No one is going to hurt you. And once your daddy gives me what I want, you get to go home. Won't that be nice?"

She tried to speak. No sound came out. She licked cracked lips and tried again. "I hope you die."

"How rude," Eric said. "Perhaps I should teach you some manners?"

Fear filled her eyes. Her bottom lip trembled.

"No?" Eric asked.

She shook her head.

"Then watch your mouth," Eric told her.

A sob escaped her chest.

Eric stood up and went to the door. "I'm going to leave my security team here," he told Fau. "If everything goes according to plan, this will be over in forty-eight hours."

"Aren't you forgetting something?" Paeng said.

Eric looked at him.

"The money," Fau interpreted.

"You'll get paid when I get paid," Eric told them.

Fau and Paeng exchanged glances but kept their mouths shut.

The head of Eric's security team, a stoic Australian by the name of Henries with red hair and freckles, directed his team into strategic positions around the quarry.

Tiger blew a bubble and popped it. He was watching the girl with hungry eyes. "This is a big deal," he said. "I should stay here and look after things."

If he left his little brother alone with the girl, Tiger would have her bent over a conveyor belt before the Bentley reached the end of the drive. "Henries can handle this," Eric said. "I need you elsewhere. I've got a shipment coming in tomorrow evening. You and your crew will have a chance to do some real work for once."

Tiger glowered.

"Get in the car."

Tiger held his ground, smacking his gum and looking petulant. Eric met his gaze and held it, daring him to disobey. Finally, Tiger shook his head and loafed to the Bentley. Eric watched him go and considered putting a bullet between his shoulder blades.

One less problem to deal with.

He waited until his brother got in the car and slammed the door, then he turned to Henries. "Do you need anything from me?" he asked.

The big Australian shook his head. "Nah. We got this under control."

Eric joined his brother in the back seat of the Bentley. The driver started the car, swung around, and started up the long gravel drive. Eric waited until they were ten minutes south, headed into Kowloon, to start making phone calls.

CHAPTER TWENTY-SIX

A FAMILIAR MINIVAN IDLED AT THE CURB WITH THE side door open. Oscar reached under Noble's jacket, relieved him of his weapon, and then waved him into the vehicle. Noble slid in behind the driver. Samantha climbed in beside him, and Oscar crowded onto the end of the seat with his pistol aimed at Samantha's belly. The heavyset driver turned to glare at Noble. The bridge of his nose was swollen and black where Noble had hit him with the binoculars. Bits of wadded-up toilet paper, stained pink with dried blood, stuck out of each nostril. The bloody tissue spoiled his attempt at intimidation. He turned back to the wheel without a word, started the van, and pulled out into traffic.

Samantha sat with her hands clasped together in her lap and her head bowed. Tears streaked her cheeks. Her hair hung in a black curtain over her face. "I'm so sorry, Jake."

"It wasn't your fault," he said. "They knew we were coming."

"Diego?" she guessed.

Noble nodded. "He must have figured he could get back in Lady Shiva's good graces by selling us out."

Oscar pressed the gun into Samantha's side. "Shut up."

The driver turned on the radio. Filipino pop music filled the van with synthesized drums and maddeningly repetitive lyrics. Noble kept his attention on the road. Jeepneys jammed up the boulevard, and pedestrians thronged the sidewalks. He knew the area. They were headed toward Makati, a Mecca of depravity and squalor at the heart of a wicked city.

He scolded himself for not dispatching Diego when he had the chance. It was sloppy. He had gotten soft, and he would pay the price for it. Worse, he had let Samantha get tangled up in this and now she would pay for his mistake as well. A knuckle of fear squeezed his guts. He'd been in tighter spots before but not by much.

Noble didn't fear death so much as what came after it. If his mother was right then eternity was heaven or hell, and Noble was headed for the wrong side of that equation. If the public education system was correct then death was nothingness, a long black non-existence. The first idea scared him, and the second bored him. Noble couldn't decide which was worse, hell or nothingness.

Before he solved the eternity question, the driver turned off Makati Avenue in the bustling red-light district down a narrow side street. Noble caught a quick look at the front of the building as they rounded the corner. The sign said *LUSH* in lurid red neon. Underneath it advertised 'Health and Relaxation Massage.'

The van squealed to a stop in back of the club. Oscar

climbed out and yanked on Samantha's arm. She stumbled from the vehicle and went down on one knee. He hauled her back to her feet, pointed the gun at Noble, and took a step back, keeping the distance. Noble scooted across the leather seat and stepped out onto cracked asphalt.

Fear etched itself on Samantha's pretty features. She stared into Noble's eyes, looking for comfort, some sort of nonverbal signal that he had the situation in hand. He tried to convey confidence with a tight nod. It seemed to give her some strength. Unfortunately, that was all he had to offer. She had no idea what they were in for. Noble did. The knuckle of fear had become a fist, twisting his guts, like someone wringing out a soapy dishrag.

The back door was solid metal. A hooded light bulb flickered and buzzed, attracting moths. They zipped and looped around the weak glow. The driver hammered on the door with an open palm.

Noble considered making a play for Oscar's weapon. It was going to be bad inside for him, and it would be worse for Samantha. All they could do to Noble was torture and kill him, but they could keep Samantha alive. Some fates were worse than death. But Oscar kept three long strides between him and Noble, and he kept the pistol pressed against Samantha's chest. Noble could rush him, but Oscar would pull the trigger and Samantha would be dead before she hit the ground. And there was still a chance—a small chance—if Noble played his cards right, he could get them both out alive.

A heavy bolt drew back with a clang, and the metal door swiveled open on well-oiled hinges. A bar of light spilled across the alley.

Noble found himself staring down the twin barrels of a sawed-off shotgun. The guy holding it was on the wrong side of sixty, shirtless with droopy man boobs, and blown out flip-flops.

At a nod from Oscar, the old man stepped aside. Samantha and Noble were herded in. The metal door slammed shut with a hollow boom like distant thunder. The sound raised goose bumps on Noble's arms. The small hairs at the back of his neck stood on end.

They were in a dingy kitchen with mold creeping between the tiles. Noodles boiled on an electric hot plate, filling the air with the aroma of cabbage and red peppers. A chipped Formica table held a half-finished mahjong game. A potbellied man in a stained white undershirt straddled a metal folding chair, watching a football game on a black-and-white portable television. A .38-caliber Smith and Wesson lay on the table. The ancient revolver was black and pitted with rust. It looked like it hadn't been cleaned or oiled since World War II. There was no use lunging for it; the thing would probably blow up in Noble's hand.

A beaded curtain led to the front rooms where Noble heard the sharp cackle of the working girls and the rich baritone of Louis Armstrong growling his way through, "What a Wonderful World." Where they'd come by the old recording or why they chose to play it in a whorehouse, who could say? Noble wondered if it would be the last song he ever heard and if there was some sort of poetry in that fact. Did it have what college literature professors called symbolism? Or was it just a crappy coincidence?

The only other door led to a sagging staircase, which they climbed all the way to the third-floor landing. The air reminded Noble of finger-painting day in kindergarten class. He faced a short hall with two doors on the left and a third straight ahead. Three surprisingly good oil paintings graced the crumbling plaster walls.

The paintings were so tasteful and so completely out of place that Noble's steps faltered. All three showed the Philippine countryside, rice paddies, and thatched roof farmhouses under blue skies boiling with white clouds.

The fat driver gave Noble a push to get him moving again. Oscar opened the first door at the top of the stairs, and his partner manhandled Noble inside.

CHAPTER TWENTY-SEVEN

Bakonawa Ramos, dressed in his bathrobe, poured a fourth cup of coffee and added a dash of bourbon. He padded through the first floor of his brownstone on Massachusetts Avenue to the front window and parted the curtains with one hand. The sun had come up on the capital city, driving back the late September chill. Pete Shaffer, from three doors down, jogged past on his morning run. Ramos kept expecting to look out and see police cars parked on his manicured lawn, but the rest of the world went on as usual.

He went to his study and dug through the desk until he found an ancient pack of Djarum Black buried down at the bottom of a drawer. They still had the sweet clove smell even if it was a little muted. More digging turned up a gold-plated Zippo engraved with his initials. He pocketed the cigarettes and the lighter and climbed the steps to Bati's bedroom.

He still thought of it as her room even though she hadn't really lived in it since leaving for Yale. It still looked like the bedroom of a high school girl. The bed had a duvet with big yellow sunflowers. Teddy bears were stacked in the corner. A powder-blue dresser was covered in the kind of jewelry marketed to teenage girls. Pictures of Bati and all her friends were stuck in the mirror frame. Ramos recalled all the sleepovers and the giggle of prepubescent girls.

Peter Rabbit and the Pokey Puppy graced the bookshelf along with high school textbooks and several religious works by C.S. Lewis and Lee Strobel. She had been in middle school when all the church stuff got started. One day she came home and asked if she could go with a friend to some kind of concert, and Ramos said yes not knowing it was a Christian concert. Soon Bati was attending Sunday services. Then Wednesday-night Bible studies. He thought it was a phase that would pass. He should have put his foot down. By the time he realized she wasn't going to outgrow her teenage convictions, it was too late.

Now he wondered if all this could have been avoided if only he had said no to that damn concert.

He plucked a picture of a smiling Bati from the mirror and sat down on the bed. This had become his routine, a ritual. He would wander through the house sipping coffee and peeking out the windows, but he always ended up in Bati's room looking at the pictures and touching the teddy bears. He hadn't shaved since he got the news. Heavy black stubble covered his face. He had dark bags under his eyes. He rarely slept and when he did, he curled up in a corner of Bati's bed. He was terrified to move anything in the room.

When he left to haunt the rest of the house, he replaced the picture in exactly the same place on the mirror frame. He felt that if he could preserve it all exactly as it had been when Bati still lived here, then he could keep her alive.

He took the Djarum Blacks from his pocket, debated with himself for several minutes, and finally stuck one in his mouth. It took several tries, but he got a flame from the Zippo, lit the cigarette, and took in a lung full of slightly stale nicotine-laced smoke.

He coughed, pounded his chest with a fist, and then had another drag. In a few moments, it was like he had never quit. He smoked that one down to the filter and lit another one from the stub. Before long, a lazy blue cloud filled the bedroom. Morning sunlight streaming in through the blinds lit the slowly swirling eddies of smoke.

His phone rang in his pocket. The sound shattered the quiet. He had turned the ringer all the way up to be sure he didn't sleep through it, not that he'd slept. Ramos flinched and nearly spilled his coffee. He placed the mug on the bedside table and put a shaking hand in the pocket of his bathrobe. The number said private caller. He took another drag from his cigarette to calm his nerves, pressed the talk button, and put the phone to his ear. "I'm listening."

"Good to hear your voice, old friend. How long has it been?"

Naked fear gripped his heart with icy fingers and refused to let go. Sweat sprang out on his forehead. Ramos cleared his throat. "Twelve years."

"That long?" Eric Tsang said. "Time flies."

Ramos stabbed his cigarette out on the bedside table.

He didn't shout or make threats. Letting his emotions control him would only complicate the situation and maybe get Bati killed. "How much is it going to cost to get my daughter back?"

"I don't want your money," Eric told him.

"Then what do you want?"

"You are going to turn over all of your operations to me and end your crusades against human trafficking."

Ramos snorted. "You're out of your mind."

"I'm not finished," Eric said. "You are also going to tell the world who you really are."

Ramos had feared something like this for ages. He lay awake nights wondering what would happen if he was ever exposed. Now, all of his worst nightmares were coming true at once. His sins had finally come back to haunt him. The threat of exposure was only trumped by a father's instinct to protect his daughter. He looked around Bati's bedroom like he might find help from the stuffed animals. They stared mutely back at him. "This crosses the line, Eric. We've always been competitors, but we've always been gentlemen about it."

"That was before you started using the CIA as your own personal police force," Eric said. "You stepped over the line first, old friend."

Ramos stood up and paced Bati's bedroom. "Look, Eric, you have my word I won't put international law enforcement onto any of your operations."

"Not good enough," Eric said. There was a pause on the other end of the phone. "You know I have a daughter now? She's seven. They grow so fast."

"What's your point?" Ramos asked.

"I lose sleep at night thinking of all the terrible things that might happen to her," Eric said.

"I want to talk to my daughter. Put her on the phone."

"I left her in the care of some mercenary friends. I'm paying them top dollar to keep her alive. How much she suffers is up to you. You have forty-eight hours to turn over all your operations to me and then tell the world who you really are. After that I'm going to let my men have their fun with your little girl and I'll mail what's left of her back to you in a shoe box."

Ramos gripped the cell phone so hard the plastic creaked. "I want to talk to her. I want to know she's all right. Put her on the phone."

"You have forty-eight hours."

"If you hurt her-" Ramos started to say, but Eric had already hung up.

He slammed the phone down on the dresser. The glass screen cracked. Ramos paced around the room with his fists clenched, breathing curses. He grabbed his cell and went to the kitchen where he poured a drink. Two fingers of bourbon helped steady his nerves.

Eric was as good as his word. If Ramos did not hand over his operations in forty-eight hours, Bati would die badly. He didn't want to think about that. It felt like a mean little rat gnawing at the lining of his stomach.

He poured another drink and went to his study. He had work to do. In forty-eight hours he would be ready for the trade off, but he had another card to play first. He picked up the phone and dialed Fredric Krakouer.

His wet workman picked up on the first ring. "Hello."

"She's in Hong Kong," Ramos told him without preamble. "Eric Tsang has her. Take my private jet to HK. It will be fueled and waiting by the time you get to Ninoy Aquino."

"I'm on my way," Krakouer said. "Before you hang up, there is something you should know. I think the CIA has operators over here looking for Bati."

Ramos pulled out his office chair and sank into it. "You think or you know?"

Krakouer hesitated. "I'm almost positive they're operators. There are two, a guy and a girl. They showed up at Diego's place earlier this evening and then again at a club owned by Lady Shiva. The boxer got the drop on the girl. They are in a meeting with Ana right now."

Ramos ran a hand through his thinning hair. If the CIA was investigating, it wouldn't take them long to put two and two together. But if Ana had the agents then she might be able to dispose of them before they caused any trouble.

"What do you want me to do?"

"I want you to do what I told you," Ramos said. "Get to Hong Kong, find out where Eric Tsang is keeping my daughter, and bring her home. If anyone gets in your way, kill them."

"Okay," Krakouer said and ended the connection.

Ramos punched in a number he hadn't dialed in years. The situation was quickly spiraling out of control. He needed to get out in front. He was dealing with people who knew his secrets. If the agents in Manila were talking with Ana, they would start making connections. Ramos couldn't take that risk. While he listened to the phone ringing on the other side of the planet, he saw a book of poems by Robert Frost on his bookshelf.

"And miles to go before I sleep," Ramos said to the empty room. "And miles to go before I sleep."

CHAPTER TWENTY-EIGHT

NOBLE HUNG FROM A HOOK IN THE CEILING. OSCAR was using him as a punching bag. They had duct-taped his wrists together and lifted his hands over the hook like a slab of beef. His toes barely scraped the threadbare rug.

Boxing gear and exercise equipment littered the makeshift gymnasium. There was a bench press loaded up with 210 pounds, a teardrop-shaped speed bag on a platform, and a rawhide jump rope tangled up on the floor. Scotch tape affixed a poster of Oscar De La Hoya in red trunks and matching gloves to the crumbling plaster wall. The room had the stale, lingering odor of a high school gym locker. Noble's gun, wallet, phone, and the small pouch with Bati's insulin syringes lay on the bench press.

Samantha had been duct-taped into a cheap rolling office chair. They had secured her wrists and then Oscar and his buddy had left her alone to focus on Noble. She had watched the first few minutes with her face pinched and tears rolling down her cheeks. She pleaded with them to stop, and when that didn't work, she shut her eyes tight and turned her face away.

Oscar was stripped to the waist, his fists wrapped, working Noble's midsection like a champ. The driver stood behind Noble, holding onto his belt loops to stop him from swaying—the way a coach would steady the bag. They had obviously done this before. Oscar kept his punches centered on Noble's stomach and ribs to cause maximum pain without destroying his ability to answer questions later. Hit a guy in the head, and you risk knocking him out or breaking his jaw. Too many blows to the head will cause the brain to swell; the pain receptors short-circuit. The victim can't feel a thing. You can wail on a guy all day long and get nothing out of him. But punch a guy in the rib cage, and he will feel it every single time.

And Noble felt it all right. Every impact sent shock waves of pain rippling through his internal organs. His ribs groaned from repeated blows, threatening to break. The hard flat smack of Oscar's fists filled his ears. Beads of sweat rolled down his face and pasted his shirt to his chest. He tried desperately to remember his training.

Between the military and the CIA, Noble had been through two courses on resisting torture. The Army had forced him to stay awake for days without food, standing in the 'stress position,' and screaming in his face. It wasn't pleasant, but he survived. The Company took things one step further, locking him in a room and giving him low voltage electric shocks. It was never enough to do any real damage, but enough to hurt like hell. Noble had endured it all knowing his life was never really in danger. Resisting interrogation at the hands of his training officers was different than holding out under genuine torture. Every-body has a breaking point. Sooner or later Noble would reach his.

They would start asking questions, and Noble didn't have the answers they were looking for. When they found that out, he and Samantha were dead. For her sake, if not his own, he had to hold out as long as possible and hope an opportunity for escape presented itself. He hung there with his lips peeled back from clenched teeth, reminding himself to breathe.

It was hard to say how long Oscar wailed on him. Noble's sense of time lagged and leapt as the pain took its toll. Eventually the door opened and Lady Shiva entered wearing a poison-green dress embroidered with a red dragon.

She was tall and whisper thin. Crow's feet had started around her eyes. Her age did nothing to detract from her cold beauty. She examined Noble with hard eyes.

The champ took a breather. Sweat matted his black hair to his head. He kept up his footwork, bouncing on the balls of his feet, and looking over his shoulder at his employer.

Lady Shiva perched herself on the bench press with a straight back. She crossed one leg over the other. The split in her dressed revealed a tantalizing glimpse of bare thigh. She gave a slight nod to Oscar. The punishment resumed. Lady Shiva watched.

Noble grunted with every impact. One of his ribs was ready to snap. He could feel it. While he played the part of the punching bag, Shiva picked up the Armscor pistol. She turned the weapon over in her hands and then set it aside.

She picked up the leather pouch. She inspected the contents. "That's enough," she said.

The beating stopped.

Noble gasped for breath. Sweat stung his eyes, forcing him to blink.

"Oscar has a prize fight next weekend," Lady Shiva said in an offhand tone.

Oscar thrust his chin at the poster taped to the wall. "I named myself after Oscar De La Hoya."

"We have high hopes for him," Shiva said.

"His right cross could use some work," Noble said. "Plant your feet more. Get your waist into it."

Oscar cocked his fist back and drilled a punch into Noble's fly ribs. The force caused his whole body to pendulum back and forth on the hook.

"Much better," Noble managed to groan out.

Samantha let out a sob.

Lady Shiva's expressionless eyes went to the girl and then back to Noble. "You are a hard man," she said. "Mr...?"

"Taft," Noble told her. "William Howard Taft."

"Twenty-seventh President of the United States," Shiva said. "I'm familiar with American history."

She waved a long-fingered hand, and Oscar rewarded Noble's lie with a flurry of blows. The last one slipped below the belt. A sickening ache spread through his guts like liquid fire. He groaned in pain.

"Admirable," Lady Shiva said.

She stood up, crossed the room, and ran her fingers through Samantha's hair. Sam ducked her head and hunched her shoulders. Shiva took a fist full of Samantha's black tresses and yanked.

Sam shrieked. Her chin came up. Her small breasts strained against her black cotton shirt.

"Americans are so very predictable," Lady Shiva said. "You think nothing of giving your own life, but when it comes to the life of an innocent..."

Lady Shiva nodded at Oscar.

The boxer back-handed Samantha across the face. The slap rocked her head to the side and left four perfect fingerprints on her pale cheek. To her credit, Samantha pressed her lips together and refused them the satisfaction of hearing her pain.

Oscar cocked his hand back for another slap.

"Enough," Noble said.

"Like I said..." The hint of a smile played across Lady Shiva's painted lips. "Predictable. That's why America hasn't won a war since the fifties. The American public can't stand to see collateral damage. They want nice, clean wars where no one ever gets hurt." She flashed her teeth at Noble. "Where is Bati Ramos?"

Noble was running out of moves. He decided to gamble. "Let the girl go, and I'll tell you."

She laughed. "Or I could let Oscar and Li take turns with her while you watch," Shiva said. Her words lacked malice. She wasn't trying to scare him. She was simply stating a fact. She would hurt Samantha until she got the truth from him. "Where is Bati Ramos?"

"I don't know," Noble said.

Lady Shiva snapped her fingers, and Oscar struck Samantha another stinging blow.

"I don't know where she is," Noble said. "I thought you

had her. Why else would I try to set up a meeting with you?"

Lady Shiva's brow pinched. "Perhaps," she said. She picked up the Armscor pistol from the bench and put the barrel against Samantha's kneecap. "Perhaps you are lying."

Samantha looked at Noble with naked terror etched on her face. Her mouth opened in a silent plea for help. Shiva's finger tightened on the trigger. The hammer inched back. He should have told her to pound sand, but he couldn't watch while Lady Shiva crippled Samantha.

"My name is Jacob Noble," he said.

Shiva's finger relaxed on the trigger. She cocked an eyebrow at him. "The truth at last. Who do you work for?"

"I used to work for the CIA," he told her.

"Now you work for Bakonawa Ramos?"

"No," he said. "I'm an independent contractor."

"A mercenary," Shiva said.

"If you like the expression."

"Where is Bati?"

"I don't know."

"Well, Mr. Noble," Shiva said. "If you don't know where Bati is then you are of no use to me."

She pointed the gun at Noble's head.

He had nowhere to go and no cards left to play. She was close enough that he could try one last, desperate attempt to kick her, but that would only buy him a few moments at best. Shiva was about to punch his ticket. He was going to step over into the unknown, and that nagging fear hit him. The question of what happens after?

The tip of Shiva's manicured finger turned white against the milled aluminum trigger. Noble squeezed his eyes shut, waiting for the thunderclap that would end his life.

He was saved by a knock at the door.

Shiva looked annoyed at the interruption. She lowered the weapon. "Enter!"

The door opened and the potbellied man from downstairs stuck his head in. He held up an old gray cordless telephone the size of a brick. Shiva's nostrils flared. She snatched the phone from his hand, and he retreated, closing the door gently.

CHAPTER TWENTY-NINE

SHIVA WAS FRUSTRATED. OSCAR HAD MADE A MISTAKE bringing these two here. They had no information and now she had to murder them both. As a rule, she tried to avoid murder whenever possible. It was messy, attracted attention, and left a trail. It would force her to change tear down shop and set up somewhere else for a while, just until the heat was off. Fortunately she had several clubs and safe houses where she could hide. She tucked the phone between her ear and shoulder. "Hello?"

"Hello, Ana."

A bitter smile curled up one side of her mouth. She had been waiting for this call. She handed the gun to Oscar. He took it and paced back and forth in front of the mercenary.

"To what to I owe the pleasure?"

"My sources tell me you are holding a man and a woman," Ramos said.

"Perhaps."

"Don't play games," Bakonawa said. "I know the boxer

got the drop on them. They're with you right now. They are CIA operatives. They need to be eliminated."

Shiva switched ears with the phone and looked over her shoulder at Jacob Noble. Sweat trailed down his face, gathered on the tip of his chin, and fell in fat droplets to the floor. One side of his shirt was untucked and his hands, bound in duct tape, were turning purple. His fingers resembled tiny eggplants. If he was still with the company, killing him would bring a world of hurt down on her head. *Was he lying when he said he no longer worked for the CIA? And what about the girl?* She sat with her head bowed and her eyes screwed shut, muttering to herself or whimpering. It was hard to tell.

"How very interesting," Shiva said.

Oscar stopped pacing, thumbed back the hammer, and pressed the barrel into Noble's cheek, forcing his head to one side. Shiva snapped her fingers. Oscar looked over his shoulder. She waved him off. His mouth pressed together in a thin line, but he took the gun out of Noble's cheek.

"Kill them both and get rid of the bodies."

"As usual, I don't think you appreciate my position," Shiva told him. She was not in the habit of taking orders from Bakonawa Ramos, and killing CIA agents was bad for business. She stayed alive by staying in the shadows. Murdering intelligence officers would invite open warfare.

"Eric Tsang has Bati," Ramos growled into the phone. He paused to let that information sink in. "We both know he'll kill her. I've got a man on his way to Hong Kong to rescue her right now, but he can't do his job with two American agents complicating the situation. Get rid of them."

Shiva paced the floor. The 'man' Ramos referred to was

Frederick Krakouer, a hot-tempered ex-marine with an alcohol problem and trouble with authority. He was the proverbial bull in a China shop. Despite all his faults, he had more of a chance of getting to Bati than any of Shiva's people. "Very well," Shiva said. "We'll do it your way."

CHAPTER THIRTY

NOBLE HUNG FROM HIS WRISTS. HE COULDN'T FEEL HIS fingers, and his ribs grated with every lungful of air. It made breathing painful. He listened to the phone conversation, trying to pick out any small detail he might use to stay alive a little while longer. He was clinging to life on a second-by-second basis.

Lady Shiva was careful with her words. She didn't give anything away or use names, but Noble didn't need both sides of the conversation to know the winds had changed. Were they blowing in his direction?

She set the phone down on the bench press, crossed her arms over her narrow chest, and considered Noble the way an astute trader might study a potential stock investment. Oscar and Li waited. Shiva picked up the insulin case and rapped it against her open palm. "The girl is diabetic?" she asked.

Noble inclined his head. Anything more would cause pain.

Shiva weighed her options. "Bati is being held by a man named Eric Tsang in Hong Kong. Do you know him?"

Noble had heard the name mentioned during intelligence briefings on human trafficking coming out of Hong Kong. Tsang was the current head of the Nine Dragons. "Doesn't ring a bell."

Oscar drove a punch into his navel.

"I might have heard of him," Noble admitted.

Oscar hit him again.

"Now I remember," Noble spoke through gritted teeth.

"None of my people have the necessary skills or subtlety to go up against a man like Tsang," Shiva said. "But you have a fighting chance."

"Why would I help you?" Noble asked. He was going to do it, of course. It was the only way he would leave this room alive, but he wasn't going to make it easy on her. He had to make Shiva think she was coercing him, instead of the other way around.

A cruel smile turned up her red lips. Her eyes went to Samantha. "Because I will be holding onto your friend until you return. She can help *entertain* my guests. Who knows? She might even enjoy it."

Samantha choked back a sob.

Noble clamped his teeth together and jerked his head forward, conveying reluctant acceptance.

Shiva's grin widened. She held up the slim box of insulin. "I will be holding onto these as well."

"You are gambling with Bati's life," Samantha said.

Shiva flashed her a withering stare. "A risk I'm willing to take."

Oscar pointed the gun at Noble. "You're going to trust this guy?"

Lady Shiva cuffed his ear with an open palm. The blow turned Oscar's head. He closed his eyes and pressed his lips together.

"Take the girl to my studio," Shiva ordered.

Oscar and Li pushed Samantha to the door. One of the wheels made a sound like a tiny mouse hunting for cheese. Samantha threw one last, desperate look over her shoulder at Noble as they steered her out of the room, and then she was gone.

Lady Shiva ran one manicured fingernail over his chest. "Other parties want you dead, Mr. Noble."

"Tell them to get in line."

She toyed with one of the buttons on his shirt. "I hope I'm not making a mistake letting you go."

"I'll find the girl, just don't hurt Samantha."

Oscar and Li returned, lifted Noble off the hook, and dropped him unceremoniously on the threadbare rug. Pain tap-danced up his spine to his brain. He groaned.

Oscar rolled him onto his back and used a switchblade to cut away the duct tape. Noble flexed his fingers, made fists, and rotated them in an effort to get some feeling back into his hands. He sat up with a grunt of effort. Six years in the Green Berets and another four with Special Operations Group had taught him how to handle pain. He was hurting but not quite as bad as he made out.

"How's this going to work?" he asked.

Lady Shiva seated herself on the bench press. "Oscar and Li are going to drive you to the airport, and all three of you will get on the first plane to Hong Kong. I expect hourly updates. If I don't get a call from Oscar every hour, I'll kill the girl. If I get a call saying you've misbehaved in any way, I will kill the girl. If you double-cross me, I'll kill the girl."

"I'm starting to see a pattern."

"You're a quick learner."

"Top of my class," Noble said. "How do I know I can trust you?"

She cocked an eyebrow. "What choice do you have?"

"Since you put it that way," Noble said. He tried to stand, but his legs gave out. He crumpled to the floor. Oscar and Li grabbed him under the arms and hauled him up.

CHAPTER THIRTY-ONE

Oscar and Li wheeled samantha into an art studio and left her alone. For several minutes she sat there, all the muscles in her body tense and her shoulders drawn up. Being held at gunpoint and slapped around had reduced her to a trembling mass of nerves on high alert. Her cheek burned, and her neck muscles ached. She waited, hardly daring to breathe, for Oscar to come back and finish what he had started.

Minutes ticked by and nothing happened. The naked terror began to subside, and Sam relaxed her muscles. Clearer thinking prevailed. A few slaps was small change compared to what Noble had been through. She took stock of her situation. She was still alive, relatively unmolested and, for the moment, unguarded.

The room was long and low with hardwood floors and sloping eaves. Dozens of oil paintings were stacked against the walls. They showed real talent. Samantha had taken an art elective at Yale, mostly because there was a cute guy in the class that she had a crush on. She didn't have any artistic ability as it turned out, but she recognized it when she saw it. These were better than average with an eye for color and movement.

An easel stood in the center of the room with a half-finished painting of the ocean and a few fishing boats. Next to it was a rolling cart cluttered with supplies. The smell of oil and solvents filled her nose.

Samantha glanced at the closed door and chewed her bottom lip. Her legs were free. She had nothing to lose. She pedaled herself toward the cart. The hard wheels of the office chair made a loud grinding noise against the hardwood floor, broken by the tiny *squeak-squeak-squeak* of one rusty wheel. She cringed but kept going, praying under her breath.

The cart had a collection of brushes in an old coffee can, half used tubes of oil paints, a mixing palette, clothes pins, and dirty wedges. Flecks of paint covered everything. Nothing looked particularly useful. Sam had been hoping for a knife or something sharp to cut the tape.

Some of the smaller brushes had handles that tapered to fine points. She maneuvered the office chair around the corner of the cart, leaned over, and tried to clench one of the slender brushes between her teeth. It took several tries, but she finally bit down on a single brush. She lifted it from the coffee can and then tried to drop the brush into her open palm and missed. It clattered to the floor.

She growled in frustration, glared at the fallen paintbrush, and then started again. She did better the second time, but that brush also ended up on the floor. Samantha tossed her hair and told herself, "Third time pays all."

She thrust her neck forward and came up with one slender brush clenched between her teeth. She dropped it into her open hand. With that done, she turned the brush and stuck the bristles into her mouth. It tasted like paint. She bent over and used the sharp end to pierce a small hole through the duct tape on her wrist.

A bright thrill of victory surged through her. A little time and a lot of effort was all that stood between her and freedom. She hunched over and drilled another hole through the duct tape, and another. Sweat beaded on her forehead, and the muscles in her neck started to cramp. Making the holes line up was difficult. She kept jabbing her own skin, but she refused to give up.

She had made a dozen tiny punctures when the door opened. Lady Shiva, in her poison-green dress with her heavy lidded eyes and long legs, entered. She looked from the fallen brushes to Samantha's restraints and snorted.

Sam straightened up and spat the paintbrush out onto the floor. Her heart hammered at the wall of her chest. The muscles in her shoulders tensed. She clenched her fists and readied herself for a slap or more hair pulling.

Shiva swung the door shut, turned on a large diffused lamp, and replaced the work in progress with a blank canvas. Sam watched in tense silence while Shiva selected a graphite pencil and started sketching lines. She worked without speaking. Occasionally her dark eyes flitted from the canvas to Sam and back.

When it was clear that Lady Shiva meant to go on sketching, Samantha discreetly tested the gray strip of duct tape around her right wrist. She hadn't even done enough to loosen the grip. She could see why men used the stuff to repair anything and everything around a house. She gave up on the tape and turned her attention to Lady Shiva instead. "Did you paint all of these?" she asked.

Shiva studied her from under those heavy painted lids. "Don't ask stupid questions."

Sam pressed her lips together.

Shiva went back to sketching. The graphite pencil made soft scratching noises on the heavy canvas. Samantha summoned up her courage. "You don't have to do this, you know?"

When Shiva didn't respond, Samantha plunged ahead. She had no idea where she was going, only that she had to try something. She did not want to end up a smack-addicted whore. "Bati and I run a shelter for women just like you."

That got Shiva's attention. Her pencil paused. "You know Bati?"

Samantha nodded. "We graduated Yale together."

"And you help her run the shelter?" Shiva asked.

"We have sewing classes and cooking classes and church services on Sunday..." she trailed off.

"The good little Christian missionary girl," Shiva said. "Will you save my soul? Are you going to tell me that I can redeem myself? Leave this all behind? And what would I do then? Get a *job*?"

"You could sell your paintings," Samantha offered timidly.

Lady Shiva threw her head back and laughed. The gesture struck Samantha as strangely familiar.

"You really are naïve," Shiva said. "We can't all go to

Yale, missionary girl. Some of us were born to poor farmers and sold as whores." She went back to sketching with quick, jerky movements. A vein pulsed in her forehead.

"Is that what happened to you?" Samantha asked.

"I was nine," Shiva said. "The first night was the worst. I bled for three days."

Samantha felt like she would vomit. Tears welled up in her eyes. She wanted to say something, but everything she thought of sounded hollow and pathetic.

"Tell me about Bati," Shiva said in a conversational tone. "Does she believe in all this God nonsense?"

"She's the one that came up with the idea of opening a shelter in Manila," Sam said. A bittersweet smile turned up her mouth and faded just as quickly. She had followed Bati over here with high hopes and grand ideas about saving women from the sex industry. Reality had set in fast. The shelter cost more than they had budgeted. Twice they had to ask Bati's dad for more money. Then there was the problem of getting women through the doors. Both Sam and Bati worked long, thankless hours, only to watch most of the girls who passed through the shelter go right back to prostitution.

Sam looked at Shiva. "Why do you want to hurt Bati? She hasn't done anything to you."

"Hurt her?" Shiva asked. Her pencil stopped. "I don't want to hurt her. I just want to meet her." Her face pinched. She seemed to think she had said too much, and she went back to drawing. She stuck her tongue firmly in the corner of her mouth while she worked.

The truth came to Samantha in a flash. The high cheekbones, the wide mouth, the heavy lidded eyes, the way she stuck out her tongue when she concentrated. "You're Bati's mother."

CHAPTER THIRTY-TWO

Noble allowed himself to be hauled back downstairs and into the minivan at gunpoint. He slid across the long seat, placing himself behind the driver. Oscar climbed in next to him, but this time Samantha wasn't between them. The boxer had Noble's own pistol pointed at his belly. The heavy bull barrel of the .45 caliber gaped like the open mouth of a train tunnel.

Li climbed in the driver's seat. He fired up the engine and battled his way through the Makati traffic before merging onto the skyway and revving the old minivan up to sixty miles an hour. Balding tires hummed against the blacktop. The worn-out transmission hiccupped twice, throwing Noble against the cracked vinyl seat.

Arc sodium lamps drew circles of light on the dark stretch of highway like tiny UFOs looking for signs of life. Each time they passed beneath a street lamp, the cabin of the minivan was momentarily lit by a pallid yellow glow before plunging back into darkness. Noble counted the seconds of shadow between pockets of light. At this speed he had roughly ten seconds between street lamps. It took his pupils less than a second to adjust to the change, which gave him a small window. He had to take out both Oscar and Li without giving either man enough time to make a phone call. He groaned and stretched, trying to work some of the soreness out of his aching abdominal muscles.

Oscar eyed him and thumbed back the hammer. The noise punctuated the steady hum of the tires. The kid was a welterweight, with reflexes born from countless hours spent in a boxing ring. Noble, on the other hand, had spent the last four years fishing. He kept screwing up his face in pain and shifting every couple of minutes until Oscar got used to him squirming in discomfort. It wasn't a hard sell.

After a mile, Oscar stopped glancing every time Noble groaned. Two miles later he barely noticed Noble's discomfort.

Fighting inside a moving vehicle is a desperate gambit, but it was now or never. Noble slowed his breathing and kept counting the seconds between darkness and light. As they passed from the spill of a street lamp back into shadow, Noble slapped the gun.

Oscar jerked the trigger.

The resulting explosion inside the minivan felt like a ball-peen hammer against Noble's eardrums. A fiery tongue leapt from the barrel. The bullet drilled a hole through the driver's seat and into Li's side, two inches below his armpit. It was a lethal wound. Li slumped against the steering wheel, and the minivan careened left across two lanes of traffic toward the concrete divider. Horns blared.

Noble latched onto the gun with his right hand and

punched Oscar in the face with his left. He was aiming for the point of Oscar's chin—what boxers call 'the button'—but hit teeth instead.

The minivan humped up onto two wheels like a dog lifting its leg on a fire hydrant. Noble was thrown into Oscar, and they both slammed into the passenger side door. The front bumper impacted the concrete barrier with a crunch. All of the windows exploded in a shower of broken glass. The minivan crashed down onto the passenger's side and ground to a halt.

The engine coughed and died. One tire continued to spin, making a whirring noise overhead. The smell of leaking petrol filled the van. Cars crept past as drivers slowed down for a better look at the carnage.

Noble and Oscar lay on the crumpled side door fighting for control of the gun, glass grinding beneath them. Both men had one hand on the pistol. Oscar snaked his free arm around Noble's neck and choked off his air supply. Noble drove his elbow into Oscar's face three times, hard and fast. Oscar's grip on the weapon relaxed, and Noble twisted it out of his hand.

He turned the .45 on Oscar and fired. Another deafening boom filled the cabin. A brass shell-casing joined the litter of broken glass. The slug punched through Oscar's shoulder. Blood splattered the crumpled passenger side door. Oscar screamed and pressed a hand over the wound.

Noble scrambled into a half-crouch and stamped his foot down on Oscar's bloody shoulder.

The boxer spit curses.

Noble eased off the pressure. "How many more guys are there in Shiva's club?"

"Two," he said.

"You and Li and the two guys in the kitchen?" Noble asked. "You expect me to believe Lady Shiva only has four trigger men?" He stomped Oscar's shoulder.

"I swear it's the truth," Oscar gasped.

"Cell phone," Noble ordered.

Oscar dug in his pocket and handed over his phone. "Just don't kill me, Okay?"

"It's your lucky day," Noble told him.

He climbed over the seats into the front.

Li was still alive. The safety belt held him in the driver's seat. His right arm hung down. Fat red drops of blood dripped from his fingertips. Noble patted his pockets, felt the lump of a mobile, and dug it out.

Li drew a ragged breath and managed to whisper, "Hospital."

"Pal, you need a miracle," Noble told him. He slipped out through the busted front windshield. Glass crunched under foot. He had a host of small cuts and scrapes, but no major injuries.

A gray Nissan was stopped in back of the overturned minivan. The driver, a middle-aged Filipino man in a rumpled blazer, opened the door and stuck his head out. "Is everyone all right?"

Noble leveled the .45 at him. "Get out."

The man shifted into park and leapt out of the vehicle.

"I'll need your jacket too."

The man shrugged out of his sport coat, handed it to Noble, and then backed up until his butt pressed against the concrete barrier. Noble took the coat and slid in behind the wheel. "You have a mobile?"

The man nodded.

"Call an ambulance," Noble said.

He deposited the handgun, the coat, and the phones he'd collected into the passenger seat, put the Nissan in gear, and swung around the crashed wreck of the minivan. At Sales Road, Noble turned off the skyway. He navigated the confusing series of switchbacks at the airport and got turned around headed north. He checked his watch. Twenty minutes had gone by since they left the club, which gave him another forty, give or take, before Shiva would expect a phone call. Noble had no doubt she would make good on her threat. He had forty minutes to get back to Makati and rescue Samantha before Shiva killed her.

CHAPTER THIRTY-THREE

THE STOLEN CAR WAS RUNNING ON FUMES BY THE TIME Noble made it back to Makati Boulevard. The Nissan hiccupped and sputtered the last few hundred meters. It died two blocks from club *LUSH*. Noble coasted into an open parking spot on the south side of the street. The back bumper hung out into traffic. People beeped their horns and swerved around.

Noble checked himself in the rearview. He felt worse than he looked. He had a small cut above his left eyebrow. The blood was already dry. Being thrown around inside the minivan had done nothing for his bruised ribs. Breathing was painful, but he could still stand up straight. He shrugged out of his torn and bloodied suit jacket and pulled on the stolen sport coat. It was wrinkled, a little musty, and a size too big, but it worked for metro Manila. He tucked his shirttails back inside his trousers and stuffed the .45 in his waistband. He left the keys in the ignition, got out, and walked.

He wanted to shoot his way up to the third floor and leave Lady Shiva's operation a smoldering wreck. The idea appealed to his sense of vengeance but would only get Samantha killed. With an experienced team to back him up, Noble wouldn't think twice about a hard take down. Instead of a highly trained squad of professional door kickers, he had a pistol with five rounds in the magazine and bruised ribs. To get Samantha out alive he would have to infiltrate and find his way up to the third floor without raising the alarm.

He passed a half dozen other sex parlors on the way. Pretty young Filipino girls in skimpy lingerie sat around looking bored. A few of them flashed fake smiles. Most pulled on cigarettes and watched the street traffic with dead eyes. Lady Shiva's club had a barker out front. He was all knees and elbows with long hair and a sad attempt at a mustache. He couldn't get into a rated R movie in America, but he was hawking prostitutes in Manila. He spotted Noble. "Hey, my friend! What are you looking for? You like girls?"

Noble slowed, not really stopping. He did his best to look nervous and intrigued at the same time. "I don't want to get in any trouble."

"Is legal in Manila," the kid lied with a smile and pointed to the open door. The snarling guitar and mumbled lyrics of an old John Lee Hooker tune had replaced Louis Armstrong. In the display window, three girls crowded onto a large antique chaise lounge, taking hits from a hookah pipe. One of the girls winked and crooked a finger.

"Really?" Noble raised his eyebrows and made a show of checking out the trio.

The barker grabbed his elbow and tugged. "What kind of girls do you like? You like young girls? I got a nice young girl just for you. Maybe you like two girls at same time? Come in, my friend. No problem. Totally legal."

Noble put on a sloppy grin and allowed himself to be dragged inside. "I suppose it couldn't hurt to take a peek."

Lady Shiva had gone for a late Victorian look. The place was packed with sturdy old furniture upholstered in busy patterns and low lighting. It could have passed for a small but classy hotel lobby, except for the half-naked women everywhere.

The harsh stink of pot smoke filled his lungs. He had smoked dope twice in his life—both times to keep his cover intact during operations. He didn't like the sluggish feeling or the way everything seemed to lag. Noble was a man who needed to feel in control of himself and his environment. He knew operators that used alcohol to take the edge off. Noble drank coffee by the gallon to stay focused.

Two of the girls gravitated over to him. Both were young and beautiful and, judging by the track marks on their arms, addicted to heroin. It was a common practice in the brothels. Club owners shoot farm girls full of smack. Most people are addicted after the first hit. After that the girls will do whatever it takes to get the next fix.

Lately, a lot of Filipino pimps were making the switch to meth. It's cheaper, just as addictive, and can be cooked up in a bathtub. Apparently Shiva wasn't keeping up with the trends.

One of the girls ran a nail over Noble's earlobe, while the other slipped a finger between the buttons on his shirt. "You strong man," she said, probing his abdominal muscles.

Her touch caused him exquisite pain, but Noble forced a smile onto his face. He chose one of the girls at random and put an arm around her waist.

Her name was Paquita. Price negotiations were short. He hedged just enough to make the interaction believable. She took him by the hand and led him upstairs. Noble did his best to keep his mind on the mission and off her swaying hips. It wasn't easy.

The affectation and refinery was reserved for the first floor. The second floor had all the charm of an hourly motel. Noble followed Paquita along an uncarpeted hall with bare bulbs overhead and peeling wallpaper. The girls had attempted to personalize their doors with construction paper and magic markers. Paquita's door had pink hearts and her name in blue. Her room had a twin mattress on a cheap metal frame and a small bedside table with a lamp.

"Ladies first," Noble said.

She bared her teeth in what was supposed to be a smile. Noble let her get just inside the room and then put her in a chokehold. He kicked the door closed with his heel.

Paquita bucked widely in an attempt to escape his grasp. She clawed his arm with her fingernails. The sport coat took most of the damage. When that didn't work, she tried to claw his face. Noble craned his head to the left to avoid her talons.

Her eyes bulged from their sockets. Her mouth opened wide for a scream. A soft whisper escaped. She stomped down with her heel. Noble moved his foot in time, and she missed. The impact rattled the lamp on the bedside table and the light flickered. Noble doubted anyone downstairs would pay attention. They probably heard thumps and bangs all night long.

The tension drained from her limbs as she used up the last of her oxygen supply. Her eyes rolled up. Her fingers lost their strength, and her feet stopped kicking. Noble tossed her limp body onto the bed. She fell in an unconscious sprawl with her hair spread across the mattress in a black fan.

She wouldn't stay out long. Certainly not long enough for him to sneak upstairs and deal with Shiva. He needed to make sure she stayed under for another ten minutes at least.

Most of the girls lived at the house and needed someplace to keep their meager belongings. Noble checked under the bed. There was a battered suitcase. Inside he found miniskirts, tank tops, lingerie, and three pairs of shoes. He also found her kit. It was a tin lunch box with Charlie Brown and Lucy on the lid. Lucy had swiped the football again. Charlie was in mid-air, a look of surprise on his face, about to come down on his back.

Inside the lunch box, Paquita had a spoon, lighter, syringe, a length of hollow tube and enough brown powder in a small Ziploc baggie to put her out of action for a while.

She moaned. The toes on her left foot, spread, curled, and relaxed. Oxygen was returning to her brain. Her fingers and toes were probably feeling like pins and needles.

Working fast, Noble shook some of the heroin into the charred and blackened spoon, and then flicked the lighter. In a few moments he had a bubbling witch's brew. He siphoned it into the syringe as Paquita was coming around. One skinny arm waved drunkenly in the air like she was fighting off an unseen attacker.

Noble grabbed the other arm just above the elbow and pinched. Her veins bulged. He jabbed the needle in and pressed the plunger. Heroin goes to work almost immediately. By the time she swam up from unconsciousness, the smack had taken effect. She giggled. Her head lolled from side to side like her neck muscles were made of rubber. Her eyelids fluttered open, and her pupils dilated. She stared at the ceiling and giggled again.

Noble patted her cheek. "Sweet dreams, kid."

CHAPTER THIRTY-FOUR

SAMANTHA'S FEAR OF LADY SHIVA WAS REPLACED BY A morbid curiosity. She strained forward in her seat in order to study the infamous Madam. It was like looking at Bati, only twenty years older. Now that she had seen it, she couldn't unsee it like one of those pictures with an image hidden inside a seemingly meaningless geometric pattern.

"How did it happen?" Sam asked.

"How does it always happen?" Shiva said without looking up from her sketch.

"I meant how is it possible? Mr. Ramos is a good man. He campaigns against human trafficking. He gave us the money to start the shelter."

"Tell me all about this *good* man." Shiva flashed Samantha a baleful look. "Who do you think bought me like cattle when I was nine? He raped me. Forced me into prostitution. He did things to me that would send you screaming back to your ivory towers and mocha lattes."

Sam swallowed a knot in her throat. She didn't need Shiva to spell out the details. She had heard the horror stories from the girls passing through the shelters. Some had started even younger than Shiva, sold into slavery by uncaring fathers and abused by countless men before being discarded like trash.

"Then I had Bati," Lady Shiva said. A sad smile flashed across her face. She rummaged through the trolley full of art supplies until she found a sharpener. She gave the pencil an angry twist, peeling off a perfect curl of wood. It dropped to the floor. "She was a beautiful little baby girl, and the only good thing that ever happened in my life. And that black-hearted bastard stole her from me."

She gave a bitter laugh and waved a hand to indicate the room around them. "This was his idea of compensation. He set me up as a madam to make up for destroying my life and stealing my baby girl."

———

Noble left Paquita in a heroin-induced slumber, locked the door behind him, and hurried to the end of the hall. A battered and scarred door led to the back staircase. He pressed his ear to the hollow core and listened. He heard only silence on the other side. He couldn't risk hanging around on the second-floor landing too long. Sooner or later one of the girls would finish up with a customer and emerge from her room. She would want to know what he was doing there. He wouldn't have a good reason for snooping around the back staircase so he held his breath and turned the knob.

The stairs were empty. He caught the distant noise of

the football match on the television. The crowd cheered as the home team scored, and the thin sound floated up from the kitchen. Noble eased the door shut, drew his pistol, and took the steps two at a time to the third floor.

If Oscar had been telling the truth then the only muscle left in the building was downstairs watching the Manila Nomads. But Noble couldn't afford any unnecessary risk so he searched the top floor starting with Oscar's gym. He threw open the door, swept the room with his pistol, found it empty, and moved on.

The next door was Lady Shiva's bedroom. It had more real estate than Oscar's gym and better furnishings. The soft scent of lavender immediately enveloped him. The leather pouch with the insulin shots lay on the dresser along with the extra magazines for Noble's weapon. He pocketed the kit and the mags and spotted a framed sketch of Oscar on the bedside table.

The picture gave Noble valuable insight into Lady Shiva. Despite her treatment of Oscar, he was more than hired muscle—more like family. Noble couldn't be sure how that might play out over the next few minutes, but he was suddenly glad he had spared Oscar's life.

He stepped back into the hall, paused in front of the last door, and heard voices. He could make out Lady Shiva's menacing purr followed by the occasional response from Samantha. The conversation was muffled and indistinct. Noble threw open the door and entered with his gun up, looking for threats.

Dozens of canvases were propped against the walls, overlapping one another. Samantha was still duct-taped into the chair. Shiva stood in front of a wooden easel with a charcoal pencil in one hand. She moved with the speed of a hunting tigress. She swept the easel out of her way with one arm. The canvas landed with a flat smack on the hardwood floor. Shiva leapt behind Samantha, using the girl as a shield, and pressed the point of the pencil into Sam's neck. She hunkered down until Noble could only see one heavy lidded eye peeking over Samantha's shoulder.

"One more step and I'll stab this pencil into her carotid artery," Shiva said.

"Go ahead," Noble told her. He centered the front sight on Shiva's exposed eye. "She's not mission vital."

Shiva showed her teeth. She dimpled Samantha's flesh with the graphite point. "I don't believe that for a second, Mr. Noble. Now put that gun down or I'll scream."

Noble turned his attention to the doorframe. He rapped the wood with his knuckle and made an approving face. "It's sturdy enough to stop a few bullets. Go ahead and call your men. I'll shoot them as they come up the steps." He put his shoulder against the molding and aimed down the hall to the stairs, then looked over his shoulder at Shiva. "Where does that leave you?"

"With a pencil in your girlfriend's neck," she said.

He shrugged. "Make up your mind quick. I've got to go to Hong Kong and save Bati. That's what we both want, right? It will be a lot easier if I don't have to shoot my way out of here."

Her jungle cat grin faltered. "You would walk out of here with the girl and leave me in peace?"

Noble jerked his head forward. "That's what I'm saying. Let the girl go, and we walk. Call for your men and I knock down the whole house of cards. The choice is yours."

Her eyes narrowed. "Oscar?"

"He's alive," Noble told her. "He'll have to take a rain check on that fight."

Shiva slowly straightened up to her full height. Her eyes never left Noble's. He let her sort through her options. It was a short list. He had her in a tight corner. Her only real choice was to let Noble walk out with Samantha and then try to relocate her headquarters before he could put Manila branch onto the club. Shiva took her time about it but finally removed the pencil from Samantha's neck.

Sam slumped in the chair and made a noise like air escaping a balloon.

As a sign of good will, Shiva took a small pair of scissors buried amid the supplies on the cart and cut through the duct tape. Sam peeled her wrists free, sprang out of the chair, and ran to Noble's side.

"Let's get out of here," she said.

Noble held up a hand. "What do you want with Bati?"

It was Samantha who answered. "She's Bati's mother."

Noble watched Shiva's reaction. She didn't deny the accusation. She replaced the scissors on the cart and calmly returned his gaze. Noble tried to wrap his head around the implications.

"And Bakonawa Ramos is the father?" he asked.

Shiva nodded. She picked up the easel and reset the legs. She replaced the canvas. Samantha's face had begun to take shape in black charcoal lines against the white background. One eye was still a blank orb with no pupil, and her nose needed nostrils, but the resemblance was there. Shiva took up her pencil, gave it three quick turns in the sharpener, and went back to drawing.

Noble stood there a moment longer, his gun trained at the floor. Ramos had an illegitimate love child with a prostitute. The information was a hell of a bargaining chip for anyone who knew. Ramos had to be worth a few million, and a scandal like that could ruin him.

"How did you find her?" Noble asked.

"I kept tabs on her for years," Shiva admitted. "It wasn't hard when her father was always in the spotlight. Then two years ago, she fell off the radar. I searched everywhere."

Shiva stopped long enough to look at Samantha and then filled in the missing eye. "I nearly gave up hope," she said. "Then one day I learned through sources that Ramos was bankrolling a Christian shelter for women. My connections in the police department put the place under surveillance. Imagine my surprise. Bati was right here in Manila, under the last name Ramirez."

Noble filled in the rest. "So you struck a deal with Diego. You'd pay off his gambling debt, and he would make sure Bati was outside the shelter at a certain time. Then you sent a couple of heavies to kidnap her."

"That's right," Shiva said.

"What happened?" Noble asked. "Eric Tsang bought off your men?"

"It would appear so," Shiva admitted.

Noble grinned. "It's hard to find good help." He grabbed Samantha's arm and steered her out the door.

"Mr. Noble?"

He paused in the doorframe.

"Will you tell your handler where to find me?"

"Yes," he said.

"How long have I got?"

"Hard to say. A few hours at most."

Shiva acknowledged that with the barest of nods.

Noble left her in the art studio working on a sketch of Samantha while he escorted the real thing down to the second floor.

CHAPTER THIRTY-FIVE

Noble steered Samantha down the back staircase to the second floor. The door to Paquita's room was still closed. By the time she came up from her heroin nap, local law would be swarming all over this place. Hopefully she would be placed in a hospital where she could rehab and, maybe, straighten out her life. Noble ushered Samantha down the main staircase to the first-floor salon. They were halfway to the door before one of the girls spotted the sleek black pistol in Noble's grip. She gave a shout and pressed herself up against a wall. It took another moment before anyone else realized what had upset her. Then everyone scrambled for cover.

Noble hurried Samantha outside.

The barker was still on the sidewalk, calling out to people passing by. He turned, saw Noble, and smiled. "Hey, my friend, you done already?"

Noble stuck the gun in the kid's face.

He raised both hands straight in the air.

"Find a new job," Noble told him.

The kid turned and took off down the sidewalk at a sprint.

Noble tucked the .45 in his waistband and hailed a passing taxi. He gave the driver the address to a motel in Tondo where he had gone in the past to lie low. The cabbie pulled into traffic. Noble didn't relax until the lights of club *LUSH* had dwindled in the rearview. He let out a breath and slouched into the seatback.

Samantha sat against the passenger side door, as far from him as possible, staring pointedly out the window. Noble was expecting gratitude. A tight hug and a kiss would be nice. But he would have settled for a simple thank you. Instead he got the silent treatment.

"Something troubling you?" he asked.

She fumed in silence for another block and then said, "You were bluffing, right? When you said I wasn't mission critical?"

Noble laughed. "I risked my life going back for you. I could have taken the first flight to Hong Kong and left you at the tender mercies of Lady Shiva."

She closed her eyes and nodded. "I'm sorry. It's just... I was so scared."

"Everyone gets scared," Noble told her. "It's what you do with it that makes the difference. And you did well."

"You didn't seem scared," Samantha said. "Even when they were beating on you."

"I was," he assured her. "I just channeled that fear into something more important."

"What?"

"Keeping you alive," Noble said.

She reached across the seat and took his hand. He almost pulled away. Falling for her had nearly gotten them both killed. She was young and pretty and cool under pressure, but Noble knew he had to walk away. They were two totally different people thrown together by circumstance. She ran a shelter for abused women. He was a hired gun, not to mention a decade older. But knowing the truth and acting on it are two different things.

He gave her hand a little squeeze.

The neon sign out front of the motel said "the Highstreet," but it could just as easily have been called the Last Resort. It was the type of place that rented by the hour, took cash, and didn't ask for an ID. Noble paid for the whole night. The room was on the second floor with a window overlooking the street. The carpeting was worn through in places. A poster on the back of the door advertised X-rated movies. The bed sheets smelled like mold and mothballs.

Samantha raised her eyebrows. "You really know how to treat a girl."

"That's me," Noble said. "A regular Casanova." He tossed the key with the orange plastic fob on the TV stand, went to the window, and checked the street.

Samantha turned on the bedside lamp.

Noble drew back from the window. "Turn that off."

"Sorry," Samantha muttered.

She pulled the chain, plunging the room back into semi-darkness. Noble went back to watching the street. He stood there several minutes until he was sure they had not been followed. Then he went around unplugging the television, phone, lamp, and anything else that had a cord.

Before Samantha could ask, Noble said, "Remote

listening devices require a power source. If an intelligence agency wants to bug a room, they piggy back the microphone onto a lamp, a telephone, anything with an electric cord."

"So unplugging all the electronics would cut the power to the listening device as well."

Noble made a gun with his thumb and forefinger. "You are a quick study, Samantha."

"My friends call me Sam," she said.

"Okay, Sam."

"How about you?" she asked. "Do your friends call you Jake, or Jacob?"

"I don't have friends." He brought out one of the phones he had collected from Shiva's henchmen and dialed.

Manny picked up after a dozen rings.

"It's me," Noble said.

Manny cleared his throat. It took him a moment, but he finally managed to form words. "Do you have any idea what time it is?"

"I need to hitch a ride to Hong Kong," Noble said.

"Try the airport," Manny told him.

"I was hoping for something a little more clandestine."

"A gun is one thing," Manny said. "A black crossing requires a lot of resources. I'll have to pull strings. People will ask questions."

"Have you got a pen and paper handy?" Noble asked.

He gave Manny the address to club *LUSH*. In the intelligence community, nothing is free. Noble needed to give a little to get a little. And it wouldn't hurt to curry favor with Manila branch.

While he spoke, Sam got his attention. She pointed to

herself, pointed out the window to a drug store across the street, and then made a walking motion with two fingers. Noble shook his head, but she was already on her way out the door.

"What am I supposed to do with this?" Manny asked.

"How would you like to be the guy that brings down Lady Shiva?"

The sleep evaporated from Manny's voice. "You're kidding?"

"She's been living in the top floor of a cat house in the red-light district," Noble told him.

"Right under our noses," Manny said.

"You'll have to move fast if you want to catch her. She knows you are coming," Noble said. "Any ideas on getting me into Hong Kong?"

"I'll see what I can do. Keep this phone handy," Manny said and hung up.

Noble dialed Matthew Burke. Through the window he watched Sam cross the street and disappear into the twenty-four-hour convenience store. Flashing signs advertised beer, cigarettes, and lotto. *What could she possibly need at two in the morning?*

Matt's baritone voice answered. "Twenty-four hour plumbing."

"It's me," Noble said. "Had to switch phones."

"Jake, tell me you have good news?"

"Okay, I have good news."

"You've got the girl?"

"No," Noble said.

"You know where she is?" Burke asked.

"Not exactly," Noble admitted. "But I know she's in

Hong Kong. What can you tell me about a triad boss named Eric Tsang?"

Noble heard Burke tap keys. "Nasty piece of work. He started out as a runner for the Nine Dragons when he was ten. Worked his way up through the organization. Now he's running the show. Our sources say he murdered the previous Dragon Head with a box cutter. He also fed an enemy through an industrial press."

"Sounds like a real charmer."

"Tsang isn't your average street thug. Our analysts say he's self-educated. Never went to school, but he's a voracious reader. Since taking over the Nine Dragons, he's expanded the operation from a minor heroin ring into prostitution, gambling extortion, trafficking, you name it. He's even got several legitimate fronts that are making honest-to-God profits. Tsang has a wife and a seven-year-old daughter. He's also got a younger brother called Tiger. Little brother is a bit of loose cannon."

Noble snorted. "There's one in every family. Any connections to Bakonawa Ramos?"

Keys tapped. "None, but he's got a team of mercenaries on his payroll. Five of them. These guys aren't doughnut-eating ex-cops padding their pensions either. Let's see." Burke read off the roll call. "Henries, Johnathan. Former Australian Special Air Service Regiment. Two tours in Afghanistan with the SASR and two more as a private contractor. Donaldson, Graham. Also former SASR. Philippe, Rene. French Foreign Legion. Served in Cambodia, Somalia, Rwanda, and Sarajevo. Lehrer, Daniel. Israeli Defense Force with ties to the Kidon. And last but not least

Fischer, Otto, a former sniper for the Kommando Spezialkräfte."

Noble bared his teeth.

"Quite a roster. If Eric Tsang has the girl, you can bet these hard cases will be guarding her," Burke said.

"Lucky me," Noble said. "Has Ramos contacted any authorities?"

"No. In fact he hasn't emerged from his house since this whole thing started. He's being awfully cagey. Any ideas why that is?"

"I'm starting to get an idea," Noble said. He switched ears with the phone. Sam emerged from the convenience store with a shopping bag dangling from her elbow.

Layers within layers.

He watched her cross the street. "I should be able to lay out a more complete picture once I've got the girl. Do me another favor."

"I live to serve," Burke said.

Noble ignored the cheek. "Dig up everything you can on a Samantha Gunn. That's Gunn with two Ns. She works with Bati at the shelter."

"I'm on it."

Noble hung up before Burke could ask any more questions. He could hear Sam in the hall outside the door. She had probably gone for food; that was the simple answer, but she had been gone long enough to make a phone call.

CHAPTER THIRTY-SIX

SAMANTHA CAME IN CARRYING A PREGNANT SHOPPING bag. She tossed the bag on the bedspread. Cardboard and paper packages murmured together.

"You didn't make any phone calls did you?" Noble asked. He sat down on the end of the bed with a painful grunt and dumped the bag. Inside was a collection of medical supplies, a pair of toothbrushes, protein bars, generic acetaminophen, and bottled water.

Sam shook her head. "My phone is on the seat of my car still parked on the street in front of club 10." She took a bottle of water, twisted the cap off, and drank half in one long swallow.

"Probably stolen by now," Noble remarked.

"The phone or the car?"

"Both," Noble said.

One side of her mouth turned up in a tired grin.

He reached for the aspirin. He shook four into his open

palm and then, with a shrug, two more. He popped all six into his mouth and swallowed.

"You should eat something," Sam said. She sat down beside him on the bed, sorted through the protein bars, and handed one to him.

He tore off the wrapper and took a bite. His mouth watered at the taste of chocolate and peanuts. He hadn't eaten since landing in Manila. He scarfed down two more bars and quaffed a bottle of water. He was so intent on the food, it was several moments before he realized Sam was watching him eat.

"What?"

She cleared her throat. "I should take a shower."

In the bathroom, she shut the door, and Noble heard the lock click into place. The water turned on. A moment later, he heard the change in the rhythm as she stepped under the stream.

He tried not to think about her in the shower. It was a tough sell. His brain wanted to stay on the image, but Noble forced his thoughts to other matters. His first order of business was replacing lost fluids. He twisted open another bottle of water and drank. He took his time.

With his hunger satisfied, the pain was setting in. Oscar had done his best to turn Noble's ribs into ground chuck. The smallest movements hurt. It would only be worse tomorrow. He sorted through the medical supplies. Sam had done a thorough job. She had bought bandages, medical tape, Neosporin, and ice packs. He applied Neosporin to the cut above his eyebrow and then stood up to remove his shirt and jacket.

Sam chose that moment to turn off the shower. She

emerged from the bathroom wrapped in a towel. Her black hair hung in limp tangles around her bare shoulders. The open window bathed her bare limbs in soft blue moonlight. Damp white cotton clung to her slender frame.

She saw him struggling out of the jacket. "Let me help."

"Not necessary," he said.

She hurried around the end of the bed and helped him free his arms from the sport coat.

"It's fine," Noble said. "Really."

"Don't be stubborn," she said.

The smell of her clean skin invaded his senses. Her fingers worked the buttons on his shirt. It was an effort to remain still. He felt like a college student posing for the freshman art class. It made him nervous and excited all at the same time. She pushed the shirt down over his shoulders.

Black and purple welts marched in ranks from his belt line to his chest. Her fingertips traced the narrow channels between his abdominal muscles. Her small chest swelled and relaxed with each breath. Bright spots of color appeared in her cheeks. A silent, intangible tension flooded the room. It felt like someone had turned the thermostat up to roughly the surface temperature of the sun.

She was closer now. Noble didn't know which of them had moved, but the distance between them shrank until he could feel her breath on his chest. She turned her face up to his. Her lips parted. "It's mostly bruising."

"Mostly," Noble said.

"We should put ice on it."

Noble could only nod in agreement.

She reached past him and sorted through the medical

supplies until she found an ice pack. She crushed it to release the cold, then placed it gently against the worst of the bruising. He drew a sharp breath through clenched teeth.

"Sorry," she said.

Noble took the ice pack out of her hand and tossed it on the floor. A trembling breath escaped her chest. Noble pulled her tight. Their lips met, slow and timid, then with more passion. They tangled up in each other's arms. Noble gave himself over completely to the passion. He let his hands slide down her narrow waist, over her hips until he was touching the bare skin of her slender thighs. He started to push the hem of the towel up.

Sam drew a sharp breath and forced him away. Conflicting emotions fought for control of her face.

"What's wrong?" Noble tried to pull her back into his embrace.

She pushed back with more force. "We can't, Jake." She held onto her towel with both hands. "I can't. I'm sorry."

The heat of the moment winked out like a candle in a hurricane. In all of his years, Noble had never encountered a more puzzling riddle. One moment she was wrapping herself around him with an urgency that boarded on desperation and the next she didn't want to be touched. He couldn't figure it out so he cleared his throat. "I should get into a shower."

She nodded, clutching her towel like he might try to take it by force. "That's a good idea."

Noble went into the bathroom, flicked on the light, and closed the door. Dead moths filled the glass belly of the overhead fixture. The weak bulb revealed moldy grout and a cheap plastic shower curtain. Samantha's clothes were folded on the back of the toilet tank. Black lace peeked out from between shirt and denims. The sight set his pulse galloping. He stripped down and left his own clothes in a pile on the floor.

CHAPTER THIRTY-SEVEN

SAM FELT LIKE SHE WOULD MELT INTO A PUDDLE ON the cheap motel carpet. She grabbed two fistfuls of hair and tugged. She could still feel Jake's strong hands exploring her body and his hungry mouth on her lips. She sat on the edge of the bed, twisted the cap off a bottle of water, and drank. It did nothing to quench the fire. She realized she had left her clothes in the bathroom only after Jake turned on the shower. She stared at the closed door.

Why had she stopped him? He probably thought she was crazy. Had she blown it completely?

She stood up, paced around the room, and then sat down again. The idea of climbing in the shower with Jake flashed through her mind and made her thighs tremble. She told herself it was the situation; she had been held at gunpoint, strapped to a chair, and slapped around by a criminal. Jake had saved her. A certain gratitude was expected, but it was more than that; she wanted to feel his kisses so badly that it was a raw ache in her chest. She wanted to spend one night wrapped up in Jake's arms, but she had made a promise her sophomore year.

Like so many college freshman, Sam had gone a little crazy. It was her first time away from home, and the freedom went to her head. She started to party, and her grades slipped. She nearly got kicked out of school. Bati convinced her to attend a campus Bible study. It was where the two of them really connected for the first time. Sam started going regularly. She turned around her flagging grades and promised herself that the next guy she slept with would be her husband.

She balled her fists in frustration. That promise felt meaningless given the circumstances. Facing the very real possibility of death, one night of pleasure seemed insignificant.

She finished off the bottle of water, went to the window, and leaned on the sill. An occasional car hummed past on the street below. She tried to focus her mind on something else. Anything else. The more she tried, the more Jake Noble, with his strong hands and eager mouth, intruded upon her thoughts until Sam was sure she'd go mad.

The answer came to her all at once. She would let Jake decide. Maybe it was stupid. Maybe she'd hate herself in the morning, but she would put the burden on him and accept whatever happened.

Sam let the towel fall to the floor and climbed, naked, into bed. Her heart hammered so hard she could feel the blood in her ears. *Would he climb under the covers and make love to her? Would he sleep on the floor?* If he ignored her and slept on the floor, what did that mean? If he made love to her, what did that mean?

She closed her eyes and waited. She felt confused and scared and not at all sure she was making the right decision.

CHAPTER THIRTY-EIGHT

Bati had to escape and to do that she needed to know everything about them and how they operated. She started by attaching names to faces. The big redheaded Australian called Henries seemed to be the leader. He gave the orders. Shortly after their well-dressed Chinese boss drove away, Henries told the German with the long rifle to find a perch—whatever that meant—and that was the last Bati had seen of the man named Otto.

The others spread out around the rock quarry. Occasionally one would pass by the open door but never the same man twice in a row and never with the same frequency. Bati tried counting the seconds between their passing and came up with different numbers each time.

Even if she could get past the soldiers, she couldn't sneak past Fau and Paeng. They were sitting on sacks of crushed gravel in the open door. Paeng was half asleep. His chin kept settling onto his chest. He would snap awake, only to nod off again. Blood from his severed finger had soaked through the bandage and dotted the floor. Bati could have *walked* past Paeng, but Fau was awake and ranting. He wasn't happy about the situation. Every few minutes his tirade climbed a few octaves and he would wave his gun around, leveling impotent threats at empty air. He was in the middle of one of these rants when Henries appeared in the doorframe like a ghost materializing out of the darkness.

Fau stopped midsentence. He looked like a teenager caught watching porn. The two men eyed each other with open hostility. Fau's handgun looked puny next to the sleek black rifle strapped across Henries's chest. Bati held her breath, hoping they would kill each other.

No such luck.

Fau dropped his gaze. The muscles in his jaw clenched. He stared sullenly at the ground. Henries waited a beat before turning his back on the kidnapper and strolling back outside. His boots crunched through the gravel, and he disappeared from sight. As soon as the Australian was out of earshot, Fau launched back into his tirade. Paeng peeled open one eye long enough to add a weak grunt then nodded off again.

While Fau ranted, Bati considered her options. She was barefoot, and her hands were zip-tied behind her back. Her only weapon was the syringe hidden under her thigh. It felt less than useless against men with guns.

She wondered if there might be another way out of the building, a back door or a window she could climb through. She peered into the dim recesses, but she couldn't see very far. It was built in the shape of an L, and Bati could only see to the corner. She scooted in that direction, hoping for a better view.

"Hey," Fau said. "What are you doing?"

"I have to pee," Bati told him. It wasn't a lie. She'd been holding it for hours.

"So pee," he said.

"Not here," she said. "Can't I go back there?"

He glanced at his partner, but Paeng's eyes were shut. Large red drops fell from his bandaged hand. Fau sighed and stood up.

Bati palmed the syringe and scrambled to her feet. "I can do it," she said.

He grabbed her by the elbow. His nails dug into her skin. Bati winced. "You're hurting me," she said.

"Shut up."

Fau marched her around the corner. Dust-covered machinery connected by a series of pipes and electrical wires crowded the long end of the building. It smelled like an attic that hadn't been aired out in years. A red metal toolbox sat atop one of the conveyor belts. A name was stenciled on the side in simplified Chinese.

Between the Chinese boss and the toolbox, Bati realized they must have taken her to the mainland. Panic set in. It felt like a metal band closing around her chest. China was huge. They could be anywhere. *Not anywhere*, she reminded herself. They had to be somewhere near the coast, probably a major shipping port. That still left a lot of possibilities. They could be in Macau, Kowloon, Shenzhen, or any number of port towns in the South China Sea.

Fau gave her a push.

Bati stumbled forward, fought for balance, and then turned to face him before he could see the syringe clutched in her hand. It forced her to expose the front of her pink panties.

He looked her over and then said, "Go ahead."

"I can't go with you watching."

He shrugged. "Then hold it."

Bati whimpered. If she tried to hold it any longer she would end up peeing down her own leg. Fau made no sign of moving, so she used her zip-tied hands to tug down her underwear and then squatted. Fau watched with a smirk. Bati clamped her eyes shut. It took an effort on her part, but she finally let go. Her stream pattered on the concrete floor. She felt immediate relief mixed with anger and humiliation. Her face burned with shame while warm urine puddled around her heels.

She finished and opened her eyes. Fau had watched the whole time. Bati straightened up and did her best to drag her panties back up with her hands zip-tied behind her back. It didn't work.

Fau deposited his handgun on top of a rusting machine and grabbed her by the hair.

Bati let out a terrified shriek. "Please don't hurt me."

He closed his mouth over hers. She tried to pull away. He held her in a steel grip. She could taste the cigarettes on his breath. She squealed and squirmed. Her struggles only seemed to excite him more. He spun her around and shoved her, face first, against the nearest machine. She felt her eyebrow split open and warm blood trickle down her cheek.

Unreasoning fear gripped her. She pushed away from the machine and lashed out with the syringe. She was aiming for his crotch, but stabbed him in the stomach instead.

He shouted, more from surprise than pain. His hand came around in a hook and hit her hard across the face. Her feet tangled, and Bati went down flat on her chest. All the air burst from her lungs.

Fau jerked the needle out of his stomach and tossed it. The disposable syringe clattered across the concrete. He knelt down behind Bati and pinned her to the ground. She heard his zipper purr open. She let out a shrill screech. She bucked her hips and lashed out with her bare feet, but he was too strong for her.

As she struggled, a single thought went through her brain, *God, please don't let this happen to me!*

A thunderclap filled the crushing facility. Blood sprayed Bati's back and hair. Fau slumped sideways. His head hit the floor with the same sound a rotten cantaloupe makes when it's dropped. His eyes were open and staring. Pulpy red matter oozed from his open skull.

Henries stood at the corner with smoke leaking from the barrel of his rifle. He lowered the weapon, crossed the floor, and pulled Bati to her feet. She started to stammer out her thanks. He didn't seem to care one way or the other. He took hold of her panties and yanked them up over her hips, covering her nakedness, then clapped a hand on the back of her neck and drove her back to the front of the building.

The Frenchman waited at the open door with his rifle across his chest and his hands folded over top of the weapon. Paeng was in a semi-conscious slump. Henries steered Bati to the open space directly in front of the rolling door. "Sit," he ordered.

She sat. "Please," she said. "Please just let me go. My father will pay you."

"Shut your mouth," he ordered. To the Frenchman, he said, "If she tries anything, bash her brains in with the butt of your rifle."

"Oui."

Henries stalked over to Paeng and kicked the sack he was napping on. The kidnapper came awake with a start, blinked, and looked around.

"Your partner is dead," Henries told him. "I killed him. Keep your hands off the sheila, or I'll kill you too. Understood?"

In reply, Paeng held up his bandaged hand, as if to ask how he could possibly molest her with a finger bitten off. He sniffed, held his ruined hand to his chest, and let his eyes droop shut. Henries stalked out, leaving Bati alone with the Frenchman.

CHAPTER THIRTY-NINE

NOBLE STOOD UNDER THE CHILLY SPRAY, ALLOWING the cold to numb his aching muscles and clear his head. He had a job to do, and fantasizing over Samantha Gunn wouldn't get it done. He needed to focus. Bati was in Hong Kong being held by the Nine Dragons triad. How and why was still a mystery, but at the very least he now had a compass heading. He turned off the shower, dried himself, and pulled his pants back on. He couldn't do anything until Manny found him a back door into HK so he had a few hours to kill. He determined to get some shuteye.

Sleep while you can was a mantra he learned in Special Forces. Missions sometimes required soldiers to stay awake for days. Noble had mistakenly thought that covert operations would move at a more relaxed pace, but the world of espionage was a lot like a battlefield. There were sleepless days spent watching and waiting, interspersed with brief periods of intense activity. Only difference was most days Noble didn't have to wear combat boots.

He exited the bathroom. Sam lay under the covers. Waves of black hair spilled across the pillow. One bare shoulder was lit by the light coming through the window.

Noble glanced from her huddled form beneath the blankets to the folded clothes on the toilet tank and chewed the inside of one cheek. Any ideas he had about sleep vanished. He moved the jumble of medical supplies and bottled waters to the television stand, then eased himself down on the bed next to her. She turned over and draped one arm across his chest.

"Jake?"

"Yes," he whispered.

"I trust you."

He hesitated, unsure what she meant by that. Did she mean that she had changed her mind about sex? Or that she trusted him not to take advantage of her while she slept next to him naked? Or that she trusted him in general? The more he thought about it, the more meanings he manufactured. He didn't know how to respond. Finally he said, "Get some sleep."

He spent the rest of the night intensely aware of her body draped against him. Sleep was impossible. Inside Noble's heart, there was a vault where he kept all the dreams that would never come true. Marriage, kids, family, and other things normal people took for granted were locked behind the heavy steel door. Life in the world of espionage didn't leave much room for romance. The CIA has an exceptionally high divorce rate. Family life is something to be enjoyed by the working class crowd—the average Joe who knows where he will be tomorrow, and next week, and next month. Special Operators sacrifice relationships on the altar of national security. Over the last four years, Noble had toyed with the idea of dialing in the combination to the safe but never summoned up the courage.

Now, lying here in the dark next to Samantha, the bolts drew back. The door swung open a fraction. Noble peeked in at all those dreams of happily ever after. He found himself entertaining wild fantasies where he and Sam were married. He imagined a house in the mountains and a couple of kids. Swing sets. Backyard barbeques.

Crazy, Noble told himself. Those things were for other people.

The mobile phone rang, and Noble's eyes snapped open. He had been drifting on the soft edge of sleep where reality starts to fold dreams into waking thought. The first ghostly gray tinge of predawn light filtered in through the curtains. The time stamp on the mobile told him it was 4:37. He tapped the talk button and put the phone to his ear. "Yeah," he said through a mouth full of cotton balls. He wanted to go back to sleep. He settled for closing his eyes.

"I had to cash in a lot of favors, but I managed to put together a black crossing," Manny said.

"I owe you."

"I'm keeping score," Manny said. "Are you familiar with the Navotas neighborhood?"

North of Manila proper, Navotas City was a finger of land, much like Manhattan, surrounded by narrow waterways. The only way on or off the island is bridge or water taxi. Unlike Manhattan, Navotas was mostly a jumble of confusing shanty towns and shipping companies.

"Much as a foreigner can be," Noble told him.

"Meet me at the bakery on the corner of Pascual and Little Samar street in one hour. I've got a plane for you."

"Wait. What kind of plane?" Noble started to explain that it had been a while since he'd been in the air, but Manny had already hung up. Noble dropped the phone down on the mattress and sat up. All the muscles in his stomach screamed with the effort of pulling himself into an upright position. He let out a groan.

The covers next to him were empty.

Samantha knelt on the floor at the foot of the bed with her forehead against the mattress, muttering under her breath. She had dressed sometime in the night.

Noble frowned. "You Okay?"

Her head nodded in the affirmative. She looked up and there was a red line printed across her forehead from the edge of the mattress. "I was praying."

Noble rolled his eyes. He got up, dug through the shopping bag for a travel-size toothpaste, and went to the bathroom where he turned on the sink. He brushed his teeth with more vigor than necessary.

Sam appeared in the doorframe and crossed her arms under her breasts. "You have something against prayer?"

He took the toothbrush out of his mouth, spit, and gazed at her reflection in the mirror. "You really believe some spirit in the sky is going to help us save Bati?"

"I believe in a higher power," she said. "I'm sorry if that offends you."

Noble snatched a hand towel off the rack and patted his face dry. "My mother is always going on about the power of prayer."

"Sounds like a smart lady."

"When the doctors told me she had cancer, I prayed." He wadded the hand towel and tossed it on the counter. He could barely form words into sentences. "I prayed. God never answered. She's dying. I haven't got the money for her treatment. Where is God when I need him?"

Sam uncrossed her arms. "I'm sorry, Jake. I didn't know."

He pushed past her and picked his shirt up from the floor. "I've got to go."

"What about me?" she asked.

Noble pulled on his shirt and started on the buttons. "I appreciate you want to help, but this isn't your fight. Shiva found out about Bati on her own. You aren't responsible. Go home and let me deal with this."

Sam opened her mouth, closed it. She paced once around the room and then seemed to lock in on an idea. "Do you speak Cantonese?"

Noble was halfway through tucking his shirt in and stopped. He spoke half a dozen languages, but Cantonese was not one of them.

Seeing his hesitation, Sam pressed her advantage. "My mother is from Hong Kong. My father met her on a business trip. I grew up speaking the language."

A native speaker would be invaluable. At least, that's what Noble told himself. Maybe he was just looking for an excuse to keep her around. He made one last, halfhearted attempt to defeat her logic. "Everyone in HK speaks English," he said.

"Gangsters talking about gangster stuff will use their native language," Sam pointed out. She had a point.

Noble finished tucking in his shirt. "Are you going to follow my orders exactly?"

She nodded vigorously. "Promise. I'll just be your interpreter."

He frowned like he was thinking it over, but he'd already made up his mind. He stuffed his gun in his waistband, gathered the sugar kit and his mobile phone, and went to the door. Samantha followed without being told. Downstairs they hailed a taxi.

It wasn't five in the morning yet, and the streets were already packed with honking cars and stalled jeepneys. They sat in a traffic jam at the corner of North Bay Boulevard and the C-3 for fifteen minutes. They finally reached Navotas shortly before six o'clock.

CHAPTER FORTY

THE BAKERY TURNED OUT TO BE A DUNKIN DONUTS. Over the last decade, dozens of the American-based franchises had sprung up all over metro Manila. Noble opened the door and let Samantha go first. His belly rumbled at the smell of warm dough and freshly roasted coffee. Behind the counter a young Filipino greeted them with a smile. Manny sat in a corner booth by the window, munching on a chocolate éclair and reading a newspaper.

"See the fat guy in the booth?" Noble told Sam. "Go introduce yourself."

"But..." Sam started to ask questions.

Noble gave her a stern face.

She pressed her lips together, walked over to Manny's table, and said hello. Noble ordered up two cups of coffee and a raspberry-filled donut. He found a certain comfort in knowing he could travel to just about any major city in Southeast Asia and still get a hot cup of Dunkin Donuts coffee. He paid, balanced Sam's pastry on top of the coffee cups, and slid into the booth beside her.

Manny had a spot of cream on his shirt and dark bags under his eyes. He hadn't shaved. A tired smile turned up his face.

"Sorry we're late," Noble said.

Manny waved away the apology. "I was just getting to know this very charming young lady. We were having a lovely conversation until you interrupted. Tell me, my friend, how did you end up on the arm of such a beautiful woman?"

"Some guys have all the luck," Noble said.

"And I thought I was the only friend you had left in the Philippines," Manny said.

Noble ignored the quip. "Did you net Lady Shiva?"

"We did." Manny grinned. "In fact, she was waiting for us. She's not talking yet. I think she has a card left to play, and she's waiting for the opportune moment."

The news concerned Noble. Shiva was crafty. Whatever she was up to, Noble would bet his boat it had to do with Bati. He peeled the plastic lid off his coffee. "There was some mention of a plane?"

"It's fueled and ready to fly." Manny's eyes went to Sam. She was busy adding a second pack of sugar to her coffee and stirring vigorously. "Will the young lady be joining you?"

Sam went right on stirring, picked up her donut with her free hand, and took a large bite like she hadn't heard a word.

Noble nodded.

"You like to take chances, my friend."

"I'm already operating off the reservation on this one."

Manny shrugged, stuffed the last bite of éclair between his lips, and spoke with his mouth full. "Time, as I understand it, is critical. So let's not waste it sitting here."

He levered his bulk out of the booth and folded his newspaper under one arm. Noble and Samantha followed him along Little Samar Street and through a confusing labyrinth of huts made from corrugated steel and castoff timber. Dirty sheets took the place of doors. Scrawny dogs and chickens had the run of the place. Some Filipinos lived their entire lives in these shanty towns. An old woman sitting on a low stool, smoking a long-stemmed pipe, watched them pass with suspicion etched in the craggy lines of her face.

Manny led the way to a rotting wooden pier bobbing on the rusty brown water of Manila Bay. At the end of the dock floated a Grumman G-21 Goose. It was an eight-passenger amphibious aircraft built before World War II. Noble would be surprised if he could get the old bird into the air.

Manny saw the expression on his face. "What did you expect? A Gulfstream?"

"I'd be better off trying to paddle this old heap to Hong Kong," Noble said.

Manny turned to Sam. "I work all night, and this is the thanks I get."

"It's lovely," she said. "Thank you."

Manny handed the folded-up newspaper to Noble. "Your friend Burke said that might come in handy."

Noble opened the newspaper and found a file folder. He thumbed through. It contained information on Eric

Tsang, his operations, and the mercenary crew working for him.

"You didn't get that from me," Manny told him. He took a set of keys from his trouser pocket and handed them to Sam.

"You going to want this back?" Noble asked.

"Preferably in one piece," Manny said. He strolled up the dock toward the shanty town. Over his shoulder, he called out, "Have fun, my two little love birds."

Sam watched him go. "He's sweet." She looked at the Grumman and let out a low whistle. "Are we going to die?"

One side of Noble's mouth turned up in a grin. He opened the hatch and motioned her inside. The interior was no better than the exterior. It looked like it had been used as a troop transport or reconnaissance plane during the war. The passenger seats had been stripped out and cargo netting hung.

Sam pinched her nose. "Smells like something crawled in here and died."

They squeezed into the cramped cockpit and buckled themselves in. Sam reached across and put the key in the starter. The twin propellers turned over with all the grace and effort of an old man trying to lift himself out of a rocking chair. The engines hiccupped twice, rumbled, and coughed up black clouds of burning oil, but finally blurred into motion.

Noble taxied the aircraft along the channel, adjusted the flaps, and increased the throttle. The fuselage vibrated. The belly of the craft skipped across the surface, throwing Noble and Sam against the safety straps. He fought the yoke back. The nose lifted into the air. The water fell away, and the rattling contraption took to the air. Noble climbed to three thousand feet, leveled out, and increased air speed to 160 knots.

Sam let out a breath and relaxed. She turned to Noble and said something. He saw her mouth move but couldn't hear the words over the roar of the engines.

He took a pair of headphones off a hook overhead, placed them over his ears, and adjusted the microphone. Sam put on the other set. "Any reason we didn't take a commercial flight?" Her voice came through the headphones grainy and a little too loud.

"Several," Noble told her. He leaned forward and lifted his jacket so she could see the pistol grip sticking out of his waistband. "Airport security frowns on that sort of thing. Besides, I don't have a legend."

"What's a legend?"

"A cover story," he explained. "I don't have a reason to be in Hong Kong."

"You told Manny you were off the reservation," Sam said, now gazing out over the bright blue waters of the South China Sea. "What does that mean?"

"It means I don't officially work for the United States Government. I wasn't lying when I told Lady Shiva I was a mercenary."

"But you used to?"

He nodded.

"What happened?"

Noble checked fuel, altitude, and heading before answering. "I was a team leader for a Special Operations Group. It's a division of the CIA that specializes in clandestine operations, top secret, totally off the books. My team was in Qatar to rescue a bunch of girls who were about to be sold as sex slaves. The op went sideways."

"What does that mean?"

"We got the girls out but a high-ranking Qatar politician was killed in the process." Noble sighed and looked out the window before continuing. "If he hadn't been in the slave trade he wouldn't be dead, but he had connections. The Qatar government couldn't officially tie it to the CIA, and they didn't have to. It was enough that they suspected. People high up wanted someone to blame. The CIA needed a fall guy."

"And that ended up being you," Sam said.

Noble nodded and descended to two thousand feet in an effort to stay below radar. Radar arrays only see what's in their line of sight. Since the earth is round, hugging the deck can keep a plane from appearing as a little green blip on a destroyer console. Of course staying under radar would not prevent a Chinese sailor on the deck of a battleship from spotting the plane. Noble scanned the horizon for dark specks that might materialize into large ships with cannon and surface to air missiles.

"And now you are a mercenary?"

"I'm still working for the same people, only now I work on commission."

"How much will you get for saving Bati?" she asked.

He hesitated, and then said, "$150,000."

Sam whistled. It came through the microphone as a piercing locomotive blast. Noble winced. They hit a patch of turbulence. The twin prop shook violently for a moment then leveled out.

Sam was lost in thought for a while. "You are doing it for your mother?"

Noble nodded.

She reached across and laid a hand on his forearm. "How bad is it?"

"Bad," Noble told her. "The doctors want to do another round of chemotherapy. If that doesn't work..." he shrugged.

"I'm sorry," she said. She changed the subject and that was fine by Noble. "How long will it take us to reach Hong Kong?"

"Three hours assuming we don't crash into the ocean first."

"What are the chances of that?"

"This old thing handles like a building with wings," Noble said.

Sam's face pinched in concern.

He smiled. "Relax. I've never crashed before."

Sam laughed and asked him where he'd learned to fly. He told her about some of his training at the Farm in Langley. They spent the next two hours in idle chitchat. He recalled some of his time in the Green Berets and then being recruited into the CIA's Special Operations Group. She told him about growing up between Hong Kong and San Diego, how she had met Bati, and some of the troubles they experienced starting the women's shelter in Manila.

They passed over the first string of green islands that lay roughly twenty kilometers south of Hong Kong. White sailing vessels speckled the blue waters below. Noble descended to a thousand feet and reduced airspeed.

The rugged green landscape of Hong Kong appeared on

the horizon just as the starboard engine let out a loud buzzing like an angry hornet. The Grumman rocked and shuddered, but the engine recovered. For a moment Noble thought everything would be fine. Then the old propeller clanked. Black smoke trailed behind the aircraft like a banner.

Sam gripped the dash. "Is that bad?"

"Yes," Noble said.

"How bad?"

"Start praying."

CHAPTER FORTY-ONE

THE GRUMMAN RATTLED SO HARD NOBLE THOUGHT the old bird would shake apart in midair. He wrestled the stick and tried to remember the procedure for emergency landings. Sam gripped the console. Her knuckles turned white. Noble attempted to restart the engine. The starboard propeller blurred into motion for a few hopeful seconds before slowing to a crawl. The stop and go caused the aircraft to buck like a wild bronco.

He shut the engine down. It died with a grateful cough. The propellers locked in place. He adjusted the flaps to compensate for the loss. Hong Kong was coming up fast. He aimed the nose at Aberdeen Channel, where two rocky outcrops of land encompassed a bay of blue water. From this distance, he could see the sun winking off the glass front of expensive high-rise condos that lined the shore.

The Grumman drifted slowly to port. Noble made another adjustment to the flaps and crimped the yoke starboard to correct the drift. South of Aberdeen Channel rose a small rocky outcrop called Ap Lei Pai, connected to the main island by a narrow stretch of beach. There were no houses or roads on Ap Lei Pai. It was a hump of green shrubs and stunted trees and the perfect place to beach the aircraft without attracting too much attention.

Noble aimed for the western side of the island where the shoreline was a soft grade covered mostly in grass and loose gravel. He had the Grumman under control now and reduced air speed in preparation for a landing. They were six kilometers out when the strain of carrying the crippled aircraft finally overwhelmed the remaining engine. The port-side motor started to scream in protest. The Grumman lurched through the air, threatening to roll over and pitch into the ocean.

Noble's lips peeled back from clenched teeth. Sweat broke out on his forehead. The veins in his neck bulged. He fought the yoke to keep the nose up. The starboard wing dipped dangerously low until the tip skimmed the water. Noble strained to correct the drift. The starboard wing came up reluctantly, and the port wing evened out. Then the craft overcorrected, and Noble had to fight it back the other way.

"Come on!" he barked.

The port engine cut out altogether. For a moment, the aircraft coasted along in utter silence. Then gravity took over. The water came up fast. Noble's heart jumped around inside his chest. His stomach clenched. He hauled back on the stick and raised the flaps. The nose went up, and the tail section sank like a dog dragging its butt on the carpet. All he could see was blue sky and ragged wisps of white cloud.

Noble knew that if they hit the water like this, the tail

section would rip off and the plane would come apart. He pushed the nose down and saw the line of the horizon directly ahead. The belly of the craft smacked water.

There was a tremendous crash. Noble's jaw cracked together hard enough to make fairy lights dance in his vision. The fuselage shook like an angry beast. The plane skipped over the surface, giving them another moment of silence before humping the water again. They were treated to another violent impact. Both of them pitched against their safety belts. Saltwater sprayed over the windscreen, blotting out their vision. When it rolled away Noble was looking at Ap Lei Pai directly ahead. Another three kilometers and they would have slammed into the rocky outcropping at speeds that would have crushed the aircraft like a tin can.

The Grumman mounted soft swells, plunged into the troughs and plowed up white foam in her wake. Momentum carried them along. They would hit the shore doing a leisurely ten knots, give or take. Not fast, but enough to put the old World War II relic out of service.

"Get your hands off that dash unless you want two broken elbows," Noble said over the sound of rushing waves.

Samantha snatched her hands away as the nose of the craft impacted the steep rocky incline of Ap Lei Pai with a shriek of buckling metal. The Grumman came to rest with the crumpled nose pointing at the sky and the tail submerged, listing hard to starboard.

Neither of them moved for several long seconds. They stared out the cracked windshield, hardly daring to believe their luck. For Noble, the adrenaline wore off, and pain set in. Being thrown repeatedly against the safety belts had done nothing for the state of his bruised ribcage. He couldn't remember the last time he'd hurt so badly. He pried his cramped hands from the wheel only by a conscious effort to straighten his fingers.

Sam covered her mouth with both hands. Her chest heaved against the restraints. Her hair was a mess.

"You okay?" Noble asked.

She nodded weakly.

Noble released his belts and pushed himself to his feet using the console for support. He had to duck his head to keep from knocking it on the low ceiling. The file folder lay scattered all over the cockpit floor. He collected pages, jamming them back into the folder. "Can you stand? We need to get as far away as possible. At least a dozen boaters saw us go down. Someone will call it in. It won't take long for the HK Coast Guard to respond. They're probably on their way already."

Sam shrugged out of the safety harness and scrambled to her feet. They staggered down the slanting deck to the hatch. Noble twisted the latch and shoved. He feared the buckled fuselage might make the door stick, but it cranked open with a cantankerous groan. He leapt out, turned around, took Samantha by the waist, and lowered her to the ground.

He cast a glance over the downed relic and felt a stab of regret. It was a sad end to an historic bird. Under different circumstances he would have enjoyed restoring the Grumman to its former glory. That was out of the question now. The nose had crumpled on the rocks. One wing had buckled and hung limp like a broken appendage. The tail section was submerged, no telling how much damage it had sustained.

Samantha saw the look on his face. "What's the matter?"

"Manny will be heart broken."

They high-stepped over low shrubs and brambles to the north side of Ap Lei Pai, where a narrow strip of white sand created a land bridge to the larger island of Ap Lei Chau. From there, they hiked along the rocky coastline past the break wall to a marina crowded with yachts, trawlers, sailboats, and catamarans. Modern high-rises lined the oceanfront boulevard.

Noble took Samantha's hand and led the way down to the marina. "Act natural."

They strolled along the docks, passed a group going the other direction, and exchanged polite greetings. Sam looked over her shoulder and waited until the group was out of earshot. "Are we stealing a boat?"

"Does that offend you?"

"I barely survived being in a plane with you. I'm not sure I want to try my luck on a boat."

Noble's face split into a grin.

"So you do know how to smile," Sam said.

"We're taking a boat because the police are going to assume that whoever crashed that plane was trying to sneak onto the island," he told her.

"So the police will be checking cars and buses," Sam said.

Noble nodded and steered her onto the deck of a forty-foot yacht called the *Glory Bound*. "This will do," he said.

Living at the marina had equipped Noble with a wide

and eclectic knowledge of boats. This particular model had an electric starter and did not require a key. The sliding glass door on the rear deck wouldn't give him too much trouble either. He took the lock picks from his wallet and had the door open in less than a minute.

"What if there are people on board?" Sam asked. "How do you know it's empty?"

"I don't," Noble admitted.

They searched below decks. The yacht proved to be vacant and in one of the aft cabins Noble found a dresser full of women's clothing. He emptied drawers out onto the bed until he turned up a black bikini.

He handed it to Sam. "Put this on."

She gave him a flat look.

"We just crashed a plane in Hong Kong," he said. "In half an hour this place is going to be a media circus. We want to look like millionaires out for a pleasure cruise, not like fleeing suspects."

Sam narrowed her eyes. "Oh, I understand. It's all part of the disguise and has nothing to do with the fact that you want to see me in a skimpy bathing suit."

"It's a tough job," Noble said. "Somebody has to make the hard sacrifices."

"It must be so difficult for you."

He shrugged, crossed his arms over his chest, and leaned in the doorframe. "I'm not in it for the accolades."

She pointed at the door. "Out."

Noble returned topside and heard the steady beat of helicopter blades. A chopper hovered over Ap Lei Pai. He cast off the lines, climbed into the wheelhouse, and engaged the starter. The engines roared to life. Ten minutes later, he was cruising south out of Aberdeen channel with Sam lying on the forward deck in the black bikini. She had found a beach towel and a Chinese Cosmo. She stretched out on her belly with her bronze skin shining in the morning sun.

Beyond the southern tip of Ap Lei Pai, Noble turned west, coasting past the wreck of the Grumman. A pair of police cruisers was inbound, headed to the crash site. Sam still had her nose in the magazine. Noble stuck his head out the window and yelled, "Hey, babe, check it out. A plane crashed."

She sat up and shielded her eyes against the sun. "Oh, gosh. I hope everyone is all right."

The police boats were passing them on the port side. One of the officers elbowed his friend and pointed at Sam. They watched her for a while and then returned their attention to the downed plane. Neither man even glanced in Noble's direction. Sam studied the scene long enough to make it convincing and then lay back down on her belly. She reached back, untied the bikini top to avoid tan lines, then put her head down and closed her eyes.

Either she was teasing him intentionally, or she had no idea the effect the sight would have on him. He chewed the inside of one cheek.

The memory of last night's rejection was the only thing stopping him from walking onto the deck and gathering her into his arms. Why had she stopped last night? And what had she meant when she said she trusted him? Noble kept turning those questions over in his mind.

He sailed north and west around Ap lei Chau into Waterfall Bay. The police cruisers dwindled from sight, and Noble throttled up to twenty-five knots. He circled the big island of Hong Kong, waving and smiling at other boaters as they passed. He found an empty slip in the Causeway Bay Typhoon Shelter. Sam changed back into her dark denims and black tank top, and together they vanished into the urban chaos of Hong Kong.

CHAPTER FORTY-TWO

BY ONE O'CLOCK THEY HAD PURCHASED NEW CLOTHES in a hip shopping mall called Times Square and then sat down for lunch at Heichinrou. It was the first time in his life Noble had to talk a girl *into* shopping. He thought Sam would be excited about a spending spree, but she didn't have the heart for it while her best friend was being held captive by triads. He convinced her they needed to change their appearance and she had, reluctantly, agreed to the delay.

Sam bought a forest green shirt with tiny cargo pockets on the sleeves and hiking shoes. Noble now wore a black shirt under a dark gray windbreaker with plenty of pockets, dark cargo pants, and trainers. The ensemble made him look like an American tourist. Part of good clandestine work is blending in; that doesn't always mean looking like a local.

After changing clothes, they had found their way to the food court. Noble had his heart set on BLT Burger, but Sam balked at the idea of eating American food in Hong Kong.

She insisted they eat Cantonese. Noble acquiesced without bothering to tell her that the first heichinrou opened in Yokohama, Japan.

While they ate, Noble checked news feeds on his mobile. He wanted to see if the police had put out a bulletin on the two people who crashed a plane and stole a 1.2-million-dollar yacht. So far it looked like the police had no description and no leads. Noble allowed himself to breathe a little easier.

They finished their food, ordered more coffee, and went over Manny's file on Eric Tsang and his associates. Tsang was at the top of the criminal food chain in Hong Kong, and the group of mercenaries he contracted as private security was top notch. Every single one of them had elite military training and combat experience.

Tsang had forged a criminal empire through intelligence, cunning, and no small measure of ruthlessness. Crusaders like Bakonawa Ramos probably cost him a fortune. Noble could understand Tsang abducting the girl, but why wasn't he leveraging her?

"None of this makes any sense," he said.

"What do you mean?"

"If Tsang has Bati, why isn't he making any demands?" Noble said. "Bakonawa Ramos, supposedly a pillar of the community, has an illegitimate love child with a Filipino hooker who tries to kidnap her own daughter. Tsang gets to the girl first. Then he just sits on her? No ransom demands?"

"None that we know of."

"You think Ramos is getting ransom demands and not telling anyone?"

Samantha shrugged. "A scandal like that would ruin him."

Noble shook his head. "I don't buy it. If my daughter were kidnapped, I would do everything in my power to bring her home, including exposing my indiscretion with a prostitute."

He sipped his coffee. "Hell, if his PR people spin it right, he could sell his one night with a hooker as the wake-up call that opened his eyes to the awfulness of human trafficking. Write a tell-all and make millions."

"I think this goes deeper than a simple indiscretion from twenty-five years ago," Sam said.

"How so?"

"The way Shiva made it sound, I think Bakonawa is up to his neck in human trafficking."

Noble leaned back in his seat, crossed his arms over his chest, and frowned. "I doubt it. I'm going to read you in on something you aren't supposed to know; Bakonawa Ramos is a CIA asset. He has been for years. He picks up info in his campaigns against human trafficking and feeds it to the Company."

"Maybe he isn't getting that info from his war on human trafficking," Sam said.

She had a point. It was possible the CIA had been so busy spying on the enemy, they had forgotten to take a good hard look at their friends.

"Think about it. Publicly, he is a respected diplomat. Behind the scenes, he makes a fortune selling girls on the black market. Who would ever suspect the guy that champions the fight against prostitution to be involved in prostitution? Maybe Ramos has been feeding the CIA info on his competition."

When she laid it out like that, it made sense. And if true, Bati's chances of survival were slim. "I hope you are wrong," he said.

"Why?"

"Because if Ramos is leading a double life as an underworld crime boss then Eric Tsang might not want money," Noble told her. He could lie, but he might as well lay it out for her. Prepare her for the worst. "He might have kidnapped Bati for revenge."

"Why are we sitting here drinking coffee? We need to get out there and find her before it's too late."

Noble held up a hand. "First of all, I'm not Superman. I have to eat. Second, information is our best weapon against a guy like Tsang. We can't go in guns blazing. We have to find the weak link."

"What do you mean?"

Noble passed her the grainy black-and-white surveillance photo of Tiger Tsang from Manny's file. "We start with his kid brother."

CHAPTER FORTY-THREE

FREDERICK KRAKOUER LANDED IN HONG KONG AT 5 a.m. and booked himself into an airport hotel for a few hours of shuteye. He needed some rest. The game had changed since learning the Triads were involved. Krakouer wanted to be in top form if he was going up against Eric Tsang. Lady Shiva was a second-rate hustler. She used a spooky name and a violent reputation to inspire fear in low-level punks. At the end of the day, she was nothing more than a whore who had worked her way up to madam. That was all she would ever be.

Eric Tsang played for keeps. He didn't make threats, and he didn't bother hiding behind a nickname. He killed anyone who crossed him, simple as that. Krakouer would not be able to throw his weight around against a heavy hitter like Tsang. Getting Bati back was going to require more than tough talk. Just getting close to a man like Tsang would prove next to impossible. He kept a low profile, rarely leaving his secure high-rise office on Canton Road. Rumor had it he slept there most nights. Fortunately his little brother was a flashy punk with too much money and not enough sense.

Tiger Tsang owned a Mahjong parlor on Ning Po Street above a shop that sold knockoff wristwatches to gullible tourists. The Mahjong parlor was Tiger's de facto base of operations.

Krakouer woke a few minutes after noon, ate a large lunch, and then took the subway into Kowloon. He found the Mahjong parlor without much trouble. Getting inside was easy enough. He passed himself off as a bored American businessman with money to burn. He offered the proprietor of the watch shop a C-note and said that a friend of a friend had told him about the game.

The old man scrutinized the American bill with rheumy eyes and then waved Krakouer through a curtain at the back of the shop. Boxes littered the stockroom shelves with names like Rolex, Omega, and Tag Heuer. The forgeries looked identical to the real thing.

At the back of the stockroom was a steep staircase. Krakouer climbed to the second floor and found a door protected by a barrel-chested man in a cheap suit. He weighed roughly three hundred pounds, had the blunted knuckles of a street brawler, and a neck the size of Krakouer's thigh.

Krakouer related his cover story, forked over another C-note, and the bruiser opened the door for him.

The floor was covered in a thin green carpet littered with cigarette butts. Cocktail waitresses in short red dresses and high heels shuttled drinks back and forth to smoking men gathered around poker tables. Several heads turned to look at the gwai lo.

Krakouer brought out a pack of cigarettes and shook one out. He flicked his lighter, took a drag, and waved away the cloud of smoke. He instinctively liked any place where he could light up. The politically correct weenies in Washington DC had managed to outlaw smoking in public. It was illegal to walk down the street and smoke a cigarette in the beltway, but he could go to Denver and fire up a joint. Go figure.

He scanned the floor. Tiger wasn't here, but it wouldn't be long before he made an appearance. Krakouer inserted himself at a table without any trouble. Gamblers are predictable. You can play as long as you have money to lose. Krakouer knew the rules of Mahjong, but like poker, knowing how to play and playing well are two different things. Thankfully, he was betting his employer's money.

He played for several hours, lost more than he won, drank six beers, and smoked half a pack of cigarettes before Tiger finally showed up.

Foreigners at the club must have been common enough. Tiger didn't spare Krakouer a second glance. He went to a table, accepted a cigarette offered by one of the other players, and joined in.

Krakouer brought out his cell phone, pretended to send a text, and then placed the device on the table in front of him. He was already bored with the game and the Chinese girls in their short dresses. But placing himself in the same room as Tiger was only half the job. The next part needed a little skill and a lot of luck. Another hour ticked slowly past until Tiger's phone rang.

It was Krakouer's turn. He made a bad play that would cost him the game and then picked up his cell. Under the guise of sending another text, he opened an app and tried to angle the microphone over his right shoulder at Tiger.

One of the benefits of working for a multi-millionaire was that it gave him access to all the best toys. Krakouer was a low-tech kind of guy in general. He believed you could do more with a well-placed kick to the balls than you could with all the high-end gadgets employed by law enforcement. However, this was one situation where technology proved useful.

The application he used was a high frequency receiver designed by defense contractors to remotely capture phone conversations. The development team had envisioned an application that would allow field agents to capture and translate conversations up to fifty yards away. In reality, the low quality microphones installed in commercial mobiles severely limited an agent. It only worked reliably from a few yards and only when it was pointed directly at the target, which made it difficult to remain inconspicuous. Krakouer aimed the phone at Tiger and moved his thumb like he was texting.

Tiger answered. He talked a little but mostly listened. The call ended. He rolled his eyes, punched in a second number, and waited for someone to pick up. The second conversation was brief. When it ended, he shook his head and went back to playing.

Krakouer's phone gave him a loading icon. He put the mobile down and smiled at the other players at his table. "Business," he said by way of explanation.

Thirty seconds later, the phone finished its work. Krakouer left it on the tabletop and casually scrolled through the dialog to text translation. It was far from perfect. The application first had to capture the conversation and then translate into English. Any words the microphone failed to capture or the program could not translate appeared as a series of jumbled characters.

> *Caller: ...@XX in tonight. I need &*## to go*
> *down there and check on the ^&*&.*
> *%$$^* to be fed and watered*
> *Receiver: I B@R&L in %XL middle of*
> *a game*
> *Caller: ##Q give a %$!!VG about your*
> *$BT@ Lot of money on that boat.*
> *^!WWL want you and three of +*?/@ **
> *(!$ on that ship before midnight*
> *Receiver: Fine*
> *END CALL*

> *The second call read:*

> *Caller: *@B& Tiger. Take three men and*
> *G%##L to the pier on Stonecutters*
> *Island. The cargo X@@ food. I will %^>*
> *there before midnight. Do not &UX$#*
> *this time.*
> *END CALL*

And just like that Krakouer had a location. He stayed long enough to lose a few more rounds, finished his drink, and excused himself.

CHAPTER FORTY-FOUR

Noble and Samantha took the Wan Chai Ferry across Victoria Harbor to Kowloon and located a car rental company. Sam gave the man behind the counter her credit card number. He gave her the keys to a gray BYD F3. The F3 was a Chinese knockoff of a Toyota Corolla. The vehicles were so close in design you could pull the BYD symbol off the front grill, slap on a Toyota badge, and drive it down any street in America. No one would look twice. This particular car had been smoked in, often. The rental company had tried to cover it up with a half dozen cardboard air fresheners shaped like giant cherries. The first thing Noble did was crank down all four windows.

According to Manny's file, Tiger ran an underground Mahjong parlor near the corner of Ning Po and Woosung Street. It catered to low-level triad enforcers and was the one place where Tiger, ever in his brother's shadow, could play big man on campus.

Sam wedged the F3 into a parking space between a flat

paneled delivery truck and a row of motor scooters. The Mahjong parlor was three doors down on the opposite side of the street. It was a bad neighborhood, made worse by the gangs. Clotheslines stretched overhead, weighed down with damp laundry. There was a Circle K on the corner. The rest of the storefronts sold knockoff electronics, cheap jewelry, and pornography. Noble counted four trading companies. Triads used them to launder dirty money.

Sam turned off the engine but left the keys in the ignition. "What do we do now?"

"Now we wait," Noble told her. "This is Tiger's haunt. He'll show up sooner or later. Every organization has a weak link, one guy that's a little too flashy, likes to party too much, or has a soft spot for the ladies."

"Like Diego's gambling problem?"

"Exactly. You find the weak link and then use it to climb the chain of command. In the case of Eric Tsang, it's his younger brother. This is the one place where Tiger gets to call the shots. He'll turn up sooner or later and then we follow him to Eric. If we are lucky, he'll lead us directly to Bati."

They propped the black-and-white surveillance photo of Tiger on the dash and settled in. Noble reclined his seat and laced his fingers together behind his head. Sam sat up straight, drumming the steering wheel with nervous fingers and watching the front of the shop.

As a Special Forces operator, Noble had spent days lying on dank jungle floors while waiting on a target, smelling the fetid vegetation with insects feasting on his flesh. Surveillance in a parked car was an easy day at the office by comparison. Not a lot of fun but not unpleasant either. It beat the hell out of being hip deep in rotting sewage or wedged into a rocky crevice.

Sam did all right for the first hour but grew increasingly restless. She added heavy sighs to her drumming fingers. Noble tried to keep the conversation interesting, but she was too worried about her friend to make small talk.

A parade of gangsters came and went. Two hours dragged by before a red Ducati roared to a stop in front of the watch shop. The driver wore a matching red helmet, a silk shirt, and leather pants.

"That's him," Noble said.

Sam sat up straight.

He reached across and laid a hand on her arm. "Relax and don't look directly at him."

She slouched. "Are you sure?"

Noble only nodded as the biker switched off the Ducati, swung his leg over, and pulled off his helmet. He had long hair, dyed red, and a pair of clunky headphones around his neck. Tiger hung the helmet on the handlebars and entered the shop, utterly unconcerned that someone might steal either helmet or bike. Everyone in this neighborhood must know who owned the Ducati. Tiger could probably leave a roll of bills on the seat and it would still be there when he came out.

"How did you know that was him?"

"You don't know much about motorcycles."

"Expensive?" she asked.

"Very."

Sam turned to face him. "I've got an idea."

"I can't wait to hear it."

"I go in, flirt with him, and lure him outside. Then you can question him."

"Or," Noble said. "We can wait."

She hammered the dash. "Bati could be dying! Tiger knows where she is. We're just going to sit here?"

"You want to walk into the middle of a triad operation and flirt with the boss?" Noble jabbed a finger at the watch shop. "Those are cold-blooded killers in there. They look like gangsters. They've got scars and tattoos. You know what you look like? You look like a Yale graduate."

She started to say something, and Noble held up a hand. "Tiger will come out," Noble told her. "When he does we'll follow him and confront him in a location where we have the advantage."

Sam crossed her arms under her breasts and stewed. Inaction was eating away at her. Fifteen minutes later she put her hand on the door latch. "I'm going for a coffee. Want one?" She said it with the same tone she might use to tell someone to burn in hell.

"Black, no sugar," Noble said.

She got out, and Noble watched her in the rearview mirror until she reached the Circle K. She came back ten minutes later with two Styrofoam cups and a bag of milk candies. They tasted exactly like what they were—milk, dried and hardened into a shape about the size of a tootsie roll. Sam held the bag out to him. He shook his head. He had tried one his first time in China. Once was enough. He peeled back the plastic lid on his coffee, blew, and sipped.

He pulled a face. It was scalding hot and so weak it could pass for water. When it came time to extract information from Tiger, Noble would make him drink Circle K coffee. He punished himself with another sip, pulled an identical face, and set the cup on the dash.

Sam straightened up in the driver's seat. Noble looked up and recognized the driver of the dark sedan who had been parked in front of Diego's building. His bald head and scar were hard to miss. He turned east on Ning Po Street.

Sam narrowed her eyes. "It's him."

"You know that guy?" Noble asked.

She nodded. "I think his name is Krakouer. He works for Bati's dad. I saw him in Manila too."

Krakouer stuffed both hands into the pockets of his black windbreaker, checked for traffic, and crossed the street, then continued east. He was a block away now.

"When were you going to tell me about this?"

"I got duct-taped to a chair and it slipped my mind," Sam said with an edge to her voice.

Noble put a hand on the door handle. "Stay with Tiger. If he leaves before I get back you follow him, but not too close. Hang back a block or two. Call me on your cell and let me know where he leads you."

"Wait..." Sam started to ask questions, but Noble was already out of the car and moving east on Ning Po Street.

CHAPTER FORTY-FIVE

NOBLE TOOK LONG STRIDES AND CLOSED THE GAP between them to fifteen meters, then slowed his pace. He hooked his thumbs in his pockets and peered into shop windows as he passed. Krakouer reached the intersection at Ning Po and Nathan Road. If he knew how to play the game, he would use the corner to check for a tail. Just in case, Noble stuck his head in the open passenger side window of a parked taxi. He told the driver he wanted to go to Victoria Park.

Cabbies in Hong Kong were supposed to run the meter, but it seldom worked that way. Instead, the driver assigned a price based on distance and how much the customer looks like they can afford to pay. If the customer has a white face, the fee automatically triples. The hand signs used to nego-tiate price made things more confusing for the hapless foreigner. The practice arose because of the sheer number of regional dialects in mainland China. A man from Nanjing, in the north, could travel south to Guangzhou and not be able to understand the local speech, but he could buy and sell using hand signals.

The cabbie made a cross with his forefingers. Noble countered with his thumb and pinkie. He watched Krakouer from the corner of his eye while haggling over the fare. Sure enough, the big bruiser glanced over his shoulder as he made the turn onto Nathan Road. Noble went back and forth with the cabbie until Krakouer disappeared around the corner and then said he had changed his mind. He hurried to the end of the street and followed Krakouer onto Nathan Road.

It didn't make sense for Ramos to pay a hired gun to find his daughter when he could have relied on the training and recourses of the CIA. If Sam was right and Krakouer worked for Ramos, then the diplomat had more to hide. And Noble was willing to bet Krakouer could shed some light.

He tailed Krakouer eight blocks north to Man Ming. Krakouer took the stairs to the Yau Ma Tei subway station. Noble muttered a curse under his breath. If he fell too far behind, he would lose the mark and if he got too close he would be spotted. Keeping the appropriate distance in a cramped subway station is next to impossible. If he had a team of trained operatives, Noble would hand off the target to the next watcher. Since he was alone, he had no choice but to follow Krakouer down the steps to the platform. His only saving grace was rush hour traffic.

It was a little after six, and the subway was packed with people on their way home after a long workday. The cacophony of voices echoed off the tile walls, sounding like a gaggle of geese around the shores of a lake. Krakouer swiped a metro card, pushed through the turnstiles, and joined the crowd waiting on a train. The ticket vendors were swamped. There was no way Noble would make it to the front of the line before the next train. He went to a map of the Hong Kong underground tacked to the station wall and scowled, acting like a confused foreigner.

The act would only work for so long. Hong Kong is not very big. The subway system is well laid out and easy to navigate. To buy time, he dug his cell phone out of his pocket and pretended to have a conversation while puzzling out the map.

One of the things Noble loved most about Chinese people is that they are so damned helpful. They understand their country can be a confusing place to outsiders, and most of them will make heroic efforts to help. Unfortunately, Noble attracted the attention of a well-meaning Chinese man eager to offer assistance. He approached Noble with a friendly smile. "Hello. I speak English."

Heads swiveled in Noble's direction. In a few moments he would have a crowd of people asking if he spoke Cantonese, how long he'd been in Hong Kong, where he was from, and what he was doing here. He had to diffuse the situation quickly.

He took the phone away from his ear, threw an arm around the man's shoulders, and pulled him close. Dropping his voice to a whisper, Noble asked, "Do you know where I can get a hooker and cocaine?"

The effect was instantaneous. The poor working stiff suddenly decided he did not speak English after all. He slipped away from Noble's grasp, apologized in Cantonese, and hurried to join the rest of the crowd on the platform.

Noble fought down a grin and went back to studying the map. Five minutes later, screaming tracks heralded the arrival of the train. The commuters shuffled to the edge of the platform. Krakouer towered head and shoulders over the crowd. The train burst from the dark tunnel with the spontaneity of a magician pulling a rabbit from his hat. The doors opened with a pneumatic sigh.

Noble pocketed his cell phone, jumped the turnstiles, and raced for the train. He wasn't alone either. Three teenagers leapt the turnstiles as well. All four piled onto the last car before the doors hissed shut. One of the kids grinned at Noble. He had spikey hair and a ring in his nose. Noble held out a fist. The kid bumped it.

Krakouer was two cars up. Noble worked his way forward until he could see his mark through the small window in the adjoining doors. They rode all the way to Rodney Road where Krakouer stepped out along with a flood of passengers. Noble waited until the doors started to close and then slipped through the gap.

He took the steps two at a time and almost lost Krakouer on the surface. The streets were a confusing web work of overpasses and underpasses, interrupted by frequent construction. From the sky, it must have looked like a tangled bowl of spaghetti. Noble scanned the sidewalks but saw heads of straight black hair everywhere he looked.

A raised pedestrian walkway passed over Connaught Road. On a hunch, Noble bounded up the steps to the overpass and spotted Krakouer halfway across. Krakouer turned at the same time, saw Noble, and broke into a jog.

Noble shouldered his way between a couple walking hand in hand. He sprinted the length of the overpass.

Instead of depositing them back on the street, the walkway made a right hand turn and entered the second level of the Citic Tower. Noble rounded the corner and bounded down the steps into a parking garage. He caught sight of his target turning east on Lung Wei Road.

Krakouer ran several blocks and turned left at the entrance to the Hong Kong convention center. The oblong white shell juts out over Victoria Harbor like a gigantic dinosaur egg ready to hatch. It's one of those futuristic buildings for which the city is so well known. It gets a few seconds of screen time in any movie set in Hong Kong. Noble was fairly certain action star Jackie Chan had been thrown off the roof once, or maybe he threw a bad guy off the roof instead. Noble couldn't quite remember. Either way, the building was famous.

A large sign outside the convention center announced the Hong Kong Manga-Con. Noble pushed through the double doors thirty seconds behind Krakouer. It was like stepping into a twelve-year-old boy's fantasy. He was surrounded by Storm Troopers, X-men, one incredibly well-built Princess Leia and two dozen Mr. Spocks. Booths and endless aisles of folding tables commanded the ground floor. Comic books, movies, and memorabilia decorated every surface. Eager fans appraised overpriced collectibles with all the enthusiasm of a fat man at a buffet table. The whole place smelled like dry ice and pulsed to the sounds of a movie score, interrupted by shouts and laughter.

Noble's lips pulled back from clenched teeth. Krakouer was either very lucky, or he had chosen the convention center in advance. It would be next to impossible to spot him in all this mess. His height no longer gave him away. There were seven-foot Darth Vaders and acrobats on stilts.

Noble strolled along a row of tables laden with everything from fiberglass light sabers that glowed to sonic screwdrivers and wall posters signed by famous people. He walked slow enough to be just another comic book geek looking for that rare back issue to complete his collection. While a vendor was busy haggling with a customer, Noble swiped a blue baseball cap emblazoned with a police box. He adjusted the Velcro strap and stuffed the hat on his head to better blend with the crowd.

His nerve endings hummed like high-tension wires. His head was on a swivel. He kept his eyes peeled for anything out of the ordinary, which was everything around here, but he zeroed in on anyone moving too fast, or anyone not moving at all.

A gray alien with a laser rifle leapt into his path. The plastic laser gun emitted an electronic warble and a red light blinked. Noble's reflexes took over. His hand was halfway to his own gun before he realized it was a kid in a mask with a fake rifle.

He snatched the laser rifle from the alien's hand and threw it down. The weapon hit the carpeted floor with a crack of breaking plastic. The alien threw his hands in the air. "What's your problem, gwai lo?" His voice sounded muffled through the rubber mask.

"Piss off, kid." Noble shoved the alien out of his way and kept moving. He took the escalator to the second floor of the convention center, passing a fairly convincing Malcom Reynolds from *Firefly*.

A balcony overlooked the ground floor. Noble stopped

long enough to scan the crowd below. There was no shortage of foreigners. Several were bald, but they were either too short or too chubby to be Krakouer. He turned his attention to the second floor where a large metal contraption looked like it might be a portal to another dimension. A section of floor had been roped off, and a heavy curtain hung behind the portal. The smell of dry ice was much stronger up here. Noble milled through the crowd near the stage. He figured Krakouer had given him the slip, but he would hang around another minute or two to be certain.

An announcer in tails and a top hat tapped a microphone to be sure it was working, then his voice boomed through the convention center. "Ladies and gentlemen, may I have your attention! Gather round, gather round. I present to you, the one, the only, *Phoenix Sunset!*"

The lights dimmed. A burst of sickly sweet smelling fog spilled across the floor, and a spotlight centered on the metal portal. A fire dancer appeared through the swirling mists. She was small with curly black hair cut short, bright eyes, and the kind of smile that steals hearts. She wore shorts and a halter-top emblazoned with tongues of fire.

Flaming globes at the end of chains leapt and twirled as she swayed across the floor. The fire formed hypnotizing patterns in the air. She was good, both beautiful and talented. Under different circumstances, Noble would have enjoyed watching her perform. But he had a job to do. He was about to turn and extricate himself from the crowd when he felt a gun barrel pushed into the small of his back.

CHAPTER FORTY-SIX

SAM HAD DOZENS OF QUESTIONS, BUT NOBLE WAS already a half block away. She watched him stick his head into the passenger's side window of a red-and-white taxi for a moment then he turned left onto Nathan Road. He was gone, and Sam was on her own. She ran a hand through her long black hair and blew out her cheeks.

No one would ever accuse Jacob Noble of being indecisive. He saw what needed to be done and did it. He was not the type of guy who sat around discussing his feelings. He certainly wasn't like any of the guys she had dated in college. He acted with masculine efficiency. It wasn't very twenty-first century. He had no interest in a exploring either his feminine side or his inner child, and he would certainly not be cuddling on the couch to watch *Dancing with the Stars*. He might not know the salad fork from the dinner fork, but he probably knew how to flush a carburetor and fix a leaky faucet.

Sam rolled up the windows, locked the doors, and

slouched down in the seat. The safety of America had spoiled her. At Yale, she and her classmates used to go on at length about the growing violence in American cities. Never mind the fact that they lived in the shelter of their parent's money. None of them had been to the Middle East or South America. When they did travel, it was to soak up the sun in Cozumel or hit the slopes in Switzerland. All the same, they acted like South Beach was South Africa. It didn't help that university professors seemed to invite the comparison.

Sam got her first wakeup call one summer when she joined Bati on a humanitarian mission to Myanmar. They were part of a group trekking food and medicine twenty miles by boat to a remote village that had been decimated by the ongoing civil war. Sam witnessed firsthand former child soldiers missing arms and legs. She had met a woman who had her breasts cut off by rampaging soldiers and seen people who had stepped on landmines.

The humanitarian mission was cut short when hostilities erupted between the current regime and a separatist group. Sam escaped to India along with the rest of the volunteers. They found out later that the entire village had been massacred. The local warlord claimed all the food and medicine they had laboriously hauled through the muck and mire as his own.

When she got back to Connecticut, she spent the first few days in shock. Then the grief set in, and she could not stop crying. After that, listening to her friends complain about the violence in American cities made her want to vomit. She lost her cool with a few of them. They shunned her when she refused to indulge in the narrative.

Sam sipped her coffee, unwrapped another milk candy, and waited. Her fear for Bati mixed together with images of mutilated Burmese children and turned into something palpable. It hardened and grew like a cancerous cell feeding on the terrible images in her mind. Whenever she managed to silence those fears, her feelings for Jake came rushing back in to fill the void.

She turned the events of last night over in her head but couldn't make sense of it. One minute he was trying to get her out of her towel and the next he didn't seem to care at all. He took a shower, lay down next to her, and went to sleep. Like nothing had happened. *He didn't even try to make a move.* She practically threw herself at him. Had she misread the whole thing? Had she made a complete fool of herself? She laid awake the whole night torn between her desire to feel his strong hands on her body and her determination to keep her promise. She kept wondering why he hadn't at least *tried* to make love to her.

She chased these thoughts around inside her brain until she felt she would go mad. She brought out her cell phone twice, determined to call him and find out once and for all what was going on between them, but never worked up the courage to press send. She had the phone in hand a third time when she heard a motorcycle roar to life.

Tiger had his helmet on. He twisted the throttle a few times. The motor responded with an energetic growl. He heeled the kickstand up, let out the clutch, and laid down on the fuel tank. The Ducati shot between a pair of parked scooters onto the street and sped to the corner where he turned onto Nathan Road.

Sam started the car, threw it in gear, and went after him.

Jake's coffee slid off the dash, landing in the floorboard. Sam winced. "Good thing I opted for the extra insurance."

She turned onto Nathan Road and spotted the red Ducati zig-zagging between cars. Tiger drove like he had something to prove. He was already two blocks away and quickly increasing his lead. Jake had told her to hang back, but Sam had no choice. She had to speed up and stay close or lose Tiger in traffic. She put her foot down, swerved around a double decker bus, and closed the gap. Twice she had to use the left shoulder to speed past a line of stopped cars. Soon they were on Container Port Road headed to Stonecutters Island.

Sam gripped the wheel hard with excitement. The island was mostly commercial shipping and the perfect place to stash a kidnap victim. She slowed down, allowing Tiger to pull ahead. At this time of night, most of the workers had already gone home. It was going to make tailing him without being spotted incredibly difficult. A flat paneled truck passed them going the other way. Sam let the distance between them grow. Tiger took the turn off. Sam slowed down even more, and by the time she made the turn, he was gone from sight.

She coasted through the silent stacks of long metal shipping containers, braking at each intersection to look for the red Ducati. The boxes seemed to go on forever. She wound her way through the maze with a cold fear hatching in her stomach. Panic filled her. "No. No," she said and banged the steering wheel with a fist.

She started to pray. If Bati died because she had let Tiger get away, Sam would live with that pain the rest of her life. She'd almost given up hope when she spotted a sleek red motorbike parked near a freighter.

The ship was docked on the north east side of the island and would be visible from Kowloon. Sam sat there several minutes trying to decide what to do. She couldn't idle between lanes of shipping containers. She had watched enough spy flicks to know she had to find a place where she could watch the boat without being seen.

She turned around and took Container Port Road back to the mainland and then looked for a place to park where she could wait and watch. It took a few minutes cruising the industrial neighborhoods near the shore, but she finally found a nice spot where she could see the freighter from across the harbor. She could make out the front wheel of Tiger's motorcycle beyond the bow of the ship. She'd know if he left, but by the time she got back to the island he would be long gone. Still, she felt this was a safer vantage point. She dialed Jake and put the phone to her ear.

CHAPTER FORTY-SEVEN

Noble's heart ping-ponged off the wall of his chest. All the muscles in his back tensed. The muzzle pressing against his kidney felt small—a .22 or .380 ACP—but at this range it would still kill. The bullet would blow a hole through something vital.

Krakouer slung an arm around Noble's shoulders and pulled him in close. The barrel pushed deeper into his back. He winced.

Krakouer wore a shark's grin. He thrust his chin at the fire dancer. "That is one fine piece of meat. I'd like an hour alone with her."

"You work for Ramos?"

"Aren't you clever," Krakouer said. "Figure that out all on your own?"

"I had help," Noble told him.

"Shiva screwed up. She was supposed to kill you."

"Don't be too hard on her. I can be a real handful."

"That's all right. I'll clean up her mess," Krakouer said. "Let's take a walk."

Krakouer pulled.

Noble held his ground and turned his attention to the fire dancer. "No thanks. Like you said, she's easy on the eyes."

She had worked her way to the edge of the dance floor. She was so close he could feel the heat from the whirling brands of fire. Her eyes rested on him for a moment, moved away, and then came back, as if she had realized something was wrong. Noble stared hard, trying to communicate with his eyes. If Krakouer pulled the trigger, the bullet would go through him and hit her. Noble tried to warn her.

"Think I won't snuff you right here?" Krakouer asked.

"Go ahead," Noble said. He was playing a dangerous game. Krakouer was a killer. Noble never doubted that. If he let himself be marched outside, Krakouer would take him to a dark alley and put a bullet in his head the same way a carpenter drives a nail. No remorse. And zero chance of survival. If Krakouer plugged him in public, paramedics would be on the scene in minutes. He would have a better chance at living. Not much better, but better.

"This is going to happen," Krakouer said. "You decide where. Do you want some innocent person to get hurt? Or do you want to be a man and walk outside?"

While he spoke, Noble was staring furiously at the dancer in the vain hope that she would recognize the unspoken warning in his eyes.

She spun the chains like a pair of flaming wagon wheels. The captivated crowd watched in silence as she drew a deep breath in through her nose, held it, and spit fire. A fireball streaked at the audience.

The crowd gasped and drew back in unison. Noble felt the heat on his face. It nearly singed his eyebrows off. He used the distraction to drive his head backwards into Krakouer's face. It was a sloppy attack but managed to mash Krakouer's lips and knock out a tooth. Noble spun on the balls of his feet and chopped at Krakouer's wrist. A .22 Walther hit the floor and got lost in a forest of legs. Noble followed up with a kick aimed at Krakouer's knee. The side of his foot impacted below the kneecap and scrapped down Krakouer's shin. His face twisted in pain.

Noble had the upper hand and pressed his advantage. He grabbed hold of Krakouer's collar with both hands and twisted, cutting off his air supply.

Krakouer kneed Noble in the crotch.

Pain exploded in his stomach and marched in waves that spread out to the rest of his body. He let go of Krakouer's collar. His knees tried to buckle. He staggered backward, fighting hard to stay on his feet.

The people closest to the fight recognized what was happening first. Heads turned. Within seconds, most of the crowd on the balcony was watching the fight. They stood on their toes and craned their necks to see.

Krakouer searched the floor for his weapon. Noble wasn't going to let him get his hands on the gun. Innocent civilians would get hurt. He pulled his pistol and ordered Krakouer to put his hands up.

The crowd screamed.

Krakouer sprinted for the edge of the balcony and

leaped the railing. He fell twenty feet and crashed through a folding table. Comic books and knickknacks scattered all over the floor. Krakouer rolled, scrambled to his feet, and ran for the exit.

CHAPTER FORTY-EIGHT

Cradling his aching groin, Noble hobbled to the railing. He caught a glimpse of Krakouer before he disappeared under the balcony. He would be long gone by the time Noble made it down the stairs. The table that Krakouer had used to break his fall was buckled in the middle. Noble wasn't going to try the same stunt. Krakouer was lucky he hadn't broken both his knees.

Noble leaned on the railing and sucked air through clenched teeth. The sick feeling in his gut was starting to evaporate. He was going to kill Krakouer the next time they met, and he had a feeling that would be sooner rather than later.

He retrieved Krakouer's fallen weapon from the floor. The crowd pushed back to let him through. The dancer had extinguished her fire and stood watching him like everyone else. Noble thanked her with a silent nod, which she returned. He stuffed the .22 Walther in his jacket pocket and limped down the stairs. He heard sirens in the distance as he exited the convention center. The loud whoops almost covered the vibration of his phone in his pocket.

Noble dug the phone out, pressed it to his ear, and covered the other ear with his free hand. His voice was raw from the shot to his groin. "What's up?"

"Jake?"

"The one and only."

"Do I hear police sirens in the background?"

"Yep."

"Are they for you?"

"Yep."

"Is this a bad time?"

"How are things on your end?" he asked.

"I think I found Bati," Sam told him. "I followed Tiger to a boat on Stonecutters Island. There's a guard on the deck."

While she spoke, Noble hustled to catch the Wan Chai ferry docked less than a hundred yards from the convention center. A flood of passengers crowded the boarding ramp. Noble pushed his way on as a half-dozen police cars shot past. He waited until he could hear again and then asked, "Did anyone see you?"

"I don't think so. I'm parked on the other side of the channel in the shadow of a building."

The sun had slipped below the horizon, and the last rays of light turned the wispy clouds orange and purple. The horn bellowed, loud and low. The ferry pulled away from the dock with sluggish determination, churning the water in its wake to white foam.

"Color me impressed," Noble said. "Text me the address and sit tight. I'm on my way."

He made his way to the top deck, leaned against the railing, and watched the last of the light dwindle from the sky. If all went well, he could have Bati in police protection by midnight. After that he would instruct Burke to wire the entire sum of money into his mother's account. Noble would be staying in Asia a couple days. He had loose ends to tie up.

The question of Ramos kept nagging him. The diplomat was bent, and Noble wanted to know how deep the corruption went. If he was involved in human trafficking, Noble was going to burn him right down to the ground.

It was dark by the time the ferry docked on the opposite shore. Across the harbor, the Hong Kong skyline reared into the heavens, a glimmering jewel-encrusted island of light so bright it blotted out the stars. Noble disembarked, found a cab, and told the driver to drop him three blocks from Hing Wah Street.

Sam had done well. She had picked a loop of road that looked across a hundred meters of dark water to a spit of land called Stonecutter's Island. She was parked on the west side of the street in the shadow of a vacant factory, slouched in the front seat with her arms folded across her chest.

Stonecutter's Island was a massive shipping yard where tankers loaded and unloaded. Freighters occupied the docks, and metal shipping containers, stacked three high, formed a silent city with narrow streets where all the residents were cheap export goods closed up inside windowless apartments. A forest of loading cranes towered over the city of boxes.

Noble rapped on the passenger window.

Sam gave a start, then unlocked the door.

He climbed in beside her.

"You snuck up on me," she said.

"I'm real good at that."

She eyed his baseball cap. "I didn't take you for a Doctor Who fan."

Noble remembered the hat, pulled it off his head, rolled down the window, and chucked it.

"What happened to Krakouer?"

"He got away." Noble nodded to the island. "What have you got here?"

"See that small freighter? Look at the bow. You can just make out the front wheel of Tiger's motorcycle."

"Good work," Noble told her. He sniffed. "It smells like coffee in here."

"Oh look! The guard is coming around now," Sam said.

He was a young street punk in a white undershirt with short-cropped hair. He had a black nylon strap over one shoulder. The waist-high gunwale blocked out his hands, but the strap would be connected to a gun.

"Tell me about him. Is it always the same guy? How often does he pass by? Does he take the same route every time?"

"It's always the same man. He passed by twice before. I didn't time how long it takes him to go around. Maybe ten minutes." She winced. "Sorry."

"Don't worry about it," he said. "You knocked this one out of the park."

She tried to hide a smile and didn't do a very good job. "So what now?" she asked. "Do we call the police?"

Noble snorted. "First they would send someone out to

investigate, then they would waste hours in hostage negotiations. Bati's best chance for survival is a fast take down."

He pulled Krakouer's .22 Walther from his pocket. "By the way, Krakouer wants to kill us both, and I'm pretty sure he knows about the ship. You might need this."

He passed the weapon over to Sam.

She took it in both hands like it were made of glass.

"There is a bullet in the chamber," Noble told her. "Just point and squeeze. If you see Krakouer, shoot first."

He shrugged out of his windbreaker and pulled off his shirt. The effort hurt his bruised ribs, but he didn't let it show. "I'm going for a swim. Your job is to keep an eye out. I'll be climbing the anchor chain, so I won't be able to see anyone on deck. If I'm on the chain and the guard comes back around, flash the headlights. Once I'm on board, I'll signal when I've neutralized all the threats. When I give the signal, you bring the car around. Can you handle that?"

She placed the Walther in the cup holder. "What if something goes wrong?"

"If I don't signal in thirty minutes then you can call the police." He removed his shoes and socks and bundled his clothes in the floorboard of the car.

Sam reached across and grabbed his hand. Stress lines formed around her eyes. She held on like she was afraid to let go.

"Hey," Noble said. He cupped her face in one hand. "This is what I came here for. It's my job. It's what I do."

She swallowed hard. "I know."

He extracted his hand from hers, opened the door, and climbed out of the car wearing only his pants with the .45 pistol tucked in his waistband. The cracked asphalt was cold against his bare feet. A gentle breeze cooled the sweat on his bare chest. He did a few calisthenics. This was hardly the first time he had stormed a tanker, but it was the first time he had done it by himself. He wondered briefly where the other members of his old team were right now. He wished they were here with him instead.

If wishes were horses, beggars would ride, Noble reminded himself. His mother was fond of that little ditty.

He scaled a chain-link fence and scrambled over slick rocks to the lapping waves of Victoria Harbor. The outside temperature was eighty-degrees Fahrenheit. The water felt ten degrees cooler. It would have been a pleasant swim under different circumstances. Noble waded out until he was waist deep and then dove head first into the waves.

CHAPTER FORTY-NINE

Noble cut through the water with long easy strokes. He covered the distance in five minutes. It wasn't an Olympic swim by far, but not bad for a thirty-two-year-old who was recently used as a punching bag.

The metal skin of the freighter groaned against rotting wood pylons. Waves lapped against the hull. Noble could hear the deep rumble of the engines below deck. He took hold of the anchor chain, found the submerged portion with his feet, and pulled himself hand over hand. His soggy trousers rained salt water, but his weapon was secure in his waistband.

He had almost reached the top when headlights flashed across the harbor. Noble stopped and hugged the chain. He strained to hear, hoping to catch the soft pad of feet as the guard passed by, but saw the man instead.

The tough stood near the stern with his forearms propped on the railing, peering across the water at Sam's rental. If he looked to his left, he would see Noble hanging from the anchor chain. Even a small movement might catch the guard's peripheral vision.

Noble's fingers began to tremble at the effort of holding onto the thick metal links. Noble reminded himself to breathe. After what felt like ten agonizing minutes, the lookout finally resumed his course. Noble waited until the sound of his footsteps passed by overhead and then scrambled up the chain and over the gunwale.

The forward deck had two large anchor hoists and a collection of cables slowly turning to rust. The pilothouse was a tall metal structure, like a saltine can turned on end, painted red and encircled by a metal catwalk. The paint was old and flaking. The catwalk looked ready to collapse. The guard rounded the corner on the starboard side, ducking his head to avoid knocking it against the overhang. He had a walkie-talkie in his left hand and a compact submachine gun in his right.

Noble paused long enough to roll up his wet pant legs and then padded after the guard. A fire axe hung next to the pilothouse door. Noble carefully lifted the axe off the hooks and turned the corner.

The guard strolled along the deck like a man out for a breath of fresh air. Climbing the anchor chain had been a waste of time and effort. This guy wasn't expecting any trouble. Noble could have walked right up the gangplank.

He turned the axe in his grip and attacked with the flat side, aiming for the soft spot above the hipbone and below the ribcage. The impact ruptured the man's kidney. He crumpled to the deck without uttering a sound.

Noble set the axe aside, flipped the dead man over, and found a MAC-10 submachine gun. The weapon wasn't much bigger than a handgun but fully automatic and chambered in 9 millimeter with a thirty-two-round magazine. It was notoriously inaccurate at long ranges, but inside the close confines of the ship, the little automatic would be deadly. Noble eased back the bolt, found a bullet in the chamber, and felt a whole lot better about his chances.

The guard didn't match any of the photos of Tsang's mercenaries. He was a low-level enforcer. His only job was using the radio if anyone approached.

Noble tossed the radio over the side. It hit the water like a stone. He could have dropped the body overboard as well, but the splash would be audible even below deck.

Armed with the MAC-10, Noble located the nearest hatch and pressed his ear against the cold metal. It was like putting a conch shell to his ear. He heard the steady thrum of the electric that powered the ship's lights and ventilation but nothing else. He pulled the door lever. The bolt disengaged with a loud *thock*. Noble winced. The hatch swung open on tired old hinges. Stairs led down into darkness. Each riser was lit by a miniscule safety bulb. He aimed the MAC-10 at the bottom of the steps and waited.

Something was not right. Leaving an untrained goon on the deck was bad enough. A mercenary leader like Henries, with combat experience, would never leave stairs unguarded. It was a natural choke point and easy to defend. Either Noble was walking into a trap, or the mercenaries were not here, which meant Bati was not here either.

He high-stepped over the raised sill and crept down the stairs. A long, narrow corridor ran the length of the vessel. Dim overhead lights added to the sinister feel. Closed hatches lined the cramped passage. White paint flaked from the metal doors, revealing patches of rust below the surface.

His training told him to clear the rooms one by one, to be sure all the threats were in front of him instead of behind him, but the rusting hinges would make too much noise. And he was a sitting duck in the middle of the hallway. He moved on bare feet to the first intersection and checked the corners. Both ended in dark cubbyholes crammed with pipes and valves. Either would have been excellent for an ambush. It was another sign that Bati was somewhere else.

He continued along the corridor. He passed two more unguarded intersections and then the hall ended at a hatch, which opened onto a large room. A huge turbine filled the space. The air smelled like burning oil. The rhythmic beat of the engine reverberated off the steel walls. Someone was moving around on the other side of the turbine. There was a light source back there, and a body crossed in front of it throwing a shadow.

Noble took cover behind a thick metal pipe. He peered through gaps in machinery. A fat man with a Beretta stuffed in the waistband of his trousers rounded the corner. A cigarette dangled from the corner of his mouth. He lifted his radio, pressed the transmit button, and spoke in Cantonese.

He waited. His brow pinched. He cast a brooding look at the ceiling like he could see through it to the deck above. He tried the radio again and got no answer. He shook his head and started toward the front of the ship.

Noble pressed back into the shadows. When the fat man passed his hiding place, he stepped out and cracked him over the head with the MAC-10. The fat man went down on one knee. Noble hit him twice more. He fell with a heavy thud on the metal floor.

Noble took the fat man's Beretta. He was a firm believer in victory through superior firepower, but he had no place to put another weapon. He ejected the magazine and the round from the chamber. The bullet bounced across the floor. He secreted the handgun and the magazine behind different parts of the engine works and left the unconscious man on the ground.

At the rear of the turbine room, another stair led deeper into the bowels of the freighter. Noble paused at the top. The ripe stink of unwashed bodies and human excrement drifted up from below. He could hear movement and someone speaking Cantonese. Too bad his interpreter sat in the car.

He lay down on his belly and peeked through the gap between the risers.

Cages, constructed of shipping pallets and chicken wire, were stacked two high and ran the length of the hold. Three or four women were crowded into each kennel. The Triads had a brutally efficient operation going. Noble had seen similar outfits before. Asian girls would be packed onto a boat and shipped to Western Europe or America where they would be forced to work in massage parlors, which acted as legal fronts for prostitution. Once the Asian girls were offloaded in the West, the kennels would be filled back up with white girls who would then be ferried to various ports in the Middle East and Asia.

This particular shipment must have just arrived because the cages were full of white faces.

Tiger Tsang and two of his enforcers were busy serving

supper. Tiger steered a trolley piled high with dented cans of beef stew. One man worked a can opener and another man pushed a can into each cage through a small opening. The women had to fight for their supper. The weak and sick didn't bother. Tiger chomped his gum and looked bored.

The enforcers both carried firepower. The one passing out cold stew had a fully automatic AK-47 slung over his shoulder. The other man had a pump-action shotgun, but he needed both hands to operate the can opener so the weapon lay on the trolley within easy reach. Tiger did not appear to be armed. He either considered himself too high up the food chain to do his own gun work, or he was concealing.

They were moving away from the stairs, with their backs to Noble. Using speed, surprise, and overwhelming violence, this fight could be over before it started. A few well-placed bursts from the MAC-10 would take all three down.

Before Noble could put his plan into action, one of the girls spotted his head between the steps. Her eyes opened wide. She pointed and squealed. She was too young to know any better. Tiger turned to look at the girl, then at the stairs. Noble pulled his head up but not fast enough.

CHAPTER FIFTY

THE NEXT FEW SECONDS WERE UTTER CHAOS. NOBLE had lost the element of surprise. He pushed himself off the floor, charged down the first three steps, and leveled the MAC-10 over the railing. Tiger shouted to his men while the screams of terrified women reverberated around the hold.

The thug with the AK-47 dropped the tin can he was holding—it hit the floor with a splat—and he swung his weapon into action. Noble centered the front site on the man's chest and squeezed the trigger. The little automatic burped. Empty shell casings leapt in a tidy arc from the ejection port. Three rounds punched through the thug's chest, driving him backward. Two more ricocheted off the floor.

Instead of falling down, Mr. AK-47 triggered a burst of automatic fire. The slugs impacted the underside of the stairs with heavy metallic splats. Noble felt a round bounce off the step directly beneath his right foot. The vibration traveled through the metal riser, sprinted up his leg and into his guts, letting him know how close he had come to getting his foot shot off. He returned fire. This time Mr. AK-47 sat down hard.

The other gorilla threw down the can opener and snatched the shotgun off the rolling cart. He thrust the weapon in the direction of the steps and jerked the trigger. The shotgun boomed. The steel pellets pinged off the wall a meter to Noble's left.

He must have gotten his weapon training from the movies. He thought aiming was unnecessary. Hollywood made out like shotguns were honest-to-god death rays and all you needed to do was casually wave the mighty carnage machine in the general vicinity of the target. In reality, the spread on a shotgun is only about the size of a dinner plate. Even a small error at a distance of twenty yards would result in a wide miss.

What Mr. Shotgun lacked in skill he made up for with enthusiasm. He racked and fired twice more, peppering the bulkhead with buckshot both times.

A sharp sting on Noble's left shoulder blade told him one of the pellets had ricocheted off the metal wall and lodged in his back. Pain and fear dumped adrenaline into his system. His heart thrummed against the wall of his chest. Blood pounded in his ears. He ignored the instinct to check and see how bad he had been hit; there would be time for that later. He sighted on Mr. Shotgun and pressed the trigger three times.

Half a dozen slugs stitched the gorilla's chest, throwing

him against the cages. He racked the shotgun in an effort to return fire, but his strength failed. He sank to one knee, tried to use the weapon as a crutch, then collapsed on top of it.

When bullets started flying, Tiger had ducked his head and disappeared between a row of cages like an alley cat slinking away at the first sign of danger. His hired muscle lay dead. Spent gunpowder gathered in smoky blue halos around lamps fixed to the ceiling. The women caterwauled and beat on their cages, begging for rescue.

Noble was moving as soon as Mr. Shotgun hit the floor. He could hear the voices of his Fort Bragg instructors in his head telling him to shoot and move. It was a concept drilled into combat troops from day one. He reached the bottom of the stairs and followed the starboard bulkhead.

Tiger was hiding somewhere among the maze of chicken wire cages. Noble had to assume he was armed. He was scared and desperate, and that made him dangerous. Noble slipped the MAC-10 on its strap over his right shoulder and drew the .45 pistol from his waistband. He wanted to limit the chances of the girls catching stray bullets. The semi-automatic pistol was more accurate.

He moved along the outside row of cages, peeking through chicken wire—past limbs and eager faces—looking for Tiger's silk shirt. The girls made his job harder. They clutched the octagonal wire and pleaded with him in a half dozen languages. Noble could barely make out the words. Between the girls and his buzzing eardrums, he wouldn't hear Tiger until it was too late. But that worked both ways; Tiger's ears had to be ringing just as bad.

Movement on the port side caught his attention. He cleared the center aisle and then darted across. When he reached the far side, he checked forward and aft. No sign of Tiger.

A gun thundered behind him. The bullet missed Noble and shattered a girl's elbow. Blood painted the wall like graffiti. She wailed and clutched her ruined arm. Noble sprinted the length of the hold. Tiger chased him with a hail of lead. Bullets hissed and snapped, killing one girl. The side of her head exploded in a red mist. Noble dodged left between the stacks. Tiger stopped shooting. Noble emerged on the center aisle in time to see Tiger running for the stairs.

Noble snapped off two rounds. He was aiming for Tiger's lower back, hoping to put a bullet through his guts. The first tore through Tiger's butt cheek. The second missed and rang off the metal bulkhead.

Tiger shouted in pain. He let go of his pistol and clamped both hands over his cheek. The 9mm Kahr bounced across the floor. Tiger went down face first. A dark red spot the size of a drink coaster soaked through his leather pants. It was a superficial wound. He would live.

Too bad, Noble thought. He deserved worse.

Two girls were injured. One lay dead. The rest huddled in their cages, terrified. Tiger whimpered and stretched out a trembling hand for the fallen gun.

"Don't do it," Noble told him. He centered his front sight on Tiger's head and thumbed back the hammer.

Tiger's bloody fingertips hovered inches from his weapon. One quick lunge and he'd have it. His lips peeled back from clenched teeth. He glowered at Noble. He wanted to go for the gun, but the will to live won out against his desire for revenge. He closed his eyes and put his head down. "My brother is going to kill you!"

"He'll try." Noble kicked the fallen pistol across the floor.

CHAPTER FIFTY-ONE

BATI COULD FEEL HERSELF WEARING DOWN LIKE A clockwork toy in need of winding. The earlier insulin shot had given her a boost but not enough. She was too far behind. She needed another injection soon to keep her from slipping into a diabetic coma. Her eyes kept slipping shut. Strange, half-formed thoughts wormed around inside her brain. Her limbs felt disconnected and foreign. It took a concentrated effort of will to move them. There was pressure behind her eyes and a buzzing inside her skull. She checked her thighs. The skin was sticky and dirt stained but still tan. No red streaks. Yet.

Each moment without insulin brought her closer to death. She could feel the grim specter hovering over her shoulder, waiting patiently for her broken body to surrender to the inevitable.

It must be some time in the early morning, one or two o'clock. An eerie silence had settled over the stone quarry. It felt like all the world was asleep. Only Bati and her captors remained. She had to escape. She told herself it was now or never.

The Frenchman, Rene, stood at the open door. Bati shifted in an effort to relieve the cramp forming in her lower back, and his compassionless eyes turned on her. They were like the eyes of a machine—cold and calculating, ruthlessly computing the situation and the most logical response. Humanity was not a factor. Bati feared to move again, even to relieve the pain, because she hated the feeling of his eyes on her.

The kidnapper with the severed finger lay slumped over a sack of crushed gravel. His face was sickly white. He hadn't moved in hours. Blood soaked through the bandage and puddled on the floor.

Bati licked dry lips. "I think that man is dead." The words squeezed out of a raw and swollen throat. The sound frightened her.

Rene ignored her.

"I think I killed that man," Bati told him. "I bit his finger off. Now he is dead."

Rene went to check on the unconscious kidnapper. He bent over and pressed two fingers into the carotid artery, turning his back on Bati in the process.

She struggled to her feet. A wave of dizziness hit and sent her reeling. Time slowed. She staggered across the bare concrete floor. "He's not dead," Rene was saying. "Just passed-" Bati lifted her foot and kicked him in the butt.

She would have kicked him harder if she had the strength, but her foot impacted with enough force to knock him off balance. He stumbled forward, tripped over the unconscious kidnapper, and sprawled face first.

Bati sprinted through the open door. Sharp gravel stabbed her bare feet. Her thighs burned with the effort of putting one foot in front of the other. It felt like running through knee-high water, like the nightmare where the harder she tried, the slower she went. She opened her mouth to scream. A horse whisper croaked out, "Help."

Bati swallowed, filled her lungs with air, and managed to shout, "Help me! Somebody help me!"

She reached the front bumper of the rusting dump truck. She had already gone farther than she thought possible. The Frenchman sprang to his feet and started after her, breathing curses every step of the way. His threats drove her on, spurring her to greater efforts. Fear opened the door to reserves she never knew existed. She dug deep and ran as fast as her failing body would go. A bright spot of hope blossomed in her chest. If she could stay ahead of Rene, maybe she could make it up the gravel drive, out of the rock quarry and find someplace to hide, someplace they would never find her.

Henries stepped directly into her path. Before she could stop or even change directions, he brought his rifle up and cracked her forehead with the butt stock. Her head snapped back. Her feet shot out from under her. She came down flat on her back, and the lights went out.

CHAPTER FIFTY-TWO

Navigation equipment and tiny blinking LED lights filled the pilothouse. The computer screens were all blank save one; it had a series of readouts containing longitude and latitude. A forgotten thermos and a dog-eared copy of a women's fitness magazine were on top of the computer banks. It was open to a glossy picture of a model in spandex shorts and a bikini top. Noble paused long enough to admire the model, then located a red emergency box affixed to the bulkhead behind the door. He took the flashlight from the box, stepped out on deck, and signaled Samantha.

Across the harbor, headlamps flashed. She pulled out, swung the car around, and drove toward the access road. Noble waited on deck near the boarding ramp. Ten minutes later, Sam pulled up. She barely got the car in park before leaping out and demanding, "Where is she? Where's Bati?"

"She's not here," Noble said. "But I've got Tiger down in the hold. He's going to tell us where to find her."

Sam's expression changed from disappointment to grim determination in the space of one long stride. She paused long enough to plant one foot on Tiger's motorcycle and push. The Ducati tumbled off the pier, hit the water with a splash, and sank below the surface.

"Petty and vindictive," Noble said as she reached the top of the gangplank. "I approve."

One corner of her mouth twitched up in the ghost of a smile. Noble motioned her to follow him and turned toward the hatch, giving Sam a view of his back.

"Is that a bullet hole?" Sam said. "Have you been shot?"

"I got hit by a ricochet."

It felt like someone had stabbed him with an icepick, but he could still move his arm. He took that as a good sign. If the buckshot had struck anything vital, he would already be woozy or unconscious. The metal bulkhead had reduced most of the velocity, and his shoulder blade must have stopped the rest. He hoped. "Is there a lot of blood?" he asked as he led the way downstairs.

"Not much. Does it hurt?" she asked.

"It will hurt worse once the adrenalin wears off."

They reached the bottom of the steps and turned down the long hall to the engine room. Sam grabbed his hand and stopped him. "We have to get you to a doctor."

"Later," he told her. "First thing is to find out where Bati is being held. I'm going to question Tiger, and I need to know you are on board."

Her lips pressed together in a hard line. "You mean torture?"

Noble took a breath. He didn't want to lose his temper. She had done well so far, but she had been duped by the media into believing that wars could be polite and orderly affairs where no one got hurt. Since Korea, America had been trying to win the hearts and minds of the enemy. That sounded good to the folks back home watching on CNN; in real life, it got soldiers killed.

"You don't get useable intel by turning up the air conditioning and forcing the bad guys to listen to Miley Cyrus."

Sam crossed her arms over her breasts and hunched her shoulders up. "It doesn't mean I have to enjoy it."

"You think I enjoy it?" he asked heatedly. "Sometimes I lose sleep over it. That's the price guys like me pay to keep people like you safe."

Her shoulders drooped. She uncrossed her arms. "I'm sorry, Jake. I didn't mean to..."

He waved it away. "Forget it."

They passed the engine turbine and the unconscious fat man. At the top of the stairs leading to the hold, Sam pulled a face and covered her mouth with one hand. "What is that smell?"

Noble paused on the top step. "This is a modern-day slaving ship. There are fifty or sixty women down there in cages, covered in their own filth. Think you can deal?"

Breathing through her mouth, Sam closed her eyes and nodded.

Before going topside, Noble had looked around for rope, cable, duct tape, or even a sturdy electrical cord to tie up Tiger. Unable to find anything useful, he decided to give the gangster a taste of his own medicine. He had located an empty cage, dragged it into the center of the aisle, and stuffed Tiger inside.

The kid lay on his side, rocking back and forth and

whimpering. One hand clutched the bullet hole in his right butt cheek. Sweat beaded on his forehead. He looked like he had been crying. "Please," Tiger begged as they appeared on the stairs. "Please, I'll give you anything you want. Name your price."

Noble wanted to laugh. He came down here ready to break fingers, but that wouldn't be necessary. For some people the threat of pain was enough. Tiger was ready to spill his guts to save his own skin. Just as well. It made Noble's job easy.

Sam stopped at the foot of the steps and placed both hands over her mouth. Her gaze moved along the row of cages filled with terrified and helpless women. Tears welled up in her eyes. Then she locked in on Tiger. The muscles stood out in her neck. She sprinted across the floor, kicked his cage, and beat on the chicken wire with her fists. "You monster! You sick perverted freak!"

Tiger curled up in an effort to stay away from the sides of the cage. Noble stood back and watched. Sam wailed on the chicken wire and threatened castration. Noble let her carry on long enough to rattle him, then threw an arm around her waist and hauled her back. "Let me handle this, okay?"

She stood there with her fists clenched and her body trembling. She stared daggers at the young Triad boss.

Noble hunkered down in front of the cage and rapped on the chicken wire with his knuckles.

Tiger uncovered his head and opened one eye. He had managed to smear blood from the bullet wound in his butt to his face and hair.

"Where is Bati?" Noble said.

"Who?"

"The girl your big brother had abducted from Manila."

"She's not here," Tiger said.

"Yeah, I can see that, genius. Where in the hell is she?"

Wounded and afraid, Tiger had trouble processing the question. His face screwed up in confusion. "I'll give you money. Anything you want, just don't hurt me."

Noble drew the .45 pistol and pointed it at Tiger's foot. He spoke slowly, enunciating each word. "Where is Bati?"

Tiger stuttered a few times, but the words finally stumbled out. "An abandoned stone quarry north of the Tai Lam Chung Reservoir. All the way at the end of Hap Song Road."

"Tell me about the mercenaries guarding her," Noble said.

"There are five. Henries is the leader." Tiger calmed down enough that he could speak without stuttering. "They are all ex-soldiers. Real hard cases."

"What kind of hardware do these mercenaries have?"

"Rifles," Tiger said. "Machineguns. Military hardware. All kinds of stuff."

"Explosives?"

He shook his head. "I don't know."

"If you are lying to me, I'll come back here."

Tiger shook his head harder, flinging drops of sweat. "I'm not lying. I swear I don't know."

Samantha laid a hand on Noble's shoulder. "Some of these girls need doctors."

"They aren't the only ones." He stood up. "Are you familiar with Tai Lam Chung Reservoir?"

She inclined her head and then looked at the rows of cages. "What about them?"

"We'll call the cops as soon as we are gone."

Sam glowered at Tiger in his cage, like she wanted another go at him. A vein throbbed in her temple. "What about him?"

"He stays," Noble said.

He retrieved the fallen AK-47. The dead thug had shot off half the magazine in the firefight. Noble bared his teeth in frustration. He would be going up against five trained mercenaries with a half empty AK-47, a half empty MAC-10, and his handgun. Not exactly an arsenal. "If ifs and buts were candies and nuts..." he said to himself.

Sam screwed up her face. "What?"

"It's one of my mother's sayings," he told her. "If ifs and buts were candies and nuts, we'd all have a Merry Christmas."

Back on deck, Noble was busy thinking about emergency medical treatment for the hole in his back and how to liberate Bati from a team of mercenaries. He didn't see the black sedan parked between rows of metal shipping containers. He and Sam were halfway down the gangplank when the headlamps snapped on.

CHAPTER FIFTY-THREE

A DARK SEDAN WAS PARKED BETWEEN SHIPPING containers with the front end pointed at the freighter. The harsh xenon headlights blinded Noble. Sam, directly behind him on the gangplank, raised a hand against the light. Noble resisted the urge to squint and block out the light; that is exactly what the driver wanted. Instead he took two long strides and leapt for the concrete dock.

He knew he was the target and wanted to put as much distance between him and Sam as possible. Bullets started flying before his feet even touched the ground. Lead slugs hissed through the air like angry hornets and pinged off the metal hull of the freighter.

Noble landed and brought the AK-47 up to his shoulder. He jackhammered the front of the dark sedan with controlled bursts of 7.62mm ammo. The sudden, violent counter-attack and the heavy crack of the AK-47 drove Krakouer down between the seats. Between bursts, he yelled to Sam, "Car! Now!"

Their rental was parked to the right of the gangplank. To reach it, they would have to cross five meters of open ground. He didn't know Sam was moving until he spotted her in his peripheral vision running for the passenger's side door of the DNY. She tugged at the handle, realized it was locked, and dug in her pocket for the keys.

Noble put enough rounds through the engine block to disable the sedan before the AK-47's bolt fell on an empty chamber.

Krakouer popped up like a murderous Jack-in-the-box. He thrust his gun out the driver's side window and fired. Bullets snapped past Noble and drilled holes in the trunk of the DNY.

Noble dropped the AK-47 and ran. The back windshield exploded. Sam jacked open the driver's side door, and Noble threw himself inside. Sam was ducked down on the passenger's side. She reached across, jammed the key in the ignition, and twisted. Noble threw the car in gear and stamped on the gas pedal. The back tires screamed, throwing up smoky white angels, then caught traction. The DNY shot forward. The front end veered wildly from side to side. Noble wrestled the steering wheel to stop them from flying off the pier and into the water.

He kept the pedal down all the way onto the bridge that would take them back to Kowloon. The back end fishtailed around the on-ramp, and then it was a straight shot across the harbor. He let the speedometer drop to 60mph and checked his rearview mirror. When he was certain they weren't being followed, he dropped down to 40mph. He couldn't risk getting pulled over. It would be hard to explain a car full of guns, bullet holes, and blood.

Sam ran both hands through her hair and took several deep breaths. "Was that Krakouer?"

"I thought it would take him longer to rearm himself," Noble said.

Sam twisted around in the passenger seat to stare out the shattered rear window. "Why is Krakouer trying to kill us?"

"Because you were right," Noble told her. "Ramos is tying up loose ends. My guess is he's got more skeletons than Arlington National Cemetery, and he'll kill anyone that gets too close to the truth."

———

Krakouer cursed. He had driven up and killed the lights in time to see the agents emerge on deck, or he would have picked a better spot for an ambush. Twice now Krakouer had the drop on the CIA's man. Twice he'd gotten away. He was either better than Krakouer gave him credit for or unbelievably lucky. Either way the long-haired surfer boy wouldn't walk away a third time.

Krakouer climbed out of the Nissan. He had spent an hour waiting on Ramos to arrange for a firearm and then stole the vehicle in his haste to reach the ship first. Bullet holes now riddled the hood. The windshield sagged like an elephant had sat on it. He slammed the door in frustration, and the starred windshield rained out of the frame.

All that work for nothing. It pissed Krakouer off.

Bati wasn't here; that much was obvious. They would never have left her on board, but there might be something to point him in the right direction.

He stalked up the gangplank, still mad at himself for not at least winging his target. In the hold, he found Tiger Tsang locked in a cage along with a cargo load of sex slaves. Tiger had been shot in the butt. Blood soaked the seat of his leather pants. His eyes were screwed shut. He shivered despite the oppressive heat.

Krakouer raked his 9mm Sig Saur across the chicken wire.

Tiger's eyes snapped open. Fear flooded his face and then recognition. "Hey. I know you. You were at my club."

"A tiger in a cage," Krakouer mused. "It's poetic."

"I'll give you fifty-thousand dollars to let me out of here."

"I've got a better idea," Krakouer said. "You tell me where your big brother is holding Bati Ramos, and I might not kill you."

"She's at the abandoned stone quarry north of Tai Lam Chung Reservoir," Tiger said. "Now let me out of here."

Krakouer aimed and put a bullet between Tiger's eyes. The shot blew the back of his head off. A mess of blood and brains sprayed across the floor. The women screamed. He holstered his piece and returned topside. The stolen Nissan refused to start. The engine block was shot full of holes. Krakouer cursed and set off on foot.

CHAPTER FIFTY-FOUR

MATTHEW BURKE SAT WITH ONE ELBOW PROPPED ON his desk and his forehead cradled in his hand. The other hand held the phone to his ear. An early morning cable had forced him out of the house without breakfast. He had three ops unfolding at the same time; his phone rang incessantly, and the D/O was demanding hourly updates. Through the glass wall of his office, he could see a clock hanging over the cubicles. It told him he had missed lunch as well. His stomach let him know about this appalling interruption in the regular schedule with a series of temper tantrums. He considered sending Dana to the vending machine in the hall for a dry turkey sandwich wrapped in cellophane. It was a sign of just how hungry he was that week-old turkey sounded appetizing.

"That is unfortunate," Burke said into the receiver. "Yes... Yes... I understand... It's not a perfect world."

The man on the other end hung up.

"Always nice talking to you," Burke said to the dead line

and put the receiver on the cradle. He snapped his fingers at Dana.

She also had a phone to her ear. She wore her blonde hair up today, and her breasts strained the material of her white blouse. "Hang on," she said into the phone. She took the receiver away from her ear. "What's up?"

Burke started to relay his request for a turkey sandwich from the machine, but the secure line on his phone lit up. The digital readout showed Noble's latest burner number. He snatched the receiver up. "Tell me what I want to hear."

"Disco is making a comeback."

"That's funny," Burke said. "You should take that act on the road. Have you got the girl?"

"No, but I've got Eric Tsang's little brother and a boat load of cargo all wrapped in a shiny bow. Some of the cargo is going to need medical treatment. I'm sure the Hong Kong police would like to get the credit for this one. Have you got anyone you trust?"

"I've got a guy inside the HK police department. He'll make sure the right people get assigned to the case," Burke said.

"Send them to Stonecutters Island," Noble said. "Search the red and gray freighter on the east dock."

Burke scribbled the directions on a yellow legal pad. "That's good work. And don't get me wrong, I appreciate it, but where are we on the girl?"

"I am on my way to pick her up right now."

Something in his voice made the small hairs on the back of Burke's neck stand on end. "You okay?"

"A double ought shotgun pellet bounced off a bulkhead

and now it's stuck in my back," Noble told him. "The pain is setting in."

The news left a sinking feeling in Burke's gut. The boys who made it into SOG were tough, the best in the business, but pain would eventually sabotage even the toughest operator. The Green Berets were often called Silent Professionals. They went about their job without all the gung-ho grandstanding of other Special Forces units. They didn't complain, and they didn't expect any thanks at the end of the day. The fact that Noble had even bothered to mention it meant the pain was getting to him.

"How bad?" Burke asked. "Can you finish the job?"

"Don't worry about me. There is something you need to know; Bati is the illegitimate love child of Bakonawa Ramos and Lady Shiva."

Burke sat up straight in his chair. "When were you going to read me in on this?"

"I'm reading you in on it now," Noble said. "But if this goes sideways, I want you to know where to start digging."

Burke let out a low whistle. "If that got out, it would end his career."

"That's the tip of the proverbial iceberg," Noble said. "His personal bodyguard, guy by the name of Krakouer, has tried to kill me twice. When this is over, we need to have a long chat with our friend, Mr. Ramos. Can you keep him from leaving the country?"

"Easier said than done. He has diplomatic immunity." Burke leaned back in his chair and stacked his feet on the desk. "I'll dig into Ramos. Your first priority is Bati. That girl has to be running out of insulin soon if she hasn't already."

"Agreed," Noble said. "What about that other thing I asked you to look up?"

Burke tabbed through open files on his computer screen until he found the right one. "Samantha Gunn. Age twenty-four. Born in San Diego, California. Father is a US citizen. Mother is from Hong Kong. Ms. Gunn has dual citizenship. She was on the women's rowing team in college, and according to her social media, she likes to ice skate. She graduated Yale. Moved to Manila. Works at the shelter run by Bati Ramos. No red flags. I don't suppose you are going to tell me why you wanted info on the BFF?"

"Later," Noble said and hung up.

Burke put the phone down. These waters kept getting murkier. Ramos had been feeding the company dirt on human-trafficking rings for nearly a decade. He had been their white knight. Finding out he had a dark past was bad enough; finding out he had sent a hitter to eliminate one of Burke's operators was unforgivable. If it was true, Ramos would pay, diplomatic immunity be damned.

His stomach issued another long, agonizing plea for food. He got up with the intention of going down the hall and purchasing one of those god-awful shrink-wrapped turkey sandwiches, maybe even two, but didn't make it to the door of his office before the phone rang.

CHAPTER FIFTY-FIVE

Noble dropped the cell phone into one of the cup holders. The movement made his shoulder ache. Sitting with his back against the seat made it worse, so he drove like an eighty-year-old man, hunched over the steering wheel with pain etched in the lines of his face. He had endured worse, but the years and the mileage were catching up. He must have looked a mess, because Sam sat in the passenger seat watching him like he might flat line at any moment.

"I'll be all right as soon as we get this shotgun pellet out of my back," he told her.

"Shouldn't we get you to a hospital?"

He shook his head. "Hospital staff is required to call the police when they get a patient with a GSW. They would ask questions we can't answer. Not yet anyway."

"Where are we going?" Sam asked. "We've been around this block four times already."

Noble pointed at a medical clinic on the corner. It was closed for the night and would have all the supplies he needed. He had been circling the neighborhood, piecing together a plan while talking to Burke on the phone. He checked his wristwatch. It was almost two in the morning. Most of the residents in this neighborhood were in bed, trying to catch a few hours' sleep before another day of work. The only people roaming the streets at this time of night were drunks staggering home. Noble had spotted a pair of them on his second lap around the clinic. Other than that, the block was deserted. He parked at the curb across the street and drummed his fingers on the steering wheel.

"Are we robbing a medical clinic?"

Noble nodded. "The list of supplies we need is relatively simple, but they have a security system."

"Can't you override it?"

"I was asleep that day in spy class."

She gave him a flat stare.

"We'll go in, get what we need, and get out before the cops show up," he said. "Average response time in Kowloon is seven minutes, unless there happens to be a cruiser in the area. That gives us four minutes to grab what we need and then collapse back on the vehicle, understood?"

Sam gathered her hair up in a ponytail, nodding. "What's on my shopping list?"

"Sterile bandages, as much gauze as you can carry, and hydrogen peroxide."

"And how are we going to get inside?"

Noble put his shoes and socks back on and then popped the trunk. The back hood unlatched with a soft thump. Sam met him at the rear of the vehicle. He raised the bullet-scarred trunk and hauled out the small tire iron that came standard with all mid-size sedans. It was less than useless for changing tires, but great for breaking windows.

He crossed the street with Sam close at his heels. She walked with her fists clenched like a boxer climbing into the ring.

One swing was all it took. The picture window rained down with a musical jingle on the linoleum floor. An alarm bell rang from deep inside the clinic. Noble used the tire iron to knock the jagged shards out of the frame. He swung one leg then the other over the waist-high sill.

Enough light filtered in from the street to navigate the small reception area. There were a half-dozen plastic chairs and an end table piled with old magazines. The door to the examination rooms was locked, but there was a pass through window for the secretary. Noble helped Sam climb through, and she opened the door from the inside.

Beyond the reception area, the only light came from red emergency exit signs. The alarm bell went on wailing. Noble rummaged through drawers for a pair of tongs, surgical tape, and a scalpel. With any luck he wouldn't need the scalpel but better safe than sorry. He collected every-thing he needed and stepped back into the hall that connected the examination rooms. Sam emerged a moment later from a door farther down with an armload of bandages and two bottles of hydrogen peroxide. The smash-and-grab had lasted less than three minutes.

They hurried back out to the rental car and dumped the supplies in the back seat. Noble climbed behind the wheel. They were six blocks away before the first police cruiser arrived at the clinic.

———

"Ouch! Christ! What are you doing back there?" Noble complained.

Sam slapped the uninjured side of his back with an open palm. "Don't use the Lord's name in vain!"

They had parked on the side of the highway. Working under the light of the interior dome, Sam was attempting to dig the shotgun pellet from his shoulder with surgical tongs. Noble sat with his back to her, looking out the driver's side window. He had both hands clenched together in his lap. Perspiration beaded on his bare skin. He could have taken painkillers, but they would slow him down, mentally and physically. For the next few hours, he needed to be sharp, so he let Sam poke around under his skin without the benefit of drugs.

Every nerve ending in his body went bright red at her slap. He drew a sharp breath. His arms and legs trembled. He mopped sweat from his face with one hand. "Just like my mother."

"I thought you were supposed to be all stoic despite the pain."

"In the movies maybe. In real life, getting a bullet pulled out hurts like hell."

"Well," she said while she worked. "I think I've got it."

The pain amped up to ten. It was everything Noble could do to keep from screaming. He clamped his teeth together and clenched his fists until his knuckles turned white. He bottled up all that hurt and turned it to anger. When the time came, he would pour it out on Eric Tsang and his hired guns.

"I got it," Sam said.

She had removed a metal ball slightly bigger than a child's BB from his back. Hard to believe something so small could cause so much pain. But the smallest things usually hurt the worst. Like going home every day to an empty house. Sam held the blood-covered pellet up in victory. It slipped from the tongs and got lost between the seats.

"Sorry," she said. "Did you want that for a souvenir?"

"Disinfect the wound, and slap on a bandage," Noble told her.

She twisted the cap off the hydrogen peroxide and poured half of the bottle over the hole in his back. Noble pounded the door panel with his fist. Sam ripped open a bandage, placed it over the wound, and affixed it with medical tape. When she finished, Noble draped himself over the steering wheel, closed his eyes, and waited for the burning to subside.

Sam scooped the cell phone out of the cup holder. "You've been shot. You've lost blood, and you don't look so good. Maybe it's time to call the police?"

Noble opened his eyes to glare at her.

"We could tell them to send a swat team."

He snatched the phone out of her hand. "We aren't calling the cops."

"Is it so important that *you* be the one to save Bati?"

"Yes!" Noble gripped the wheel with his left hand and spoke through clenched teeth. "My mother needs another round of chemotherapy. Are *you* going to pay for it?"

She laid a hand on his forearm. "Okay. Calm down."

He pinched the bridge of his nose between thumb and forefinger. "I need that money, understand?"

"And what happens if you get killed?" Sam asked.

"Burke will make sure she is taken care of."

She took his hand in both of hers and brought it to her lips. "I was thinking a little closer to home. What happens to Bati? What happens to me?"

The pain and fatigue was catching up with him. He wanted to close his eyes and go to sleep for a very long time. "You want to call the police, go ahead. By the time they fart around trying to negotiate for her release, Bati will be dead. Like it or not; we're the best chance she has. Now, are you in or out?"

"You know I'm in."

He moved his arm through a few slow rotations and winced. It hurt like hell, but he could still fight. He took his shirt from the floorboard—damn if it didn't smell like coffee —and Sam helped thread his wounded arm through the sleeve. He used his phone to pull up Hong Kong on Google earth and zoomed in on the quarry. The satellite photos were recent enough to show the dig, but Noble wouldn't know how accurate it was until he laid eyes on the site. He panned around and found an old logging road that ran north of the quarry. He could use it to approach from the back. He started the car and put it in drive.

The race was on. They had wasted time breaking into the clinic and pulling out the shotgun pellet. Krakouer would have used that same time to locate another vehicle. He could be in back of them or in front. Noble would have to be ready for anything.

CHAPTER FIFTY-SIX

Eric Tsang stood in front of the floor-to-ceiling windows of his high-rise office, a tumbler of fifty-year-old Glenfiddich in one hand, gazing across Victoria Harbor at the lights of Hong Kong. The hour hand on his gold Rolex was inching toward three o'clock. He should be sleeping, but the glittering jewel of the city beckoned to him. He loosened his tie, opened the top button on his shirt, and kicked off his shoes. He was waiting for the phone to ring. It wouldn't be long now. Ramos might be a criminal and a career conman, but he loved his daughter. As a father, Eric knew no price was too high for the safe return of daddy's little girl.

With his closest competitor out of business, Tsang could expand into the Philippines and from there into the Middle East. He would pipeline American girls into Saudi Arabia and Asian girls into Tampa, Florida. Arabs liked white meat, and Americans liked dark. Eric would make everyone happy. Business was good.

He gulped the last finger of Glenfiddich. It burned down his throat and into his stomach. On his way to the wet bar for a second, his phone vibrated in his pocket. He put down the glass tumbler and brought out the cell. Instead of Ramos's number, it was Lieutenant Chung of the Hong Kong police department.

Fear tickled the base of his skull. He put the phone to his ear. "It's late, Lieutenant. It must be important."

"I'm sorry about the hour, Mr. Tsang," Chung said. There was a brief pause. "I'm afraid I have bad news."

"I'm listening."

"We found your brother shot dead in a cargo ship on Stonecutters Island less than an hour ago."

A sharp pang of hurt and guilt formed in Eric's chest. He never should have left him in charge of the shipment. Tiger was careless. Eric sat down on the leather sofa and put his head in his hand. How would he explain this to their mother?

"Are you sure it's Tiger?"

"They have a positive ID," Chung said. "Uniforms found four dead bodies and a hold full of kidnapped girls. I wanted you to hear it from me first, before..."

"Before what?"

"He's your brother. By morning, investigators will be crawling all over your personal life."

"What do I pay you for?" Eric said.

"I'm not in charge of the case," Chung said. "Even if I was, I can't cover up a boat load of dead bodies and sex slaves."

Eric closed his eyes, leaned back in the sofa, and took a deep breath. "Who is in charge?"

"Captain Wong."

Eric rubbed his chin and exhaled. Captain Wong had been trying to dig up dirt on Eric for years. He was a crusader and refused to be bought off. What had happened on the ship? Was it the police? Ramos? Another Triad gang? Eric felt the first hint of panic clawing at his sense of calm.

"Is the boat in your name?" Chung asked.

"A shell company," Tsang told him.

"I'd distance yourself from that company as quickly as possible."

"I don't need legal advice. I've got lawyers for that."

"Perhaps you should be talking to them," Chung said.

Eric pressed the disconnect button. This was a complete disaster. Chung was right. He needed to be talking to his lawyers, working on damage control, but he needed to make another phone call first.

Worse than the prospect of having to tell his mother that her youngest son was dead, was the prospect that Tiger might have talked before he took a bullet.

Eric dialed Henries and waited entirely too long for the mercenary to pick up.

"Mr. Tsang. Bit late isn't it?"

"Your location is compromised," Eric told him. "Kill the girl. Get rid of the body. Make sure there is no evidence."

CHAPTER FIFTY-SEVEN

THE BATTLE-SCARRED DNY RUMBLED ALONG THE DIRT road, tossing Noble and Sam around inside. The suspension rattled and groaned. Noble followed the logging road around a soft shoulder and applied the brakes. Trees lined both sides of the lane. Stars winked in a long ribbon of black velvet sky overhead.

If the navigation app on his phone was accurate, then the stone quarry lay directly south, through a hundred meters of forest. Noble set the parking brake and turned the key. The engine ticked as it cooled. He turned to Sam. "We need to be quiet and, no pressure or anything, but our lives depend on it."

"Thanks," she said. "No pressure at all."

They left the car in the middle of the logging road and plunged into the woods. The trees formed a vault overhead, shutting out the light and forcing them to navigate in total darkness. There was only shadow and deeper shadow. And,

Noble reminded himself, Hong Kong was home to several deadly species of snakes, the King Cobra among them. He almost whispered this fact to Samantha but decided against it. By the time either of them saw a snake, it would be too late to do anything about it. Best not to worry her.

Noble reached back and took her hand so they would not get separated. She gave a little squeeze, grateful for the support. They went slow to avoid getting turned around in the dark or making too much noise. Every lung full of air was tinged with the pungent aroma of dank soil. It took them ten minutes to go less than a hundred meters.

Bright shafts penetrated the forest ahead, creating silhouettes of the trees. The mining operation that worked the site had abandoned large banks of arc sodium lights along with much of the equipment when they closed down the dig. The mercenaries were using the stadium lighting to illuminate their surroundings, giving themselves a tactical advantage. Noble hunkered at the tree line and took stock of the situation.

The quarry was shaped like a gigantic light bulb; a long, sloping access road coming up from the south widened out into a deep circular depression scooped from the earth as if by the hand of God. The steep walls bore the scars of the dynamite used to blast the crater. The floor of the quarry was loose rubble and soft shale. A massive dump truck was parked near a crushing facility shaped like an L and constructed of corrugated steel. A pair of Mercedes-Benz G class trucks with dark tinted windows was parked in the middle of the dig. The lamps were all wired to a construction trailer parked atop the ridgeline thirty meters to Noble's left. A portable

Craftsman generator next to the trailer emitted a throaty rumble.

One of the mercenaries was a German sniper. He would be concealed in the tree line with a view down the access road. Between the low light and dense foliage, he could be a dozen paces in either direction, and Noble would never know it. The idea sent a chill capering up Noble's spine. But if the sniper had seen them, they'd already be dead. It was a strangely comforting fact.

Even with the construction lights in his eyes, Noble could see three of the mercenaries from his vantage point. One knelt behind an overturned ore cart near the access road. The second had taken cover behind a large boulder. The third stood near the rear bumper of the rusted dump truck talking on a cell phone. That would be the leader, Henries, giving updates to his employer. If Noble had a decent rifle with a scope, he could kill all three from this distance.

Between the three he could see and the sniper hiding among the trees, there was one left. The fifth mercenary would be inside the crushing facility where he could keep an eye on the prisoner. The two kidnappers were likely inside as well, and Noble had to assume they were armed.

All in all, the mercenary leader had done well with limited resources. Between the gunmen in the quarry, the lights along the ridgeline, and the sniper, anyone coming up the access road would get shredded long before they reached the crushing facility.

In Special Operations Group, Noble had spent weeks, sometimes months, planning operations and analyzing every angle of attack and counter attack. But he didn't have weeks. He had to neutralize the mercenaries, grab Bati, and get out before Krakouer showed up to complicate things. With no time to formulate a plan, Noble would have to win this fight on instinct, improvisation, and a lot of luck.

The sniper was the problem. Noble needed at least two team members. One to extract Bati and one to eliminate the sniper.

He looked at Samantha. She was hunkered at the base of a tree and craning her neck to see into the pit. Her lower lip was pinched between her teeth. Her brow furrowed. The idea of putting her in harm's way formed a tight knot in his gut and forced him to examine his feelings for her. He had to admit it went beyond simple attraction. He tried to put a label on it but rejected the word love. Besides, she had turned him down last night in the hotel room. Why did he always fall for the ones who weren't interested in him?

Whatever these feelings were, they were getting in the way of the job. He leaned close and dropped his voice below a whisper. "I need your help."

She took a deep breath. "What do I have to do?"

"There is a sniper hidden along the ridgeline," Noble told her.

Sam tensed. The chords in her neck stood out. She peered around like she might spot him behind the nearest bush.

"He'll stay hidden until he has a target. I'm going to draw him out. When he breaks cover, it's up to you. All of his attention will be on me. You'll be able to sneak up in back of him."

Sam was already shaking her head. "What if I can't? What if I can't pull the trigger?"

"Then I die and so does Bati."

Her lips pressed together. Lines formed around her eyes. Noble could see the storm below the surface. He knew it was asking her to commit the unthinkable—killing another human being. For some people, it was impossible. But removing the sniper was the lynchpin of this entire operation.

He gripped the back of her neck and pulled her close. "It's a hell of a thing. But I need you. Bati needs you."

"What if I miss?"

"You won't," Noble told her. "Listen to me. He won't be able to hear a damn thing over the sound of the firefight. You sneak right up behind him until you are so close you can't miss. Put your arms out straight, hold the pistol in both hands, and pull the trigger. Keep pulling the trigger until he stops moving. Understand?"

She let out a trembling breath. "Okay."

Noble turned her face up to his, so he could look her in the eye. He needed to know she could actually pull the trigger. He was taking a desperate risk. A thousand things could go wrong. If she screwed it up, all three of them would die. "Let me hear you say it."

She swallowed hard. "I'm going to sneak up behind him, hold the gun in both hands... and shoot him."

"Again."

"I'm going to sneak up behind him and shoot him."

"One more time."

"I'm going to sneak up behind him and shoot him," Sam said with more confidence. "To save Bati."

Noble nodded, satisfied. He didn't like the idea of sending an inexperienced asset against a trained sniper, but if she failed he wouldn't have long to lament his mistake.

There were a thousand things he wanted to say and no time to say them. He had done the best he could. He turned his attention to the construction trailer. Crossing the open ground to the generator would feel like crossing a minefield. He would be totally exposed, but he had to turn out the lights or this thing would never get off the ground. He let out a nervous breath. "Wish me luck."

"Wait," Sam grabbed his hand and held on. "We should pray."

"You want to pray?"

She nodded.

"About killing people?"

She gave him a flat look.

Anger brewed below the surface. God, if he existed, never answered any of Noble's prayers. He didn't need God's help. He didn't want it. Noble made his own way in the world. Sam, on the other hand, believed. If she needed to feel that some sort of supernatural providence was working for her then it would be worth the few extra seconds. Noble told himself he was doing it for her sake. "Make it quick."

She closed her eyes and turned her face up to the sky. "Lord, we need your help. Give us victory over our enemies. Protect us and deliver us. And Lord, please heal Jake's mother. Give her a miracle. Amen."

Short and sweet. Noble would have preferred she left his mother out of it, but at least it was quick. She opened her eyes and gave his hands a squeeze. "Be careful."

"I'm always careful," he said. "I'd rather be lucky."

All soldiers were careful. Even the best could catch a bullet. Any one of them would tell you it was better to be lucky. Noble pressed the slide of his pistol halfway back and saw the soft copper gleam of a round nestled in the chamber. He thumbed the safety off and crept through the underbrush to the tree line.

CHAPTER FIFTY-EIGHT

Bati lay on the stone floor with her eyes shut and tears streaking her cheeks. A swollen purple welt on her forehead oozed pus. The slightest sound made her head feel like it would split right down the middle. Small movements sent electric jolts racing up her spine. It was everything she could do to deal with the pain. It needed all her concentration.

She was back in the crushing facility. Henries and Rene had carried her back inside and dropped her on the floor after the Australian had smashed her with the butt of his rifle. She was awake by then but kept her eyes closed for fear of further reprisals.

The Frenchman was so close she could feel him. He shifted his weight. His boots scraped the layer of grit on the concrete floor. His gear rattled. Occasionally he would fetch a heavy sigh. Bati didn't look. She didn't move. She didn't want him to know she was awake.

Wrapped up in all the pain and fear were questions—

questions Bati had long been afraid to ask. She had grown up in luxury, enjoyed special treatment at school, and met heads of state. Her father, after all, was Bakonawa Ramos. Before she was even old enough to know what a diplomat was, people would tell her how proud she should be of her father. And she was. Everywhere she went, people praised him and his work against human trafficking. There were fundraisers, galas, and award ceremonies. Bati had a good life.

Despite all that, by the time she was a senior in high school, she had developed lingering doubts about daddy's business. There was nothing she could point to specifically. It was a hundred little things. Maybe it was the whispered phone conversations late at night, or the overly lavish life-style, but Bati began to suspect that not all of his deals were above board. At first she tried to explain it away, and when she couldn't do that any longer, she chose to ignore it. As much as she hated to admit it, Bati enjoyed their expensive lifestyle as much as Daddy. Besides, she reasoned, he was working for the greater good. If that required a few less-than legitimate deals then the ends justified the means.

Now, lying here, feeling her faulty body shutting down for lack of insulin, Bati realized the sins she had tried so hard to ignore were finally coming to light. Was God punishing her? Was this the price for turning a blind eye? A tortured sob issued from her raw throat and a fresh wave of tears welled up.

She heard boots in the gravel and then Henries saying, "I just got off the phone with the boss. We are shutting this operation down."

"What about her?" Rene asked.

Bati peeled open one eye in time to see Henries shake his head.

"Shame," Rene said.

"Hold the fort while I take care of business," Henries said.

They were going to kill her. Bati's heart squeezed painfully hard. The air caught in her lungs. She sat up and shook her head. "Please don't," she begged. "Please don't kill me."

"On your feet," Henries said. He grabbed her arm and yanked her up.

Bati screamed. The big Australian dragged her toward the back of the crushing facility. She struggled wildly despite the pain it caused her head. She kicked and screeched and when that didn't work, she bit him. Her teeth clamped down on his muscular shoulder.

Henries shouted in pain and his grip relaxed.

Bati wrenched her arm free and ran. Her only thought was to find a dark corner and hide.

Henries cursed and started after her, but at that moment, the rumble of the generator hiccupped. The throaty roar rose in pitch to an overburdened shriek. The lights around the quarry flickered. Henries stopped. He looked at Rene. The Frenchman shrugged.

CHAPTER FIFTY-NINE

NOBLE MOVED SILENTLY THROUGH THE UNDERBRUSH. An itch formed between his shoulder blades with every step. The sniper was out here somewhere. Noble kept expecting to hear a rifle crack and feel a bullet perforate his heart. A twig snapped under his foot. He paused, watching and listening. His eyes strained to penetrate the shadows. After what felt like minutes, he forced himself to keep going. He made it to the edge of the tree line in back of the trailer without getting shot.

Now for the hard part.

Less than four meters separated him from the Craftsman generator, but it was four meters of open ground lit by the spill from the towering construction lamps. He would be exposed every step of the way. If the sniper happened to be looking in that direction, Noble was going to die.

The longer he thought about it, the harder it would be

to take that first step. He forced the fear to the back of his mind and broke cover.

He crossed the open ground to the generator. It was a big thirty-five-horsepower job with a plastic fuel tank on the top and a pull chord. He could hit the off switch, but that would give away his location; he wanted to keep the element of surprise as long as possible. Instead he twisted off the fuel cap, tossed it, and then turned the generator on end. Gasoline glugged out through the opening and formed a dark puddle on the bare earth. The engine started to knock and hiccup. The sound of the motor climbed several octaves. The lights dimmed and then flared back to life.

Noble took off running up the wooded incline. He crashed through the underbrush, heedless of the noise. Bare branches raked his face and sleeves. He emerged onto the dirt lane with the DNY parked ten meters to his right.

The next part of Noble's plan relied heavily on luck. There was no way to know how long the generator would keep laboring. It might have cut out already. Soon as the lights died, the mercenaries would be keyed up for a fight. He sprinted to the car, threw himself behind the steering wheel, and got the vehicle turned around.

He drove at reckless speeds with the headlamps off. The suspension slammed through divots and launched over humps. He needed to reach the quarry as fast as possible. If he killed the car in the process, so be it. He could take one of the Mercedes vans after the fight, always assuming there was an afterward. At the intersection, he fishtailed the DNY onto the blacktop. The front passenger side tire was shredding and made a telltale hum.

Noble stamped the gas and almost missed the access

road. He spun the wheel. The DNY slewed around the corner onto the gravel drive, kicking up a cloud of dust in its wake. Along the ridgeline, the arc sodium construction lights dimmed, waxed bright, and dimmed again. The mercenaries turned their attention to the trailer and the struggling generator. Noble was halfway down the access road when the work lamps winked out.

Perfect.

Grace or good luck—Noble didn't care to speculate— had given him a chance to level one hell of a surprise on his enemy. He took full advantage. His lips pressed together in a savage line. His brow furrowed. He pushed the pedal to the floorboard, coaxing the last bit of horsepower from the engine, and switched on the headlights at the same time. The motor emitted a throaty growl, and twin beams pierced the darkness.

The diversion had bought him a few precious seconds. The mercenaries heard the engine and saw the headlights. Someone yelled, "Contact front!"

Automatic fire echoed around the quarry. Bullets smacked the hood, starred the windshield, and chewed through the front tires.

Noble scrunched down in the driver's seat and aimed the car at the overturned ore cart. The headrest exploded in a shower of foam confetti. A bullet drilled through the seat less than an inch from Noble's head.

He cramped the steering wheel, stamped the brake, and pulled the parking lever at the same time, sending the DNY into a sideways skid. The vehicle slewed across the stony ground, pushing a wave of dirt and gravel ahead of it. The mercenary behind the cart realized what was about to happen and ran for safety. He wasn't fast enough. The left side of the car impacted the metal bucket and sent it tumbling. The mercenary crashed across the front hood of the vehicle in a splay of arms and legs. The DNY reared up on two wheels, hung there a moment, and then settled back onto all four with a bang.

A hailstorm of bullets blew out the windows. Shattered glass flew in every direction. Noble scrambled across the seats and pushed open the passenger side door. He belly crawled out of the vehicle and sheltered behind the rear wheel well while the mercenaries hammered the car with small arms fire.

CHAPTER SIXTY

SAM HUNKERED IN THE SHADOWS AND WAITED. NOBLE had tipped the generator on its side and run, leaving her alone. Even from thirty meters, she could hear the Craftsman struggle. It would not be long now. She put her back to a tree, reached a trembling hand into her jacket pocket, and brought out the pistol. The nickel plating winked in the faltering light from the construction lamps. It was surprisingly heavy for such a small gun. She cradled the weapon in both hands, pointed it straight down at the ground between her knees, and practiced lining up the sights. She locked her arms out—because Jake had made a point of it—and realized that it made the sights line up naturally.

The generator began to bang and wheeze. It had run quite a bit longer than she had expected, tipped on its end like that, but now it was burning through the last of the petrol. It was do or die time. Unfortunately, Sam wasn't the only one who would die if she failed.

With the portable power generator in its death throes, she closed her eyes one last time and asked God for strength.

The generator cut out. The lights went dark.

Her heart beat so hard she could hear blood pulsing in her ears. Her legs shook. The gun suddenly felt like it weighed no more than a paperback novel. She had studied enough biology to know that adrenaline was giving her strength, causing the muscles to contract harder and for longer periods of time. It was how mothers lifted cars off children. Tomorrow her whole body would ache, but for now, she felt capable of leaping tall buildings in a single bound. Eat your heart out, Superman.

A second after the construction lights went out, a pair of headlights blazed into existence. The DNY hurtled along the gravel access road, kicking up a plume of dust in its wake. The night erupted with the deadly rhythm of automatic weapons. Sam's breath caught in her chest as the soldiers peppered the car with bullets. She watched, transfixed. It was impossible to believe anyone could survive.

A loud whipcrack yanked her out of her daze. Less than sixty meters to her right, a man in a black military vest and denims crouched at the lip of the quarry. He had a long rifle with a scope balanced atop his left knee. All of his attention was on the car. He fired again. A brass shell casing leaped from the breach, trailing smoke.

DNY turned into a slide, impacted the overturned ore cart, and sent one of the mercenaries sailing over the hood. The car ground to a stop, and the mercenary landed in a tangle of broken limbs. The passenger side door opened. Jake must have piled out on the far side.

The sniper fired round after round, keeping Jake pinned behind the car. He couldn't move until Sam did her part. She knew Jake was counting on her, but she was rooted to the spot, paralyzed. The moment she moved, the sniper would see her. He would turn the big rifle on her, and the last thing she would hear was the awful thunder-clap before the bullet tore through her brain. It took every ounce of courage she had, but Sam managed to take a step.

The fear broke as soon as she moved. She dodged through the trees and underbrush, snapping twigs and crunching leaves. Noble was right; she could barely hear over the cacophony of gunfire. And if she couldn't hear, neither could the sniper.

She got within five meters and considered taking the shot. She pushed the gun out in front of her and sighted on his torso just below his left armpit. Her index finger tight-ened on the trigger, but she heard Jake's voice in her head telling her to get as close as she could.

She bared her teeth. Her nostrils flared. It felt like step-ping into a cage with a hungry lion, but Sam crept through the woods and stepped out of the tree line close enough to spit on him.

He stopped firing long enough to drop the magazine out of his weapon and push in another. He gave the full maga-zine a hard slap to be sure it seated, then shouldered the weapon.

Sam raised the .22 Walther in both hands and aimed at the back of his head, but she didn't pull the trigger. "Put it down, or I'll shoot!"

He tensed and, slowly, turned his head to peer over his

left shoulder. One corner of his mouth turned up in a sneer. He spoke with a German accent. "You will not shoot me."

The weapon trembled in Sam's grip. It was an effort to keep her knees from buckling. She had to remind herself to breathe. "Don't force me."

His eyes narrowed. Seconds stretched into hours. He swung the rifle around.

The weapon jumped in Sam's hands. She was aiming for his head. The bullet drilled a dime-size hole through his Adam's apple and exploded out the back of his neck. He made a surprised face and crumpled like a plastic statue melting in a microwave.

She hadn't known she was pulling the trigger until she felt the gun jerk. Now the sniper lay dead at her feet. And just like that, it was done. She refused to look at the dead man.

Down in the quarry, Jake conducted a one-man war against the enemy. For Sam it was like having a bird's eye view on the D-day invasion. From her vantage point, she could see a mercenary crouched behind a large boulder. His back was to her, totally exposed. Sam realized she could fire down into the pit with impunity. She was safe on the ridge, and the sniper had loaded a new magazine into his weapon.

She dropped the pistol, stretched out on her belly, and slid the rifle out from under the dead man. It must have weighed seven pounds. Sam let the barrel rest on the rock ledge. She adjusted the butt stock in her shoulder, placed her finger on the trigger, and peeped through the scope.

The sniper had made it look easy. At first she tried putting her eye directly against the scope, but all she could see were her own eyelashes. She pulled her head back a bit and saw a half-moon. After some side-to-side adjustment, she got a clear sight picture. She could see the rocky floor of the quarry and a pair of cross hairs along with a red dot in the center. There were several hash marks and numbers that Sam did not understand, but the red dot was pretty self-explanatory.

When she pivoted in search of the mercenary, it screwed up her view through the scope. It took her several tries, peering over top of the rifle to locate the mercenary and then putting her eye back to the scope before she got the man in her sights. When she finally connected the two, she placed the red dot on his back and pulled the trigger.

There was no hesitation this time. She wanted the fight to be over. Simple as that. Unfortunately her bullet smacked the rock a half meter to the mercenary's right.

He turned and hosed the ridgeline with a burst from his automatic weapon. Bullets embedded themselves in the rock wall and zipped around Sam's head like a swarm of bees. She buried her face in the dirt and breathed in a lung full of dust. Her throat clutched. Tears welled up in her eyes. She wracked out a long, painful cough.

CHAPTER SIXTY-ONE

NOBLE WAS PINNED BEHIND THE BACK TIRE WHILE THE mercenaries drilled round after round into the vehicle. They were using overwhelming firepower to quickly shift the momentum of the battle in their favor. Lead chewed through the fiberglass door panels and shredded the seats. Within seconds, Noble had gone from offense to defense. He was usually on the other side of this equation.

He had to engage and keep the pressure on, or they would use their numbers to outflank him. He fired the MAC10 through the blown-out windows in the direction of the crushing facility. Three short bursts finished off the magazine. Noble dropped the empty weapon in the dirt.

The sharp crack of a long-range rifle echoed like thunder across the quarry. A bullet hissed past his ear, forcing him back down. He bared his teeth. *Where was Sam?* Surely she had marked his position by now. Hopefully she hadn't choked.

The twisted body of the mercenary that Noble had run

over lay in the gravel two meters from the front bumper. His arms and legs were bent at wrong angles. Dark red blood covered one side of his face, but he was still alive. A pink bubble formed at the corner of his lips as he tried to speak. His weapon, an H&K 410 assault rifle, lay underneath him.

Noble decided to make a play for the gun. It would give the sniper something to shoot at and give Sam a chance to sneak up on him.

He inched along the back of the car toward the rear bumper. One of the mercenaries was sheltered behind a large rock. Noble stepped out, aimed his pistol at the boulder, and hammered it with two quick rounds, forcing the shooter to take cover and drawing the sniper's attention to the rear of the wrecked DNY. A bullet whined off the trunk.

Noble ran in a crouch to the front bumper and lunged for the assault rifle. He grabbed it by the barrel and tried to reverse directions, but the 410 was on a single-point sling secured around the man's neck.

A bullet kicked up a cloud of debris two centimeters from Noble's foot. There was no time to remove the harness. The sniper, if he was any good at all, would not miss again. With a curse, Noble flexed the muscles in his back and legs in an effort to drag the mercenary behind the car. He reached cover in time to avoid the next shot. The headlight exploded.

The sniper wasn't satisfied with driving Noble behind the car. He winged several bullets off the hood as a warning. Noble sat down hard in the dirt and went to work removing the 410 from around the dead man's neck. In the time it took him to do that, the sharp crack of the sniper's rifle fell silent.

Hope blossomed. Had Samantha pulled it off?

He stuck his head up long enough to draw fire and heard the purr of automatics but not the distant crack of the rifle. Noble felt a flash of fierce pride. She had come through. The girl had guts.

The sniper was out of the battle. Noble checked the action on the 410 and found a round in the chamber. The odds were turning in his favor. He moved to the rear of the DNY intent on engaging the remaining enemies and heard the sniper rifle crack.

The sound turned his blood to ice. He had an image of Sam lying dead up on the ridgeline. The thought left a sick, sinking feeling in his heart.

He glanced through the shattered windshield. What he saw filled him with savage excitement. The mercenary behind the boulder broke cover and sprayed the top of the ridge with a full auto burst.

Noble knew immediately what had happened. Sam had used the sniper's rifle to take a shot at the mercenary's exposed back. She missed but drove him into the open. Noble aimed the 410 through the blown-out windows and squeezed the trigger. The assault rifle chewed out three rounds with a satisfying buzz. The man arched his back, collapsed to his knees, and went over face first.

Three out of the five mercenaries were dead. The remaining two were in the crushing facility, but they weren't content to stay put. One leaned out the open door and fired while Henries sprinted to the abandoned dump truck for a better angle on Noble.

The two kidnappers had yet to put in an appearance. Maybe they had already taken their money and split. Noble leaned out and fired at the redhead behind the dump truck. The 5.56mm rounds smacked off the steel hood in a display of sparks.

From behind the dump truck Noble heard an Australian accent yell, "Reloading."

The shooter in the crushing facility forced Noble to take cover with a series of short, controlled bursts while Henries slapped a fresh magazine into his weapon. Then they took turns hammering the DNY, preventing Noble from mounting any sort of counter-attack. Exactly what he was afraid of. One man would keep him pinned while the other moved. They would surround him. He couldn't defend from two directions at once.

The dead mercenary at Noble's feet wore a chest rig. Noble ripped open one of the Velcro pockets and found a full magazine inside. He performed a tactical reload, swapping the partial magazine for the full. He kept the half spent mag in his left hand, ready for use.

He had a full weapon but nothing to shoot at. Both mercenaries had good cover, and they kept him pinned with a hailstorm of lead like angry hornets stinging the driver's side of the DNY. Noble remembered the cartoons where the blue dog with a sheriff's badge on his chest and a white cowboy hat took cover behind a rock. The outlaw, usually a bulldog with a cigar and a black hat, would carve away at the rock with a spray of bullets and the resulting statue was the Venus de Milo. Noble doubted the DNY would be a famous work of art when the fight was over, but he was running out of car to hide behind.

Sam came through again, once more turning the tide in his favor. That beautiful, gutsy woman had relocated along the ridgeline to give herself a better angle on Henries. She winged a shot off the truck, inches from the Australian's head.

She couldn't shoot worth a damn, but Henries didn't know that. He could probably stand there all day and let her plink away at him without taking a bullet, but she had come close enough to scare him. He pulled a hand grenade from his chest rig. He yanked the pin and lobbed it at the DNY, then sprinted to the door of the crushing facility while the other mercenary covered his retreat.

CHAPTER SIXTY-TWO

BATI CURLED UP IN A BALL, TRYING TO MAKE HERSELF as small as possible. Fear immobilized her. It sounded like World War III outside. The thunderclap of automatic weapons clawed at her sanity. She let out a scream that dissolved into hysterical sobs. One thought worked its way through the panic; she did not want to die here. Not like this.

She had a chance to reach the toolbox while her captors were distracted. With any luck, she would find a knife or scissors to free her hands. She wobbled to her feet and stumbled deeper into the facility, trying to retrace her steps. Her knees threatened to give out. Her head spun. The floor pitched like a ship on a high sea. She reached the spot where she had crouched to pee. The kidnapper lay dead on the floor. His brains had congealed into a sticky paste. Bati staggered to the conveyor belt and knocked the dusty toolbox off with an elbow. It landed on its end with a bang, and the lid popped open, disgorging tools.

Bati allowed her tired legs to buckle and sat down hard. She spotted a pair of tin snips. They were old and covered in grease, but they would do the job. She turned around and patted blindly at the pile until her fingers closed over the snips, then she went to work trying to slip the blades over the plastic zip tie.

Several times she thought she had the tin snips in place and squeezed the handles. Each time the blades closed on empty air. Bati whined in frustration. Outside the battle raged on. She tried again and felt the blades meet resistance. She squeezed. The tin snips snapped through the plastic and pinched her skin.

She winced. She had a small cut on the inside of her left wrist and bruising from the plastic tie, but her hands were finally free. She rubbed her wrists. Her fingers were pins and needles. She waggled them like a sorcerer trying to conjure fire in an effort to get the blood flowing.

When her hands and fingers were working again, she used the conveyor belt to pull herself up. She wanted nothing more than to lie down and drift off to sleep but knew if she let her eyes close that she would never wake up. She pulled herself along the conveyor belt to the tall machine where the kidnapper had left his handgun. She reached one trembling hand up and felt around. Her fingers closed over the barrel.

CHAPTER SIXTY-THREE

THE SMALL GREEN GLOBE ARCED THROUGH THE AIR. Noble watched it bounce in the gravel near the front bumper and roll to a stop. The passenger side door was still open. He threw himself across the front seats. The grenade exploded with a heavy *whomp*. Shrapnel blistered the side of the car. The concussion blew the last remaining shards of glass out of the window frames, shredded the tires, and hammered Noble's eardrums.

He squeezed his eyes shut and shook his head to clear it. Being that close to the explosion was disorienting and might have caused permanent hearing damage. Only time would tell. At the moment, he was more worried about getting back into the fight. He needed to engage before they could lob any more grenades in his direction or storm the car. He rolled onto his side, stuck the H&K 410 over the dash, and fired blind.

Henries sprinted to the open door of the crushing facility. The rescuer tried to cut him down with a spray of bullets. A round sizzled past his ear. He hunched his shoulders up and ducked his head.

Rene, crouch behind sacks of crushed gravel, covered his retreat with three short bursts from his AR15. He ejected an empty magazine— the aluminum case clattered across the floor— and seated another mag with a slap.

Henries stopped inside the door and took a knee next to Rene. Everything had gone to pot with alarming speed, but then, that's how it usually happens in a gunfight. One minute you had the upper hand and the next you were scrambling to stay alive. Graham, Daniel, and Otto were all dead. Henries had barely escaped the sniper's bullet. It wouldn't take the man long to relocate to a spot on the ridgeline that afforded him an angle on the door. The attackers now had the initiative. He and Rene were cornered. Their only bargaining chip was the girl.

"Stay away from the door," Henries said. "They've got a sniper up on the ridge. He's good too. Nearly took my head off."

Rene thumbed his selector to single shot and fired three rounds at the car. "I hope you have a plan. I'm running out of ammo."

"I'm not going to die for the likes of Eric Tsang," Henries said. "They want the girl. Let's see if we can use her to buy our way out of here."

Rene nodded in agreement. "I'll hold them off while you go and fetch her. Don't be long."

Henries slipped a full magazine from his tactical vest and passed it to Rene before going in search of the girl. He had already lost two-thirds of his team. He had no intention of dying here.

————

Noble crawled feet first from the bullet-riddled DNY and hustled around to the tail end of the vehicle, keeping as much metal between him and the two remaining mercenaries as possible. He leaned around the busted taillight and stitched the front of the building with bullets.

His enemies responded in kind, but they had a limited angle on the DNY from their position inside the open door. If Noble could force them behind cover long enough, he could make it around the side of the building where a conveyor belt entered through a square opening big enough to admit a man. He would have to cross a lot of open ground, but he wouldn't do any good hiding behind the bumper of a shot-up car.

He waited for them to fire and then broke cover. He shouldered the 410 and triggered short salvos while moving, hammering the corrugated steel door. The 410's bolt locked back on an empty chamber as he reached the overturned ore cart. He took a knee behind the sturdy metal container long enough to swap mags and then sprinted for the side of the building. A trail of lead chased him, kicking up little puffs of dirt in his wake. He made the corner, leapt onto the stalled conveyor belt, and ducked through the opening.

Silence descended on the quarry. After all the shooting and explosions, the quiet felt deafening and unnatural. Noble hopped off the conveyor belt and moved to his left, into an envelope of darkness.

The facility was designed to pulverize rock from the quarry into increasingly smaller chunks until finally the pebbled rock could be loaded into bags and shipped. The conveyor belt led to a giant crusher. From there, several more belts branched out to different-sized machines scattered throughout the rest of the building. The place was a maze of crisscrossing conveyors and motors. Electrical wires snared up the floor. Fine powder filled the air and made Noble want to sneeze. It would be a cruel twist of fate to survive everything else only to sneeze and get shot in the dark. He ran a finger under his nose until the urge passed.

He stuck close to the wall and made his way counterclockwise around the building. Working alone meant watching every angle at once, or trying to anyway. Without a team to watch his back, Noble felt naked. The small hairs on the back of his neck stood on end. He slid through the gap between two large crushing units and then ducked a belt.

Starlight filtered in through collapsed sections of roof, spinning a crazy web of light and shadow. Noble went slow, using dark pockets to stay hidden. He caught movement on his right, stopped, and trained his weapon on an alley formed by two control panels. He glimpsed a bald man with a barrel chest and an AR15 going the other direction.

The mercenary was out of sight before Noble could pull the trigger. He strained his ears to the sound of boots on the gritty concrete floor. The muzzle of an AR15 appeared around the far side of the control panel a moment later. Noble waited for his enemy to break cover and then tightened his finger on the trigger. Five rounds hit center mass, driving the mercenary backward. He slammed into a crusher, slid to the floor, and coughed up a dark mouthful of blood.

———

Bati could barely lift the gun. Walking was out of the question. She put her back to the nearest machine and slid down until her butt touched the floor. It was impossible to say how long she sat there. Time slowed to a crawl. Her eyelids grew heavy and slid shut. She fought, opening her eyes as wide as she could, but it was a wasted effort. Without her even realizing it, her lids drooped closed again. She was balanced on the edge of sleep, when an automatic weapon shattered the silence.

Her eyes snapped open.

Henries stood in front of her. The distance between them seemed to change and shift. Bati knew her brain was playing tricks on her. He approached, but every step he took happened in slow motion. She raised the gun. Her arm felt impossibly long. She jerked the trigger. The weapon boomed. The mercenary dove behind a bank of heavy equipment.

———

Henries saw her hand come up holding the pistol and threw himself behind cover. He knew right away where she had gotten the gun— the dead kidnapper. He should have searched the area for the man's pistol. It was a stupid mistake. He put his back to the machine, closed his eyes, and told himself to stay calm.

He pushed the transmit button on his radio. "Rene."

Silence was his only answer.

His team was dead.

How had things gone so monumentally wrong?

They had taken work with Tsang because the money was good and playing bodyguard was easy work... in the beginning. Somehow they had ended up doing the kingpin's dirty work. Henries should have known it would end badly. Lie down with dogs and you wake up with fleas.

The girl was his only bargaining chip now. He raised his voice so she could hear. "Put that gun down before you get yourself hurt. You hear?"

When she didn't respond, Henries stuck his head around the corner. She looked ready to pass out, but her arm came up. Henries jerked his head back. A bullet hissed past. He bared his teeth in frustration.

"I don't want to hurt you," Henries told her. "Don't force me. Put that gun down, before I take it away and cram it right up your..."

He felt a cold muzzle press against the side of his neck.

CHAPTER SIXTY-FOUR

Noble took off in the direction of the shots. He covered half the distance before he heard Henries telling the girl to put the gun down. Bati must have gotten her hands on a weapon and was using it to hold the mercenary at bay. Smart girl.

Noble slowed his pace and checked his corners. He spotted the big Australian with his back to a crusher, trying unsuccessfully to convince Bati to give up the gun. She looked done in. Her black hair was a tangled mess. She could barely lift the 9mm Beretta in her hand. Her skin was sickly white, and she had dark bags under both eyes. She wouldn't be able to hold him off much longer, but she wouldn't have to. Henries had not seen Noble yet. He was looking over his left shoulder; all of his attention was centered on the girl.

Noble let the H&K 410 dangle at the end of its sling and drew his pistol. He crept through the shadows to Henries's right side and pressed the barrel of the gun into the man's neck. Henries stopped mid-sentence. He released his rifle and slowly raised both hands. "All right, mate," he said. "You win. Take the girl and go."

"I'll do that. Thanks," Noble said and pulled the trigger.

Henries went over on his side like a felled tree. He was dead before he hit the ground. It was cold and brutal and all business. Noble could have let Henries walk, but why take the risk? The mercenary could find a hiding place and plug Noble in the back as soon as his guard was down. Noble couldn't care for Bati and watch Henries at the same time, so the Australian drew the short straw.

With him out of the way, Noble peeked around the crusher at Bati. Her face pinched. She seemed to be trying to make sense of what had just happened. "Bati Ramos, my name is Jacob Noble. I'm here to take you home."

Her mouth opened but no words came out. Her chin dropped to her chest and her eyelids drooped.

"Bati, I have an insulin syringe in my pocket. I want to give it to you. First you have to promise not to shoot me."

She let go of the handgun. It hit the floor with a metal clunk.

Noble stepped into the open with his hands out to either side trying to look non-threatening. He didn't want to alarm her. Bati was tired, scared, sick, and probably more than a little confused at this point. There was no predicting what she might do.

She drew a shallow breath. "Please help me," she said in a small voice.

That was all he needed. Noble holstered the .45, pulled the plastic case from his cargo pocket, and knelt beside her. The seal broke with an audible snap. Noble drew out one of four syringes and used his teeth to remove the plastic cap. He jabbed the needle into her thigh, pushed the plunger, and held his breath.

The wait lasted a lifetime. He placed two fingers on her wrist, monitoring a weak and erratic heartbeat. Several long minutes ticked by before her pulse gradually found a rhythm. He gently tilted her head back to make breathing easier. She stopped laboring for air. Her eyelids peeled open, and the pupils dilated. Her cracked lips parted, and she tried to speak.

"Take it easy," Noble said. "You are going to be all right now. It's over. I'm going to take you home."

"Did... Daddy... send you?"

"No."

Her eyes closed, but she was still awake and some of her color had returned. Tears gathered under her black lashes. "Hospital."

"That's our next stop," Noble told her.

CHAPTER SIXTY-FIVE

SAM CARRIED THE RIFLE ALONG THE RIDGELINE TO A spot that afforded her a view inside the open door of the crushing facility. She stretched out on her belly, adjusted the rifle against her shoulder, and placed the crosshairs on the entrance. She was getting better at finding a target through the scope, but every time she pulled the trigger, it ruined her aim.

A thin film of sweat covered her body from head to toe. She could feel it pasting her shirt to her back. Her hair hung in limp tangles. Her toes squished inside her hiking shoes. She had a cramp in her lower back, and her forearms were burning. Combat was nerve wracking and physically exhausting.

The hollow boom of gunshots echoed inside the crushing facility. Sam watched the door through the scope and prayed that Jake would emerge with Bati instead of the mercenaries. Every passing second made her stomach twist.

She pushed a damp lock of hair out of her eyes. "Come on, Jake."

Feet crunched in the loose shale behind her. She heard a pistol cock. Every muscle in her body went rigid. The breath caught in her lungs. Fear flooded her belly like hot oil, and panic clawed at the edge of her thoughts. Trying to roll over with the rifle was out of the question. The German tried that, and he was dead. Sam put the weapon down, held out her hands in surrender, and looked over her shoulder.

Frederick Krakouer stood behind her with a grin on his scarred face and a gun in his fist. "I'd hate to kill a sweet thing like you. Stand up nice and slow. Try anything and I'll put a bullet through your spine."

Samantha placed her hands flat on the gravel and eased herself up off the ground. Krakouer took a handful of her hair and jerked her head back, pushing his gun into the small of her back.

Sam winced. "Why are you doing this?"

"Just business," Krakouer told her. "Let's go down and say hello to your boyfriend."

He marched her along the ridgeline to the access road and down the gravel drive.

———

Bati's pulse was stronger now, but she still looked weak. Noble considered giving her another jab of insulin. It might bring her back or overdose her. Hard to say. He wasn't a medical doctor, and he was too close to the money to take any unnecessary risks. At the very least, she seemed lucid.

"Bati," Noble said. "I'm going to pick you up now, okay?"

She nodded her head. "Okay."

He scooped her up in both arms. She weighed a hundred pounds, give or take. As a Green Beret, Noble had lugged backpacks that weighed more. He stepped over Henries's body and carried Bati outside.

Samantha stood next to the Mercedes vans with tears streaking her cheeks. Krakouer was behind her, one hand tangled in her hair. He wore a cocky grin on his disfigured face.

Noble stopped in his tracks.

Sam's chin trembled. "I'm sorry, Jake."

"Don't be," he told her. "You did great."

"Touching," Krakouer said. "Put the girl down." He jammed his gun deeper into Sam's back to make his point.

She drew a sharp breath.

Noble felt helpless. He couldn't do anything with Bati in his arms. "If I turn Bati over, will you let Samantha go?"

"I promise I'll kill her if you don't."

"Don't do it, Jake," Sam said. And she meant it, too. She was pale and terrified but ready to die for her friend.

Noble locked eyes with her. The kiss they had shared played through his mind on repeat. If she died, he would spend the rest of his life seeing her face every time he closed his eyes. He would remember the kiss in agonizing detail. A quiet desperation filled him. His throat cramped. He had to force the words out. "Krakouer, listen, we are both professionals doing a job. She's a civilian. Let her go."

"From one professional to another, I'll blow her guts out if you don't put the girl down and back away."

Noble was out of options. He knelt, placed Bati gently on the ground, and stepped back with his hands out to either side.

"Toss the gun," Krakouer said, indicating the H&K 410 hanging around Noble's neck.

Using his left hand, Noble pulled the sling over his head, held it out at arm's length and dropped it. The 410 hit the ground with a clunk. He still had the .45 caliber concealed in his waistband.

Bati let out a sob.

"Smart move," Krakouer said.

Samantha caught Noble's eye. A sad smile formed on her face. She was telegraphing her intention without saying a word. She cared more for Bati than she did her own life. Noble caught her meaning loud and clear. If he could, he would have told her not to do it. He would have told her to play it safe and stay alive. He would have told her that it would destroy him to watch her die. But he couldn't say a word. Sam made her decision, and Noble could capitalize on it or let her sacrifice herself for nothing.

They both moved at the same time.

Sam swung her left arm behind her, smashing Krakouer's gun hand and twisted her hips at the same time. Noble took one long stride to his left and reached for his pistol.

Krakouer's gun barked.

The round exploded out of Sam's stomach an inch above her hip bone. She screamed, clapped both hands over the wound, and doubled over.

Noble centered the front sight on Krakouer's chest and emptied the magazine. The slide locked back. Noble dropped the spent mag and had a full one in before Krakouer hit the ground. He rushed to Sam's side, pausing long enough to put a bullet into Krakouer's skull.

She lay in a fetal position, both hands covered in deep red blood. Sweat beaded on her forehead. She took short, panicked breaths and spoke through clenched teeth. "Bati? ...Okay?"

"She's fine," Noble assured her.

He needed to know how bad she was hit. He had helped patch his share of bullet holes over the years, but those were soldiers—hard men who knew the risks. This was a beautiful woman that he was falling for. He holstered his pistol and tried to compartmentalize his feelings. Emotions would only get in the way. He turned her so that he could see the entry wound. Sam screamed in pain. Noble muttered an apology and peeled up her blood-soaked t-shirt.

The bullet had entered two finger widths to the right of her backbone. It looked like an oblong hole. A trickle of blood dribbled from the wound. Noble exhaled a shaky sigh of relief. Krakouer had missed the spine. The bullet was in and out. The surgeon would have a tough time stitching her intestines back together, but she would live.

"You crazy, beautiful, courageous woman," Noble said. It was hard to keep the emotion out of his voice. "You are going to be all right."

"It hurts really bad," Sam said. She trembled violently.

"Gut shots are painful, but you aren't going to die," he said. He left her on her side and went to the nearest Mercedes.

The doors were unlocked, and the keys were in the ignition. Noble expected as much. The mercenaries would not leave the keys with one man in case they had to extract on short notice and the guy with the keys was dead or missing. Noble popped the trunk. In back he found a white plastic box with a red cross emblazoned on the cover, a roll of duct tape, several assault rifles, and ammo. He took the medical kit.

Bati had crawled on hands and knees over to Sam, and she was putting pressure on the wound. She knelt with her bare knees on the stony ground and both hands pushing down on Sam's side. "There is a lot of blood," Bati said.

"There always is." Noble popped open the med kit and found a package of powdered quick coagulant. He ripped it open and shook some on both the entrance and exit wounds. Sam arched her back and screamed.

"That's going to sting," Noble told her after the fact. He ripped open two bandages, placed them over the bullet holes and then secured them with a roll of medical tape. She needed a surgical team, but the bandages would slow the bleeding long enough to get her to Kowloon General Hospital.

He ran and opened the passenger side door of the Mercedes, tipped the seat back as far as it would go and then went back for Sam. She screamed when he picked her up. Noble told her to stay strong and placed her gently in the passenger seat, then he secured her seat belt. After Sam was settled in, he scooped up Bati and deposited her across the back seat. He climbed behind the wheel, put the Mercedes in gear, and stamped on the gas. The back tires threw up a spit of dirt and gravel.

CHAPTER SIXTY-SIX

Eric Tsang spent most of the morning on the phone, stopping just long enough to brew a pot of coffee. He called all of his lieutenants with instructions to destroy any sensitive material that could be used by prosecutors and then he called his lawyers. Beyond the floor-to-ceiling windows of his high-rise office, the first pale light of a new day banished the darkness. Having insulated himself from the fallout at the docks as best he could, he dialed Henries for an update.

He paced the floor in his bare feet. The phone rang several times with no answer and then went to voicemail. Eric cursed and redialed with the same results. He was about to try a third time when there was a knock on his office door.

"Hong Kong Police! Open the door, Mr. Tsang. We have a warrant."

Eric put the phone in his pocket, slipped his feet inside his hand-stitched loafers, and rolled his pant legs down before answering the door. Captain Wong along with a half-dozen patrolmen stood in the hall.

The Captain handed Eric a sheaf of folded documents. "You are under arrest, Mr. Tsang."

"On what charges, Captain?"

Wong pointed to the documents in Eric's hands. "You are holding them."

Eric shook open the papers and scanned the arrest warrant. Wong had charged him with everything from kidnapping, human trafficking and smuggling, to illegal waste disposal. At the very least this was going to cost Eric several million in legal fees.

He motioned to his suit coat draped over his desk chair. "Do you mind if I put on my jacket?"

"Actually, I do mind," the Captain said. "Turn around and place your hands on your head."

Eric bore the indignity of being frisked and placed in handcuffs. It wasn't the first time he had been arrested and probably wouldn't be the last. But it was a serious blow to his operation. He was going find the people responsible and make them pay.

CHAPTER SIXTY-SEVEN

Three days later, Noble entered Kowloon Hospital through the visitor's entrance and rode the elevator to the third floor. Sam was in room 314. Noble stopped in front of the viewing window. Bati was already inside, sitting next to Sam's bed, looking considerably better than the last time Noble had seen her. She and Sam had their hands clasped together and their heads bowed in prayer. Sam wore a heart monitor on her left forefinger and an IV drip in her right arm.

Flower bouquets covered a tray table, along with a number of get-well cards and an open Bible. Noble waited until their eyes opened before letting himself in. Both women greeted him with bright smiles.

"There's the hero," Sam said.

Noble tried to suppress a grin, but it broke through.

"You're handsome when you smile," she said. "You should do it more often."

He took the second visitor chair. "How you feeling?"

She pointed to her feet. "Look." Her toes wiggled beneath the blanket. "The doctor says I should be on my feet in another week or two."

"That's great news." Noble took her hand in his. Their eyes met. She smiled. The silent tension grew until Noble wasn't sure what to say next.

Bati broke the spell by clearing her throat. "We were just praying for your mother," she said.

The smile ran away from Noble's face. He took a breath, nodded, and managed to say, "Thank you."

The dark empty place inside of him gave a painful twist. Bati had survived. Samantha would heal. But Noble had to go home and watch his mother die. All the money in the world could only buy her a small chance.

Sam saw the hurt in his eyes. "Don't lose hope."

Noble didn't know what to say to that. Maybe it didn't require a response. Instead he turned his attention to Bati. "You and I have a meeting."

Sam gave Bati a tight smile. "You'll do fine."

Bati took a deep breath. "I'm ready."

She and Noble went outside and climbed into a rented Hyundai. They rode in silence. Noble battled the Kowloon traffic to the tunnel. In the artificial glow of the neon lights, Bati finally said, "Sam's a special girl."

"Yes, she is."

"She deserves someone special," Bati said.

Noble felt like she had just stabbed him in the heart with a shard of ice. Without coming right out and saying it, she wanted him to know his place. Sure, he had saved both their lives, but at the end of the day, he wasn't marriage material. Sam deserved a guy that wore neckties to church on Sunday morning. Someone with a job and a stock portfolio. His throat constricted. "I understand."

She turned to face him. "Do you?"

He nodded.

They emerged from the tunnel into the morning sunlight and drove to a secure location arranged ahead of time by the Hong Kong branch. Noble parked at the curb in front of a high-rise office building with a travel agency on the ground floor. He pulled the parking brake and cut the engine. Traffic hummed by on the boulevard. Bati sat in the passenger seat fretting at her nails.

"You don't have to go through with it," he told her.

"But you will be able to stop a major trafficking ring if I do?"

"It will certainly help."

She fixed her hair back into a ponytail, took a deep breath, and climbed out of the car. Noble escorted her through the travel agency and up to the third floor. The elevator door opened on a carpeted hall with bare walls and harsh lighting.

Matthew Burke, dressed in a tan sport coat and slacks with loafers, waited outside an unmarked door. He grinned, grabbed Noble's hand, and pumped it. Noble felt like his shoulder would come right out of socket.

"You did real good," Burke said. "Real good. That was an impressive bit of business you pulled off. Some of the higher-ups are talking about giving you carte blanche and turning you loose on the bad guys."

"Express your gratitude by making sure the funds go into the right account," Noble told him.

Burke laughed and gave him a slap on the back, then

turned to Bati. "And you must be Ms. Bati Ramos. I'm glad we finally get to meet in person." He took both of her hands in his and placed a kiss on her cheek.

Bati blushed, flattered by the treatment.

His expression changed from jovial to serious. "Everything is arranged. You can leave any time you want."

"Thank you," she said.

Burke placed a hand on the door latch. "You ready?"

She hitched her shoulders up. "Ready as I'm going to be."

Burke gave her a wink and opened the door.

CHAPTER SIXTY-EIGHT

The room was furnished with a folding table and two chairs. Lady Shiva occupied one of the chairs. She wore a red dress and lipstick to match. Her hair was pulled up. She sat with a straight back and her hands folded calmly in her lap. She looked up when the door opened. Her lips pressed together.

Bati faced her mother for the first time in her life. She stood there for several long seconds feeling like she had stepped out of her body and into a surreal dream world. But this was no dream. She rallied her thoughts, squared her shoulders, and stepped into the room.

Noble and Burke followed.

"Hello, Bati," Shiva said. "You look just like your picture."

Bati said nothing. She took the seat across from her mother, folded her hands, and then unfolded them.

"I'm not what you were expecting," Shiva said with a nervous smile.

Bati shook her head. "No. Er... yes. I'm not sure," she admitted. "I didn't even know you were alive until three days ago."

"I know all about you," Shiva said. "I kept an eye on you. I even sent a few birthday presents..." She trailed off. "But I guess your father never let you have them."

Bati thought about that. "He gave me a stuffed bunny for my seventh birthday. He said it was from a great aunt back in Manila."

Shiva's face lit up at the mention of the bunny. "I bought him at Trinoma."

"Mister Nuffles," Bati said with a laugh. "I call him Mister Nuffles. I still have him."

A single tear formed at the corner of Lady Shiva's eye, balanced on the end of her long lashes, and then spilled down her cheek. "You were the greatest thing that ever happened to me. I'm sorry I could not be there for you growing up. Your father wouldn't allow it. I still remember holding you in my arms the day you were born. You were a tiny little life." She smiled and motioned at Bati. "Now look at you. All grown up."

Bati twisted her hands together in her lap. "What's your real name?"

Shiva had to swallow a lump in her throat. "Ana. Just Ana. I don't remember my family name. I was too young."

They lapsed into silence.

Shiva sniffed and swallowed. "I don't expect you to understand what I do. I'm not proud of it. I didn't have any other choice. You probably hate me, but I had to meet you. I wanted you to know..."

"Know what?"

"That I love you," Shiva said.

Bati said nothing for a long time. Tears leaked down her cheeks in silent rivers. She needed a tissue. She ran a hand under her nose. "I don't hate you," she said at last. She leaned forward. "If you really love me, then you'll tell these men what they want to know."

Shiva nodded.

Bati stood up and went to the door.

Burke opened it and followed her out into the hall.

————

Noble took Bati's vacated seat. "We kept our end of the deal," he said. "Now it's your turn."

He took a cell phone from his pocket, opened a voice-recording app, and placed the device on the table between them. Shiva scooted her chair up, placed her hands on the tabletop, laced her fingers together, and started to talk. She provided details on all of Ramos's operations. For thirty years he had been running the largest human trafficking ring in South East Asia and using the CIA to take out his competition. It was genius, really. On the outside, he was a respected diplomat campaigning for an end to slavery. Behind the scenes, he made a fortune in the sex-slave industry, and the CIA had been his dupe all along.

When she finished, Shiva sat back in her chair. "What happens to Ramos now?"

Noble ended the recording, pocketed the cell phone, and stood up. "The United States can't arrest him. He's a diplomat, but we've got enough to cancel his status and send him back to the Philippines.

"Your government doesn't really care about sex trafficking, but they want the rest of the world to think they do, and this will be international news. The Philippine government will make an example of Ramos in order to look good on the world stage," Noble told her.

Shiva arched an eyebrow. "What about me?"

"I'm a man of my word. You get a pass," Noble said. "For now."

"For now," Shiva said. "But I know men like you. You won't rest until you've caught me."

Noble stopped with his hand on the latch. "I may catch up with you one day soon."

"What if I find you first?" she asked.

"It will be the last thing you ever do," Noble told her and walked out.

Burke waited in the hall. "Did you get it?"

Noble handed over the cell phone. "It's all here."

CHAPTER SIXTY-NINE

BAKONAWA RAMOS SAT DOWN AT HIS DESK, PULLED OUT stationery with his letterhead on it, and penned a message to his daughter. In the letter he did not bother to explain his actions or ask for forgiveness. He simply told her that he loved her and that he wanted her to have a wonderful life free of worry. He signed it at the bottom.

With that done, he lit a Djarum Black and poured bourbon over ice. He took a swallow and reflected on his life. Several times over the years, he had considered dismantling his criminal enterprise and transforming himself into the man he claimed to be. It had been tempting. His various charitable foundations generated millions. He could have lived comfortably by skimming a small portion, but there was always more money to be made from prostitution. He wondered how things might have turned out if he had walked away.

He finished his drink and smoked the clove down to the

filter. Then he took a model 33 Glock from his desk drawer, put it under his chin, and fired a .357 round into his brain. He was dead before the weapon hit the Turkish rug.

CHAPTER SEVENTY

Noble pulled his 1970 Buick GSX hardtop into the parking lot at Saint Anthony's, found a spot in the shade, and entered through the emergency room doors. Most of the hard plastic chairs were empty today, but the smell of disinfectant remained. He rode the elevator to the second floor. Dr. Lansky stood at the nursing station, giving directions to a pair of young interns. Noble waited.

The doctor saw him and held up a finger. He finished instructing the interns, dismissed them, and offered his hand to Noble. "I have good news," he said with a grin.

Noble could hardly believe his ears. He must have misheard. "Good news?"

"It's still early." Lansky patted the air with both hands. "But we are seeing positive results. This latest round of chemo looks promising."

Noble stood rooted to the spot. For the first time in years, he felt like he would break down and cry, or dance a jig, maybe both. He managed to marshal his thoughts. "How is that possible?"

Lansky shrugged. "I wish I could give you a more scientific explanation. We still don't know everything there is to know about the human body. Some people recover against all odds, while others expire from curable diseases. I'd call it a miracle if I believed in that sort of thing. Either way, it's always nice to give good news."

Noble could only nod.

"She's awake if you'd like to see her," Lansky said.

A call came over the intercom, and the doctor had to hurry off.

Noble paced the hospital corridor letting the information sink in. The doctor's words echoed inside his head. *Positive results. Looks promising. A miracle if I believed in that sort of thing.* He stopped in front of his mother's door. He needed to see her, but first he took out his cell phone and sent a text to Samantha. It was two words.

Keep praying.

THE END

CAN'T WAIT FOR MORE
JAKE NOBLE?

Sign up for the Jake Noble Fan Club and get, SIDE JOBS: Volume 1, The Heist for FREE! This story is available exclusively to my mailing list.

https://williammillerauthor.com/fan-club/

DID YOU ENJOY THE BOOK?

Please take a moment to leave a review on Amazon. Readers depend on reviews when choosing what to read next and authors depend on them to sell books. An honest review is like leaving your waiter a hundred dollar tip. The best part is, it doesn't cost you a dime!

ABOUT THE AUTHOR

I was born and raised in sunny Saint Petersburg, FL on a steady diet of action movies and fantasy novels. After 9/11, I left a career in photography to join the United States Army. Since then, I have travelled the world and done everything from teaching English in China to driving a fork-lift. I studied creative writing at Eckerd College and wrote four hard-boiled mysteries for Delight Games before releasing the first Jake Noble book. When not writing, I can be found indoor rock climbing, playing the guitar, and haunting smoke-filled jazz clubs in downtown Saint Pete. I'm currently at work on another Jake Noble thriller. You can follow me on my website WilliamMillerAuthor.com

AFTERWORD

While the events and characters in *Noble Man* are fictitious and not meant to represent anyone, living or dead, the issues are very real. Illegal profits from human trafficking are estimated to exceed 30 billion dollars a year. Between 21 and 30 million people are enslaved as of this writing. The majority of the people bought and sold are women. In the United States alone, there are an estimated 100,000 children sold into sexual slavery every year. Most are never heard from again.

It is the purpose of this book to raise awareness and funds to end slavery. A portion of the proceeds from the sale of this book go to Veterans For Child Rescue, a non-profit organization making a difference in the battle against human trafficking. I sincerely hope you will join me in giving generously. Together we can make a difference.

But more than money is needed. Human trafficking is merely a symptom of a much larger moral cancer in the heart of society. It is a corruption that cannot be cured by organizations, governments, or even heroes like Jake Noble. In this author's humble opinion, prayer is our best weapon.

Keep Praying.

Turn the page for a sample chapter from the next Jake Noble thriller.

NOBLE VENGEANCE

by
WILLIAM MILLER

CHAPTER ONE

Jesús Torres had roughly an hour to live. He entered the recently remodeled Buenavista railway station a few minutes after one o'clock. A summer heatwave was turning the streets of Mexico City into rivers of shimmering asphalt. Inside the station, the air conditioners worked overtime. A voice announced arrivals and departures over a grainy loud speaker. Sound echoed in the cavernous hall. Torres passed the ticket booths and terminals packed with sweaty travelers, to a row of long-term storage lockers.

He dug a USB drive from the pocket of his faded denims, opened locker 314, glanced around the bustling terminal, and then hid the thumb drive inside, using the narrow ledge above the door hinge. He closed the locker, removed the key and gave it a tug to be sure it was locked.

Next he located a row of payphones near the restrooms. He took one look at the bulky, orange card readers and his lips peeled back from clenched teeth. For someone in his line of work, a credit card is like a homing beacon.

He stood there in silent debate. The only other person using the payphones was a middle-aged woman. She kept waving a hand in the air, sighing, rolling her eyes.

"Screw it," Torres said and reached into his back pocket for his wallet. He picked up the receiver, pushed his card into the slot and then waited for a dial tone.

"*Hola*." Machado said with the raspy baritone that comes from a lifetime of heavy drinking .

"It's me," Torres said in Spanish. "You have something I want."

"*Sí, amigo*. She has a lot of spirit."

Torres heard a scream in the background. His heart squeezed inside his chest. His knuckles turned white. "*Cabrón!*"

The woman on the next phone over shot him a dirty look.

"My men have been entertaining her for days," Machado said. "I was starting to wonder if you would ever call."

Torres squeezed his eyes shut. If she could scream, she was still alive. That's all that mattered. Machado was trying to push his buttons, force him to make a mistake. He told himself to breathe. She was still alive and he had a chance to save her.

"Let's trade," Torres said. "Me for the girl."

"I'm more interested in the files you stole from me."

"That's part of the bargain," Torres assured him. "Turn her loose and you get the files. Don't, and they go public."

"We pay a terrible price for the women we love," Machado chuckled. "When and where?"

Fighting to keep his voice steady, Torres said, "The airfield. One hour. Bring the girl."

"We have a deal," Machado said.

Torres slammed the receiver and walked out of the train station into the blazing midday sun. His eyes narrowed against the light. He clutched the locker key in his fist. First thing he needed was a post office.

Pick up Noble Vengeance on Amazon.com

Made in the USA
Lexington, KY
30 August 2019